CUTIE AND THE BEAST

CIPHER OFFICE BOOK #3

M.E. CARTER

WWW.SMARTYPANTSROMANCE.COM

COPYRIGHT

Made in the United States of America

Print Edition

ISBN: 978-1-949202-47-2

DEDICATION

Dedicated to the Smartypants Romance authors of Launch #2. I can't wait to get our tattoos! Karla goes first!!

CHAPTER ONE

ABEL

"Good mornings, sweets." I snuggle into her long dark curls to kiss her forehead when *THWACK!* "Son of a..." I stop myself before cussing in front of my kid, but damn. She got me right in the nose and that shit stings.

"Sorry, Daddy," my sweet baby girl says groggily, while I rub my schnoz and make sure it's not bleeding. "I dreamed you were Mommy."

"And in this dream, you were practicing your kickboxing on her?"

Her eyes close while she innocently says, "You told me to take out my aggression appropriately."

She's not wrong. I'd said it in response to Mabel's therapist deciding the best way to take her anger out about her mother leaving us was to be more Zen. Those weren't her exact words. It was closer to, "*Mabel needs to learn how to channel her anger into more appropriate activities. Journaling or painting, for example.*" I resisted rolling my eyes until we got home, and we never went back. Not only could we not find a time that worked with my schedule, I decided to implement my own form of calm.

When Mabel starts getting agitated or angry about May's abandonment, I let her take some swings on the punching bags at the gym where I work while we talk it out. It seems to work. She gets out some negativity and hyper-kid energy, then moves on with her day. But apparently, she's been listening to me a little too carefully if it's bleeding over into her dreams.

"Maybe cut back on the kickboxing dreams there, killer. You socked me right in the honker."

Mabel giggles and reaches up to grab my nose. Squeezing it twice, she makes a honking sound each time. Then her arm flops back down on her blue polka dot bedspread and she tries to snuggle back in bed.

I don't blame her. Mornings have been brutal since May left to go live with her agent boyfriend in New York; he was going to help her become a successful model. Never mind that she was already thirty and had zero experience. *"The modeling world is changing, Abel,"* she'd told me. *"Doors are opening as we speak, and I'm going to walk right through them."*

As far as I know, the only door she'd walked through was the front door of our small, three-bedroom townhome on her way to the airport. That was close to six months ago and, with the exception of being served divorce papers, we've only heard from her sparingly. Mostly through online chats that are centered around her life, and very little about her child's.

It was a rough transition at first. Mabel didn't understand how her mother could just up and leave, coupled with a lot of justified anger about it. I couldn't understand how I'd missed all the signs it was coming, coupled with *my* justified anger.

To make matters worse, there was the huge fire at Weight Expectations, the gym where I work, which closed the facility for several months. Sure, we all got farmed out to different locations, which was better than the alternative—a pink slip. But when part of your income depends on commission and the clients you've built up over the years end up scattered around the city, you find yourself dipping into savings more heavily than anticipated.

Fortunately, that season is over, and I have a brand-spanking-new building to call my home away from home. But mornings haven't quite smoothed over yet.

"Come on, baby. We've got to get a move on." I scoop Mabel up, wrap the heavy blanket around her, and carry her to the living room where I proceed to maneuver myself into an assortment of yoga poses until I have her, my gym bag, her school bag, and her clothing bag dangling safely from my arms. Well, Mabel isn't dangling, though at one point when my gym bag fell from the couch to the floor, it was a close call. Thank goodness I make a living working out, or there is no way I'd be able to hold it all at once.

Finally situated with all our daily supplies, I head out the door and step into the blustering winter weather, hence the reason why the child is dressed as a giant burrito in my arms. I lock the door as quickly as possible behind me, and race us to the waiting car.

"Mornin', Abel." A steaming cup of black coffee is handed to me between the dark blue bucket seats of the 2008 Ford Escort as soon as the passenger side door closes behind me. Actually, steaming might be a stretch. It's thirty-nine degrees outside, not factoring in the wind chill. And it's been sitting in a car for a while. Lukewarm is more accurate. But it's a cup of joe. No matter the temperature, it still hits the spot. Especially since old Betsy refused to work again this morning. No matter how sweet I talk to her, or how many times I bang on her, my favorite coffee maker refuses to brew anything. I really should spring for a new one, but I'm sentimental about the old gal. Besides, when she does work, her coffee making skills are the best I've ever had. But when she doesn't? Let's just say, thank God for Marv's sweet wife and her bleeding heart.

"Ah, Marv. You're an angel."

He scoffs at my praise, but I truly couldn't get to work safely and on time without him. Weight Expectations is only three city blocks away from our home, so it's not hard to walk to work. That's what I used to do when I was co-parenting: take off for a quick morning jog to warm up my body before putting it through the grind with my clients.

Now that I'm a single dad, though, there is no way Mabel can run with me. Actually, she probably would. My girl is very much an athlete like her father. But four forty-five a.m. is too early for her. Hell, it's too early for me, but I've discovered the most dedicated clients (and by dedicated, I mean most consistent with their payments) are early risers who need to be at work on time. Plus, it's late fall. In Chicago. When the wind blows, it goes straight through to your bones. If it was only me, I'd suffer through it to save the daily five-dollar fee, plus tip. But it's not.

Besides, I enjoy Marv. Our conversations are short and to the point due to our time constraints, but over the weeks, we've learned a lot about each other. He's privy to the reasons I'm now raising a little girl on my own, and I've learned he is really bored in his retirement. When his wife threatened to divorce him if he didn't find something to do with this time, he started his ride-share business. It's a win/win for both of us. He has taken it upon himself to be here every day with his wife's freshly brewed coffee in hand, and I don't have to carry Mabel in the freezing cold.

"Got Christmas ready for the little one?" Marv keeps his eyes on the road, hands at ten and two, his thinning gray hair combed all the way back, not a single strand out of place.

"Working on it. She wants a puppy." Marv chuckles at her request. I, on the other hand, don't find it amusing. "It's a shame Santa can't bring a puppy on a sleigh because he might fall out."

"Oh yeah. Shame," Marv says, still clearly amused.

"Your grandbabies coming in town for the holidays this year?" I don't know their names or how many there are. But Marv keeps a few snapshots taped to his dash, which is how they came up in conversation in the first place. I know they live down south somewhere with their mom, his daughter. And I know they don't visit as often as he would like. That's as far as we've gotten. Considering we've spoken for all of sixty minutes, all in three-minute spurts, I feel pretty informed.

"Get here on the twenty-third," he answers with a smile. Pulling to a stop in front of the gym, Marv ends this conversation the same way he does every day. "We're here. Need help getting out?"

I guzzle the remaining liquid and I respond the same way I do every day. "I'm good. Thank you, Marv. Let the missus know the coffee was great." He takes the now-empty cup from me and I recommence with my balancing act to get Mabel and me inside. Gina from the front desk sees us coming and lets us in quickly.

"Morning, Gina."

She harrumphs her response, eyes still barely open. Gina is not a morning person. Not many people are, but she is so far from being able to function before nine, I still can't figure out why she works this shift. Every morning, she gets here at four thirty, turns on all the lights and air or heat depending on the time of year, and brews coffee for the employees. She's supposed to make sure the locker rooms are all stocked with things like toilet paper and soap in the shower, but I'm 95 percent positive she skips that part to get the coffee done as soon as possible. Getting stuck on the toilet until someone can rescue me by throwing a roll over the stall wall isn't fun, but it's still preferable to Gina biting my head off because she's not caffeinated.

I wind around treadmills and free weights and make my way to the shared desk all the personal trainers use. Morgan has beaten me here like always, and she immediately jumps up to move the chair and unroll a yoga mat on the floor under the desk.

"Thanks," I say while she helps me maneuver the bags and the kid-sized burrito onto the floor. "Man, it's cold in here."

"That's because it's practically nighttime still. The heaters haven't kicked on yet." She hands me the small pillow we keep in a tote next to the desk, and I gently lift Mabel's head to put it under her. "Why don't you change your shift so you can come in after she's at school? Wouldn't it be easier?"

"Ah, Morgan. How quickly you've forgotten what the early years were like with your kids."

In her early fifties, she is our newest trainer. A former client of mine, she's been coming here for years, but when her kids went off to college, she decided a career change was in order. Now, instead of being my client, she's my shadow, at least until she gets a few hours under her belt.

Standing up and stretching my back, I drop the bags on the chair to clock in.

"I didn't forget," Morgan argues. "I blocked them out. I'm pretty sure those were the years my boys thought bodily functions were funny."

"They are funny," I retort. "We just stop admitting it in front of women once we hit puberty."

"Thank goodness." Morgan drops down on another chair and begins swiveling back and forth. "I don't know how many more times I could have broken up a fight when one of them farted over the other one's cereal."

"Oh yeah. Total guy thing. My cousins got in a fistfight at Thanksgiving dinner one year over that." I start chuckling at the memory I haven't thought of in years. "My parents didn't know what had happened until they looked over and one of them had the other by the throat." The visual images make me laugh so hard, I suddenly have tears in my eyes and I'm trying to catch my breath. "I was sitting right there"—I laugh again—"and Andrew literally launched himself over the table"—another laugh—"and wrapped his hands around Timothy's neck." I wipe a stray tear. "My sister was around six years old, and she was munching on a drumstick, looking back and forth at them as Timothy's face turned bright red."

I find this trip down memory lane to be incredibly entertaining. Judging by the look on Morgan's face, she does not. Sure enough, she quirks an eyebrow at me. "It's all fun and games when you're the cousin watching WWE go down in front of you. But you just wait. Someday you'll have two kids, and when they throw down at the church crawfish boil and knock over the picnic table, it won't be so amusing."

"First of all, there won't be two kids, so I'm not worried," I respond, still pulling myself together. "Second, it was your kids at the crawfish boil, wasn't it?"

"Do you know how hard red juice is to get out of clothes?" I burst out laughing again at the pent-up anger she's held on to for fifteen years or so. Even she can't stop from smiling as she bitches.

"I washed those damn clothes at least a dozen times, and they never made it back to white. I finally said screw it. They can wear orange until they grow out of them."

"I'll remember that next time we go to a crawfish boil, which will probably be never, since it's not a Chicago thing."

"Not anymore," she retorts. "We ruined it for everyone."

I don't realize how loud we're being until a small voice interrupts us.

"What's so funny, Daddy?"

My giant burrito looks up at me from under the desk, her brown eyes wide with interest.

"Nothing, baby." I bend down and brush her hair back, tucking her back in. "Go back to sleep. You have school, and you don't want to be too tired."

Mabel lets out a deep sigh and snuggles back into her blanket. It's the biggest, fluffiest one we own. Not only does it help insulate her from the wind, it usually muffles most of the noise around her.

"Again, why don't you change your shift so you don't have to bring her here this early in the morning?" This time, Morgan whispers.

"Because it's easier on both of us if she can sleep here for a couple of hours before school than it is to try and find someone to watch her after school for more hours."

"Can't she stay in the childcare center here when it opens?"

I shrug and put my bags in my designated locker behind the desk. "Dinah said she could, but only for a few hours in the afternoon. They don't want to turn it into a daycare center for employees, and there is something about how they aren't licensed to keep kids much longer than that. I don't want to take advantage of it. I need to be able to use it if I get in a bind."

She nods and pushes off the armrests to stand and stretch. "Makes sense. But if you ever need anything, you have my number."

"And it's much appreciated. If Mabel gets sick and I need someone to cover my classes, you'll be the first one I call."

"Okay, well I'm gonna hit the treadmill to warm up a bit."

7

"Sounds good."

Morgan steps around me and, not for the first time, I'm grateful for her. Between Morgan, the two other early morning trainers, and me, someone is always sitting at the desk for the hour and a half Mabel is sleeping underneath. Is it ideal to do things this way? No. But it has stayed under the radar and clients aren't aware anything is amiss, so the bosses haven't said anything. I've been very lucky in that aspect.

I grab my notes for today's clients and begin to prep. Not every trainer has one, but I prefer keeping a binder with profiles for each client. It helps me keep track of their goals, where their starting point is, and what their progress looks like. When they get discouraged, it's nice to have the numbers right in front of me so I can remind them of how far they've come. It's a good motivator for them and me.

First up today is Trevor Mendola. He's a monster of a man and one of the most jovial clients I have. He's not a huge talker, but man does he push his body to extremes. At first, he was trying to get back in shape after letting himself go post-college. It's the same struggle a lot of former football players deal with. For years, they work out for hours every day and eat an exorbitant number of calories. Then suddenly, their college ball career is over and they aren't burning off all that food anymore, but still eating the same amount. It's not always pretty.

But once Trevor discovered weightlifting, he was hooked. He's not as hard core as a bodybuilder would be, but he's definitely found a new obsession in the three years we've been working together.

I continue looking over my notes, planning out some new exercises for my various clients and classes. I'm so engrossed in my work, I don't realize we're open for business until I hear, "Beeeeeeeeast," being yelled in my direction. That's become my nickname in recent years, ever since I broke the gym record for pounds squatted. I had a plaque on the wall and everything for my accomplishment. It's not there anymore—lost in the fire. Frankly, I'm relieved. It was a terrible picture.

Looking up, Trevor is headed my direction, a smile on his face. Briefly, I wonder how he got past Gina without his face being ripped off for being a morning person.

"What's up, Trevor?" I stand up and walk around the desk, greeting him with a quick handshake and pat on the shoulder. "You ready to get started?"

"Hell yeah. I've had a protein shake and a glass of water. I'm pumped to shred these muscles. It's back day, right?"

"Yep. I wanna go old school with you today. No fancy equipment, just using your body weight. Lots of reps."

"Sounds great." I knew he'd say that. The good thing about Trevor is I could tell him we're going to scale a building for our workout and he'd be willing to do it. The bad thing about Trevor is I could tell him we're going to scale a building for our workout and he'd be willing to do it. Two sides. Same coin.

"All right. Head on over to the treadmill to warm up, and I'll get everything ready to go. Meet me in the weight room when you're done."

He nods and trots over to the machines, greeting everyone he passes. Most of them still look like they haven't woken up yet. Such is the curse of early morning workouts.

I, on the other hand, head over to the designated workout area to grab some kettlebells. I wish I had another cup of coffee to keep me energized, but I don't have time to worry about it anymore.

The day is just beginning. Time to get a move on.

CHAPTER TWO

ELLIOTT

"What in the world is this?"

I cringe and pretend not to hear her, knowing exactly what my mother is talking about. It's been a point of contention for a while...

The coffee table in the living room.

She has one of those formal tables that opens up to an oval shape, but when you fold the sides down, it's a rectangle. For whatever reason, my mother, Rose Donovan, wants the sides up. Always up. No ifs, ands, or buts... leave the sides up!

Yes, it makes the table bigger and looks lovely, but unfortunately, I have an eight-year-old daughter who loves to use that coffee table as her dance partner. In particular, she uses it to support her body weight whenever she has the desire to kick her heels up in the air. Fifty pounds of partial handstand is not what the table was designed to withstand, and no matter how many times she has gotten in trouble, Ainsley never learns. Or, as we parents call it, she has "selective learning".

She has been grounded from the living room, grounded from the television, sent to her room, and lost dessert. I've even gone as far as to take her favorite Jojo Siwa bow away from her, which created a massively dramatic crisis. But even the thought of not having her giant hair accessory doesn't seem to stop this kid when the music moves her.

So, to ensure the table doesn't break while I find which disciplinary measure will work with my child, I've taken to folding the table down. Seems logical, right?

Not with my mother.

Don't get me wrong, I understand her position. We invaded her space three years ago when I ended up in a nasty divorce and needed to get back on my financial feet, so it's up to us to be respectful of her space and her things.

But again, Ainsley is eight. She's lived here since she was five. While I very much feel like a guest in this house, my daughter doesn't. This is just her home where she lives with her mother and her Gigi, and where all her kid-related learning happens—including unintended natural consequences like broken tables.

"I don't want these wings down. I want them up," Mom passively aggressively says toward the floor, pretending to be muttering under her breath as she puts the table back in a different position. But I'm fully aware these words are actually for my benefit. "Honestly. I don't know why people can't leave my things alone."

I give up. She'll keep bitching if I don't explain my reasoning. She'll probably keep bitching anyway, but at least she can tell her friends all about the fight we got in about it. They love *tsk*ing and consoling her about how unfortunate it is that her empty-nest phase was invaded by her ungrateful daughter and grandchild. Or at least that's how I imagine their conversations go. The reality is probably much milder, but when you live in a constant state of negativity, those anxious thoughts make me hyperaware of every little thing we do wrong. Even when I'm not wrong, just preventing.

"I put them down, Ma," I call from the kitchen while slicing up some cantaloupe. It was a little overripe when I picked it up at the store earlier but not too ripe to eat. Considering it's the closest we're going to get to summer fruit in the dead of winter, I'll make the sacrifice. "You know Ainsley keeps putting all her weight on that table."

"Well, I wish you would get her to stop."

I take a deep breath, trying to control my emotions. "I know," I mutter. "You remind me of it daily."

Mom comes into the room and begins rummaging around for the Tupperware lid while I continue my knife work. It's disturbingly therapeutic every time I have to bang the blade into the juicy flesh. Either I need to move out soon, or I need to be locked up. "Honestly, Elliott. I wish you would leave my things the way I want them. This is my home, and I should be the one who decides how the furniture is placed."

"I understand that, and I'm trying to be sensitive to it. But you can't have it both ways, Mom. I'm working with Ainsley on being respectful of your furniture, but I'm also trying to keep it from breaking until she finally learns."

Mom sighs and puts the lid next to the dish I'm filling. "I know you are, honey. And I don't mean to sound negative."

I love my mother. I do. The minute she found out my marriage was falling apart, she offered up her home. No matter what part of Chicago you live in, this is an expensive city and being a single mom is no easy financial task. Especially if you're in your early forties and have been out of the work force for ten years. The middle-aged discrimination thing we were warned about? I'm finding it to be true. It doesn't matter that I have almost a dozen years in social services work. I'm not the prime candidate. And the jobs I have been offered? Well, let's just say I can't provide for a child on twenty-five grand a year. Especially in the summer with exorbitant childcare costs.

So yes, I'm grateful my mom opened her home to us, but we are all at the point where we need some space. And we need it sooner rather than later.

"I know, Mom," I reply, gathering up all the cantaloupe rinds while she holds the trash can next to my workspace so I can toss them in. "But I'm really trying. I remind Ainsley constantly to keep her hands off the table, but she forgets. Would you rather be inconvenienced by putting the wings up when people come over? Or would you prefer it to break?"

"I'd prefer neither, to be honest."

I bite my tongue from popping off with a sarcastic retort and settle on, "Again, I understand. But you're not in a position to choose that yet. Hopefully soon."

Her eyes light up. "Oh, that's right! Your interview is today. When is it?"

"Um," I glance at the clock over the stove. "I need to leave here in about forty-five minutes if I'm going to make it on time. Do you remember I need you to pick up Ainsley from school?"

"Of course, I remember," she says with a flick of her hand. "Ainsley wrote it on my calendar herself."

I can't even fight the smile at that one. While my mother and I have settled into a strained relationship over the last couple of years, she and my daughter have gotten much closer. I joke that they've become best friends, but in a way, it's true. Gigi is the first person she wants to show her school artwork to. Gigi is the one she wants to take her swimming. And she must always, always sit next to Gigi at the dinner table. If nothing else, I love that about this time in my life. Those memories are priceless. Even if the bickering between us two adults is not.

"I hope she used pencil this time."

"It was a pen. Which is still preferable to the time she used a permanent marker. No amount of white-out would fix the date on the other side. I'm still not sure if I was a little early or a little late to my doctor's appointment the following week."

Snapping the Tupperware lid closed, I begin the process of cleaning all the sticky juice off the counter. It's the last task left to complete before changing for my interview.

I applied for a position in the childcare center of Weight Expectations, a local gym. The hours are okay—if I get it, I won't go in until ten and I'll leave at dinnertime every day—but I can take my lunch break to pick up Ainsley from school and bring her back with me since it's only a couple of hours. The pay is comparable to jobs that don't provide a childcare perk. Plus, there are benefits. Actual health insurance benefits. I haven't had those since the divorce, so it was a pleasant surprise.

Because nothing says middle age is coming like being excited to finally schedule your annual pap smear and mammogram.

"Be happy you could see the time well enough to get there within the fifteen-minute range, so they still saw you." I rinse the now-dirty washcloth under the warm water, anxious to get ready to leave. Thank goodness all I have to do is change and brush my teeth. Not that I need to dress up or anything; I don't think they expect people working with children to show up in a pantsuit. At least, I hope not. "If the Sharpie had moved a centimeter to the left you would have been out of luck," I joke, but Mom isn't biting.

"Seriously, Elliott. You weren't destructive at all as a child. "

Destructive is a bit of a stretch considering we've left nothing but normal wear and tear in our wake. But I'm honestly kind of surprised she doesn't have plastic coverings over all her furniture, so I guess in her mind, it does seem like we tear everything up.

"I don't understand how she's so different from you."

I shrug noncommittally even though her words actually sting. "I have a different parenting style than you do, Mom. I'm choosing the battles I think are important to fight."

"And my table isn't an important fight?"

And here we go again. The argument that will never die. I supposed I shouldn't be surprised. The inability to let go has been a point of contention my entire life.

Don't get me wrong—my parents were actually fantastic when I was growing up. We went on family vacations and I did activities. We were involved in the community together, and it wasn't uncommon for one of them to come have lunch with me at school.

But what they never realized, and what I've never said, is I always felt like I was walking on eggshells around them. It wasn't because I was afraid I would be abused; it was because I was always trying to be "good enough" for them. Critical words were common and negative talk was the norm.

As a child, I didn't realize anything was wrong. I was actively taught to respect my elders and that's what I did. I don't regret my respect for authority. Quite the contrary.

But when I started seeing the way the negative talk affected Ainsley, when I really started paying attention to the look on her face when my mother would speak to her the same way, it finally clicked.

That day I realized I needed to make an active effort to watch my own tone and not say positive things in a negative way. That's not a slam on my parents. My parents were wonderful. But my job is to be a better parent than they were. It's the way the world works. You build upon the knowledge of those before you.

"I don't know, Mom, but I don't have time to discuss it now." Drying my now-clean hands on the dishtowel, I quickly deflect. "I need to go get dressed so I can leave. I really want this interview to go well."

Interpret: I need to get some money so we can get out of there.

I don't say that, of course. Too many eggshells, even for this forty-something woman.

"Me too, honey. Go," she says kindly, genuinely excited for me to start rebuilding my life. She needs space as much as we do. "I'll finish up in here, so you don't have to worry about it."

I don't bother pointing out to her I've already finished everything, opting instead to race up the stairs of the small brownstone we all live in. It's the same house I grew up in all those years ago.

But maybe with a little bit of luck, and this badly needed income, Ainsley won't consider it her childhood home too. It's time. We're ready to make a fresh start.

CHAPTER THREE

ABEL

"Get it, Beast! Get it!"

I blow my breath out as I push my body up, lifting myself plus the two hundred fifty pounds that balance on my shoulders. As I get to the top, the yelling begins again.

"One more, Beast! One more!"

I take three quick breaths and slowly lower myself back down to a squat position.

Customer-wise, it's slow at the gym right now, mostly because of the time of day. It's after lunch, but before the end of the work day. Lots of older folks come in at this time, so the free weights are usually free. It's the perfect time of day for me to get in my own good, hard workout, which I'm almost done with.

This is my last squat. After this, I've got stretching, a quick shower, and then it's off to get Mabel from school so I can spend the rest of the day focusing on my dad duties. But right now? Right now I'm working out all my stress.

"Push, Abel! Go! Almost there!"

I reach the top and feel some of the pressure come off my back as my fellow trainer and lifting partner, Joey, helps me get to the squat rack and put the bar back.

As soon as it's secure and the danger of me dropping the weights on us is no longer a concern, Joey slaps me on the back.

"Nice job today, Abel. You haven't pushed that much weight that easily in a couple of months."

I squirt some water in my mouth before answering. "I think all the life changes jacked up my body for a while. But I'm feeling more settled now. Maybe that's it."

"Seriously," he replies, tossing his towel into the bin as we head toward the stretching tables. "Harder to focus on training when you've been putting out so many fires for this long. And I don't mean the kind that burn the gym down."

"Ha, ha," I retort sarcastically. Joey is always trying to pun things up around here. Sometimes it works. Sometimes it doesn't. Mostly, it doesn't.

"You wanna be on top or bottom today?"

One of our regular Golden Girls takes a step back and looks at us, mouth agape. If she knew Joey was talking about who was going to stretch first, she wouldn't be so shocked. But, of course, that's why he phrases otherwise-innocent sentences the way he does.

I punch him in the chest, making him lose his breath with an "oomph." "What'd you do that for?" he complains.

Setting my foot on the table, I push myself into a runner's stretch and make a point of breathing deep. The shred of my muscles feels great, but so does pushing them to be more flexible.

"I know you say things for the shock value, but it'd be nice if you don't give someone a heart attack while I'm trying to get out the door."

Taking his sweet ass time, Joey finally gets into position to begin his own stretch. "That's awfully selfish of you. You'd just let her lie on the floor with only me to revive her?"

Rolling my eyes, I switch legs. "Must be nice to only have to think about what you and your fancy man-bun have to do every day." I swipe at his hair, making him bat at my hands. He hates it when people touch his lovely locks, so naturally, I make a habit of doing it often and making commentary about it when I do. "But some of us have other responsibilities."

"Oh, that's right. Little Miss Mabel." He acts like he forgot, but he's full of shit. My kid and my friend have this weird relationship where she's always trying to punch him in the junk and he always thinks it's hilarious. I don't get it, but hey, my girl is perfecting her kick-ass self-defense moves on someone other than me, so I've got no complaints. "Have you taken her to a bar yet? She'd be a total babe magnet."

I roll my eyes and consider messing with his hair again. "I'm not using my kid as a pawn to get laid."

"Your loss. When my nephew was a baby, I would get numbers from the hottest chicks anywhere I went. It was awesome."

"Did you tell them he was your nephew, or did you pretend you were a poor single dad?"

He shrugs and switches legs. "I can't keep someone from making assumptions."

"That's because you're a dick."

"Maybe. But I'm a dick who got some action." He gestures for me to climb onto the table and lie on my back for partner-assisted stretches. Looks like he decided for us.

Stretching my leg up, Joey leans into the back of my knee and pushes, making sure to support my rest of my leg.

We take a solid fifteen to stretch, which is not as long as we should be doing it, but I'm running out of time quickly. In fact, I barely make it through my shower before it's time to head over to the school for pickup.

In my haste to not be late, I barrel right into a woman coming through the front door.

Grabbing her arms to steady her from falling, I apologize profusely. "I'm sorry! I didn't see you. Are you all right?"

Smiling tightly, the blonde isn't thrilled a random stranger practically ran her over. But she's polite anyway. "I'll be fine."

"Are you sure? You aren't hurt?" I don't think she is, but sometimes I don't know my own strength.

This time her smile is a little more genuine. "I'm sure. You sure are in a rush."

Letting go of her arms, I feel like she needs an explanation other than me racing around like an idiot. "I'm the one parent who has a tendency to be late for school pickup. The lady at the front desk gives me a nasty evil glare if she has to call me."

This woman, whose name I still haven't bothered to ask, laughs and I'm struck by how cute she is. She's definitely a few years older than I am, but not by much. There's nothing about her that necessarily stands out in a crowd, but her smile is genuine. This is a woman who likes to laugh and have fun. I always gravitate toward those people, which gives me a fleeting thought: I should have noticed my ex-wife hardly ever smiled for real. Laughing was even rarer unless it was at someone else's expense. Those should have been easy indicators she wasn't the one for me.

"Parker Elementary?" the blonde asks.

"Yeah." I give her a quizzical look. "How did you know?"

"Do *not* mess with Ms. Alexander's routine. She will cut a bitch."

My laugh comes easily, and I find myself hoping this woman is a new member. She's funny. I love it when clients have a sense of humor. Offering her my hand, I introduce myself. "I'm Abel. Trainer here at Weight Expectations and father of Mabel in second grade."

She places her cold hand in mine. "Elliott. Interviewee for the childcare position and mother of Ainsley, also in second grade."

"Ah! Well it's nice to meet you. Fingers crossed I'll see you here later as a fellow employee. And if not here, at Parker Elementary as a fellow parent. Hopefully not in Ms. Alexander's line of sight."

Elliott holds up her gloved hands and crosses her fingers around each other. "Wish me luck. Now run fast."

I salute her goodbye for some unknown reason and pull my beanie low on my head, jogging my way to the school. It's not far, only a few city-blocks away, but by the time I get there, children are spilling out of the building and parents are greeting them with hugs and kisses. Most of the adults are understandably women. Not many stay-at-home dads out there, at least none I've run into. A man can hope, though. Some of these women and their "come hither" looks can get a bit creepy, and I'm used to gym rats hitting on me. They've got nothing on a lonely PTA mom. Or at least the one looking at me right now.

Pretend you don't see her, Abel. Play dead. Well, not dead. But whatever you do, do not look her way!

Of course, that means my eyes glance over, the traitors. Said mom is licking her lips while looking at me like I'm a piece of meat. And there's no way she can convince me there is hot chocolate in her fancy thermos cup. My money is on a hot toddy.

Quickly turning my attention away before she gets any ideas—well, more ideas than she already has—I search the crowd for my kiddo. It takes a minute to realize she's not here. Dammit. That means I have to go inside.

I hustle up the steps, praying to the gods of education that I don't run into Ms. Alexander. The creaky door isn't helping my attempt at being stealth. But it does give Mabel a heads up that I'm here. She's leaning against the brick wall, glaring at me. I assume I'm about to get an earful from Miss Sassy-pants. It's the same look her mother used to give me when I was in trouble.

But I'm not going to think about May now. I've got a child to focus on, and getting us out of the building is high on my priority list.

"Hey kiddo. How was your day?"

Pushing herself off the brick with her foot, she continues with *the stare*. "You're late, Daddy."

"I am not. Look at all these parents who are just now getting their kids." I wave my hand around, gesturing to the two or three remaining moms who are probably only there because they're volunteers.

"Ms. Alexander said she was going to have to call you again if you didn't get here in two minutes, and if it happens again, she'll have to give you a talkin' to."

"A 'talking to,' huh?" I wave up at the woman in question, so she sees its me and not some random stranger stealing my child away. The scowl I get in return sends shivers down my spine. Looking down at Mabel, I have to concede her point. "Okay, I get it. I'll be a little earlier from now on."

Satisfied with my answer, Mabel takes my hand as we leave and begin the walk back.

"Does she always look like that?" I ask once we get to the bottom of the stairs and out of earshot.

"Like she's constimated?"

I struggle to hold back a laugh. "Constipated?"

"That's what I said."

"No, it's not. And don't say that about people. It's not nice."

In her little-girl attempts at skipping through the brown slush that coats the sidewalks, she successfully ignores my reprimand. "Yes, she always looks that way. It's why I don't want her to call you. Because then I have to sit in the chair in her office and look at her looking constimated."

"Stop saying that, Mabel."

She sighs and I swear she rolls her eyes; but ever my sassy girl, she turns her head slightly so I don't know for sure.

"What are we doing today, Daddy? Are we going to the gym?" Turning to face me as we walk, she shifts into a sideways gallop. It's pretty impressive considering I haven't slowed down to accommodate her at all.

Chuckling, I'm glad I'm about to make up for being later than she wanted at pickup. "We're just going to swing by to get our stuff."

"Yay!" she yells and jumps up and down.

"Just to get our stuff, Mabel. Don't even think about pulling out the boxing gloves." She pouts her bottom lip as far as it will go, a true act of attempted manipulation. "I'm serious, Mabel. I have stuff to do at home, and you have homework."

She groans in disappointment before sighing again. "Fiiiine. Is Joey going to be there at least?"

"He's always there."

"True dat."

What did she say?

I don't ask, shaking my head in amusement. I've always loved my daughter. She is the absolute joy of my life. But this age is my favorite so far. She's funny and witty, and it's fun watching her learn about the world around her.

Plus, I'm off diaper duty. Thank the Lord.

Skipping ahead of me, Mabel uses her body weight to brace her feet to the ground and pulls on the door of the gym. It only moves an inch or two before I grab it above her head and help her open in the rest of the way, eliciting yet another glare. I really need to crack down on that somehow.

"Hi, Mabel!"

"Hi, Natalie!" she responds with a wave to the front desk receptionist before racing away, probably to spar with Joey.

"How are you, Abel?" Natalie gives me that same creepy look the PTA mom gives me. It unnerves me, but since we work opposite shifts, I'm less inclined to avoid her at all costs.

"I'm good. Thanks for asking." Then, I follow behind my daughter, ready to grab all our stuff and get the hell out of my workplace.

My more important job is just beginning for the day.

CHAPTER FOUR

ELLIOTT

"What makes you want to work at Weight Expectations?" The general manager and new owner of this facility gives me an intimidating look over the rim of her black glasses. "Seems to me you're a bit overqualified for this position."

Keely Maze is a tiny woman, barely reaching five feet, but with her sharp pixie cut, severe makeup, and bulging biceps that flex naturally as she holds my résumé, there is no doubt in my mind she could kick my booty.

I also don't think she'd appreciate me telling her the truth: after two years of searching, I realized I need to stop focusing on a job in my field and start looking at family-friendly positions. They are few and far between and don't come close to paying what a family needs to survive. But at this point, I'm getting desperate to get out of my mother's house. Maybe if I save up enough money—and possibly hit the lottery—I can slowly crawl out of this hole we seem to be stuck in.

Then again, Keely also gives the vibe she doesn't like things sugar-coated.

Steeling myself as I weigh my choices, I give in to the full truth. What do I have to lose at this point?

"Full transparency, I need a job I can work around my daughter's schedule. I didn't plan to be a single mom, but it's what life threw at me, and I'm making the best of it." Keely hasn't moved a muscle. I take that as a good sign and continue. "Yes, I have a degree in social work, but I also have different priorities now. My degree may make it seem like I'm overqualified, but what it really says is I'm hard working, reliable, and can make quick decisions without waiting for someone else to solve problems. And it means I'm empathetic, which you need when working with children."

That elicits a quirked eyebrow. I choose to believe it's a positive reaction.

"My goal isn't to come in and step on anyone's toes, or even necessarily to ladder-climb. I want this to be mutually beneficial— you have a quality employee and I can provide for my child."

Done with my speech, I slowly breathe out the rest of the air in my lungs, hoping she doesn't notice my nerves. Considering her eyes have never left mine, I doubt I'm successful.

Dropping my résumé on her desk, Keely leans back in her chair and taps her pen on the desk a few times, still staring at me. It's unnerving, but I refuse to back down. I've put it all out there. She either accepts it or she doesn't.

I really hope she does though.

Finally, she stops tapping. "Do you know how many women I know in your position right now? Degreed women who have been left high and dry with children by a man who just leaves to live his life?"

I'm not sure where she's going with this, but she sounds deeply offended by the plight of so many women.

"The difference in the ones who make it and the ones who don't," she continues, "is how they handle it." Leaning forward, she clasps her hands together and rests her arms on the desk. "Your answer impresses me, Elliott. And now that I've taken over at this facility, I want to build an impressive team. One that moms rave about when this gym comes up on social media. Is that you?"

Oddly, I understand exactly what she's talking about. I'm in a social media group or two, and moms can be vicious if they don't like something.

"The only thing I can guarantee you is my absolute best. I tend to be social, so hopefully that will make the parents comfortable leaving their children with me. And I'm pretty even-tempered, so I'll be fine with the kids."

She cocks her head. "What if one of the kids is a little brat? How are going to handle that?"

"My kid *is* the brat. I haven't beaten her yet."

I'm not positive, but I think Keely looks amused by my candor.

"What if the parent thinks you're the problem?"

I can't help it. I laugh. Loudly. Keely looks a bit taken aback, so I quickly try to control my emotions. "I'm sorry," I say, wiping the tears under my eyes. "It's just, we've lived with my mother for the last three years and she has no problem telling me what a bad mom I am because of Ainsley's behavior. I'm so good at biting my tongue, it's a wonder I can still eat an ice cream cone."

Keely's mouth twists to the side as she tries to suppress a smile. I'm almost embarrassed I've divulged that part of my life in an interview, but really, if I can live with my mother and my child and remain standing, there is nothing the people at this facility can throw my way.

In my mother's defense, I recognize she has extremely high anxiety and is a verbal processor like I am. Which means she can't let go of stress until she says out loud whatever is bothering her. Unfortunately, "out loud" means I always hear it, and over the years, I concluded I am a disappointment most of the time. I don't want Ainsley to feel the same way. I want her to grow up knowing she can talk to me about anything. I want her to always feel good about herself and know she's important. I want her to want to be friends with me as an adult.

So, I watch my tone and give her lots of space to learn things as a child, which my mother doesn't seem to understand. Regardless, though, the difference of opinion has apparently given me skills I can utilize here, so I guess it's not a total bad thing.

Keely quickly and pointedly places her hands on the desk and pushes to a standing position. "Well, let's go meet the rest of the childcare staff and see what you think."

I scramble to my feet and follow her out the door. For as short as her legs are, she's quick. I bet those calf muscles are from running. I wouldn't be surprised if she ran in those sky-high heels, as graceful as she is in them.

Hmm. I wonder if a gym membership is one of the perks of this job.

I also wonder why I care, because I am certainly not going to use it. I'll be one of those people who has it "just in case." In case of what, I don't know.

Pulling open one of the glass doors, Keely swiftly enters a large room filled with toys and children. So. Many. Children.

"As you can see, this is our prime time for childcare," she explains loudly, trying to be heard over the roar of screaming children. "The after-school crowd is just getting here, which is why we need additional staff in the afternoons."

The area we're in is set up like a foyer with cubbies for shoes lining the walls. Keely opens a half door for us to step into the chaos. That actually might be downplaying what's going on. Madness is more like it.

At first glance, I see three or four workers, each holding at least one baby, one of them with a crying toddler hanging on her as well. Someone else is around the corner in a gym space where some older kids are playing basketball. A little playhouse has so many kids stuffed inside that it looks like a clown car. And more older kids are racing through the room, playing what appears to be a version of tag. Only it's a tackle version.

But what's most noticeable is the noise. So. Much. Noise. The squealing, the yelling, the laughing... most of it is happy noise, but there's no way to tell. It's not organized chaos, it's just chaos. And from the looks on the workers' faces, they're drowning.

On instinct, I do what I would normally do in this situation, regardless if I'm stepping over a line or not. I put my fingers in my mouth and blow.

The shriek of my whistle is loud and an older boy, who happens to be running by me at the time, is knocked off balance by the sound.

Throwing his hand over his ear as he falls, he cries out. I ignore him. If I know anything about boys his age, they fall over all the time. It comes with growing up.

Besides that one small mishap, the result is exactly what I was hoping for—silence. Even the crying toddler looks stunned.

Once I have everyone's attention, I have to decide what to do with it. Welp, I've come this far. I might as well keep going.

"If you are in elementary school, raise your hand," I say in my booming mom-voice. It's not angry, it just reverberates. My theater teachers all through school said I was a natural for the stage because my voice projects. I say it just comes in handy for these kinds of situations.

A dozen hands around the room go up, and more come around the corner from the gym. All of them are sweaty and probably smell a bit, but it's time to put them to work getting everything under control.

"Can you all please come sit down in front of me?"

They look at each other and the adults they already know before doing as they're told. I'm surprised Keely hasn't stopped me yet, but I suspect she was hoping to get things under control in here and is waiting to see where I'm going with all this.

Once all the children are seated, I continue. "I know you guys just got out of school and want to play, but we need to do it in a way that's safe for everyone. Do you see all the babies around here?" The kids look around and many of them seem surprised when they notice all the littles in the room. It's as if they never paid attention before. "They're much smaller than you. If you run by you could knock them over. Or if there are too many of you in the playhouse, they could get squished. But I have an idea on how we can have fun *and* stay safe. Are you guys interested?"

Everyone nods except the boy I accidentally deafened. He's still got his finger in his ear, a sour look on his face. "Can I go play basketball?"

"How many of you want to play basketball in the other room?"

A few hands go up and I dismiss them, reminding them to walk to their destination until they are safely away from the other kids. The woman in who was with them in that room before smiles and nods at me in appreciation before returning to her station.

Turning back to the kids, I continue. "How many of you love babies?"

"I love babies," a dark haired, freckle-faced girl says. "My baby sister is here."

"Where is she?"

The girl points to one of the babies that is being held by the woman who also has the toddler attached to her. I walk over and gesture to the infant. She hands the adorable tot to me, and I immediately put her in an Exersaucer. "I bet your baby sister misses you, so come play with her. I bet she likes Peek-A-Boo, or even better, dancing." The girl immediately runs over to her sister, giving her a big kiss on the forehead and starts singing to her. The baby is obviously delighted because she begins jumping up and down. The worker smiles and stretches her arms. Poor woman was probably starting to cramp in the joints.

One by one, I give each school-aged child a "job," and within minutes, everyone is playing happily. Even the crying toddler is laughing while knocking over the tower that is continually being rebuilt by two boys just to be destroyed again and again.

"I don't know who you are," a tall, dark-haired woman says to me, "but I sure hope you're applying for the afternoon manager position."

My eyes widen. "Manager! I don't think I'm qualified for that. I was just hoping to help out."

"Oh no," the woman says and looks at Keely. "You may as well throw away the other résumés. I think we've found her." She then turns back to me and puts out her hand. "I'm Dinah. I'm the director of the childcare center here and manage the mornings. Our afternoon manager left a few weeks ago to direct a different facility. We were considering hiring within the company, but after that display, I think we're shifting things around a bit."

This is concerning to me. "No, no, no." I hold up my hands and back up a step. "I don't want to make anyone mad. Everyone here has seniority, and I'm sure they want the job too."

"That's not the way it works," Keely chimes in. "To avoid that kind of animosity, any manager is usually promoted from a different facility, unless we find someone from outside. We promote within the company, but not in-house. So, the job is yours if you want it."

My jaw drops. "Really?"

Keely and Dinah look at each other and nod. "Really. Come on," Keely says. "Let's go back to my office and go over the logistics of it."

I nod, still stunned by this turn of event. I came in today to interview for a childcare worker position, and I'm walking out the new afternoon childcare manager.

I may be out of my mother's house sooner than I thought.

CHAPTER FIVE

ABEL

A dulting sucks sometimes. For the most part, I don't mind the responsibility that goes along with the freedom. But some days, I wish I didn't have to be the decision-maker in the family. It would be nice if I could pass the buck to someone else every once in a while and relieve some of the pressure. But hey, at least I wasn't late for school pick up again today. Small victories, right?

"Hey Mabel," I call to my daughter as she skips ahead of me on our trek to the gym post-school once again, the pom-pom on the top of her hat bouncing along with her. "Are you old enough to pull your own weight around here yet?"

She stops in her tracks and turns around, narrowing her eyes at me like she doesn't trust my intensions. Smart girl.

"Does that mean I have to get a job?"

"Yep."

She purses her lips and thinks for a second. "Do I get to make the rules?"

I laugh. I should have known there wouldn't be a yes or no answer from my daughter. Always a motive with that one. "Depends on what the rules are."

She begins ticking off her fingers. "No school ever again. No baths unless I want one. I get to kickbox every day." I knew that one was coming, but she's not done. "And we have to have ice cream for breakfast. No vegetable omelets."

I find myself considering her demands. They are small prices to pay for not dealing with my latest crisis…

The mortgage.

When May and I bought our small townhouse, we were in a different financial place. Providing for a family with two incomes is very different than doing it with only one. Now that I think about it, it was actually more like one and a half. May was pretty successful selling some high-end brand of makeup from home, but she didn't put a whole lot of effort into the business side. She's a beautiful woman and really knew how to contour, so of course people wanted to know her secret. She was stopped on the street so often I eventually convinced her to create her own YouTube channel, and she ended up with a few advertisers.

It's also how she was "discovered" by her current boyfriend-slash-manager-slash-homewrecker.

Regardless, that additional income is how we qualified for the loan. Money was still tight, sure, but we could breathe and even put a little away in savings.

Then May left, the gym burned down, the clientele I had built was dispersed all over town and it was the perfect combination of events to throw me into a downward financial spiral. I try not to think about it too much, but every time I transfer money out of my saving account to pay my mortgage, I'm reminded how little we have left.

Something has to give. And soon.

Unfortunately, I don't think Mabel's up to the challenge of figuring it out quite yet.

"Sorry, Squirt." I ruffle her hair as I catch up to her. "If you don't go to school, I go to jail, so I guess the job isn't yours quite yet."

She bats my hand away and murmurs, "Your loss," before turning around and running the last few paces to the entrance.

I grab the door to help her pull it open and receive a dirty look from Mabel in return. Apparently, chivalry means nothing to an eight-year-old girl who is determined to do it all on her own.

"Hey Mabel," I say before she runs off, "I need to talk to a few people. Let's go to the daycare before we go find Joey, okay?"

She throws her head back and huffs in disappointment but complies. I'm not sure when second graders became melodramatic, but my daughter has it down pat.

"Is everything okay, Abel?" I look up to see Natalie, concern written all over her face. Not sure why she thinks anything is wrong, but with how much she stares my direction, I suppose it's not unreasonable to assume she knows all my tells. That's not necessarily a good thing, and probably something I need to explore at a later date, but right now she might actually be useful to my plight.

"Hey Natalie, do you have a boyfriend?"

She sucks in a breath, and before I even realize what a poor choice of words I used, she's shaking her head vehemently. "No! I'm single and ready to mingle. Why? Do you have a girlfriend?"

I know I'm about to disappoint her, but I ignore the question just in case. "I'm actually wondering if you know any single men who might need a roommate. I've got an empty bedroom, and I thought it might help me off-set my mortgage."

"Oh." Just as I suspect, she deflates right before my eyes. "I thought... never mind," she says with a shake of her head.

Sorry, Natalie, I think to myself. *I'm sure you're lovely, but no.*

"Anyway," she continues, looking back up at me, total indifference suddenly written on her face. That was a quick about-face. "I have a few guy friends. I'll ask around. If I get a chance."

I knock on the counter once and nod. "Thanks. I really appreciate it. Come on, Mabel. Let's go talk to Dinah. See ya."

Natalie ignores me as Mabel grabs my hand. "I think she wants to be your girlfriend, Daddy."

I was hoping my daughter had missed that, but I shouldn't be terribly surprised by her powers of observation.

"You saw that, huh?"

She crinkles her nose. "I tried really hard not to."

Shaking my head in amusement, we walk into the childcare center. This time, I let her open the door. Not only is it lighter, but she's not battling the wind either. Before I can make it through the doorway, she's off into the play area, running around like a loon with the others.

I don't know how anyone works in here. I would go bonkers. I'm pretty sure Dinah is halfway there already.

Speaking of... "Hey Abel." I find her sitting behind the check-in desk, probably still printing out stickers to put on kids' backs. "Is Mabel gonna stay a while?"

"Nah. Just long enough for me to talk to you, actually."

Her expression changes as she shifts her attention from the computer to me. "That doesn't sound good. What's up?"

Why can everyone tell something's on my mind? Is my face really that expressive? No one has ever told me that before, so it's a little disconcerting. But I don't want to think about it now.

Instead, I lean against the desk. "You have a pulse on most of the members here."

Her shoulders move in a tiny shrug. "Yeah, I guess."

"Do you happen to know of a guy looking for a roommate, er housemate? You know what I mean. Maybe someone wanting to rent a room?"

She nods in understanding of my latest dilemma. "Looking to cut down on your bills?"

"Something like that."

"That's a good idea. I know a lot of single people who are looking to find a nicer place for less money than Chicago rent can offer."

Suddenly, I feel more hopeful than I did five minutes ago. "You do?"

"Yeah. I mean, I don't know anyone off the top of my head right now, but I talk to dozens of parents every day. I can put some feelers out. Have you looked online at any ads?"

I blow out a breath. This is where it gets sticky. "I haven't. I have a kid, ya know? I don't want to pick some random person. I know I probably won't know whoever moves in, but I feel like the odds are better I'll get a decent tenant if I start with people we know."

"Why are you looking for a man then?"

I turn and look at her quizzically. "What do you mean?"

"I'm about to sound really offensive," she starts, putting her hands up and me on alert. "But you're mostly concerned about having someone that isn't weird around Mabel, right?"

"Yeah."

"Why not look for a female tenant? Not all men are pervs, but statistically you have better odds with a woman."

I open my mouth to respond, but the more I think about it, the more it makes sense. I have nothing against men. Hell, I'm a guy. And if it was Joey moving in, I'd have no problem with it. But it won't be Joey, so maybe I would have a problem. "I guess when I was thinking about someone moving in, it wasn't computing that this person would be living with my daughter too."

"It's from working in the mornings now. Your brain doesn't work in the afternoons anymore," Dinah teases.

"Tell me about it."

"Listen—hang on. Hey!" she yells across the room at some boys who have decided to take up wrestling in the middle of the room. "You guys get off each other. Miss Elliott is on the way, and she'll make you do the boring jobs."

Jobs? Since when do we have child labor around here?

The boys ignore her but have apparently finished up their WWE match anyway and are lying on their backs, arms spread wide, breathing heavily.

"Those boys are the worst," Dinah admits to me quietly. "They're close to aging out of the room, and I can't wait until their parents have to watch them instead of me."

I chuckle. "That bad, huh?"

"You have no idea. Everyone in Chicago hates winter because of how cold it is, right?" I nod. "I love it because it's not summer break when my work life goes to hell. One of these days, they're going to approve my time off request before realizing its during spring break week. I'm getting too old for this."

I laugh and rub my face while she speaks. She's not wrong. Even Mabel comes home bitching about the chaos in here during the summer. It's why she usually stayed home with May.

Shit. I have to figure out what I'm going to do with her this summer now that May is gone. More adulting. Mabel needs to hurry up and wear the pants in this family.

"Anyway, back to your issue."

"I'm glad my problems are giving you a reprieve from your own."

"And I appreciate it tremendously. Anyway," she continues, "what about a woman? How were you going to do the living arrangements?"

I shrug. "I hadn't put much thought into it, but I assumed I'd give up the master bedroom. I can charge a little extra for them having an en suite, and it's down the hall from the other two rooms. Keeps Mabel and me closer together."

Dinah is nodding rapidly now, a smirk on her face. I've seen this look before. I think she might actually have a solution to my problem.

"I have an idea." Yep. Once again, Dinah may have come through for me. I shouldn't be surprised. She's always been the most reliable person I know. "But I need to pitch it to the other person first. Are you sticking around for a while?"

"I wasn't planning on it, but I can go over some of my notes for tomorrow if I need to."

Once again, she nods vigorously, only this time she's splitting her focus between me and the two brats who are at it again. "Hey!" she yells and then thinks better of it. "You know what? I don't care. Let them get hurt. Natural consequences and all that." Turning her focus back to me, she says, "Come back in about thirty minutes. Leave Mabel. She'll be fine. Let me see if I can get you the information you need."

Smiling wide at this turn of events, I can't help but feel some relief. "Thanks, Dinah. And if you need a temporary bouncer, let me know."

"Pffft. I'm not putting you in the middle of those two. I like you too much."

Laughing, I turn to leave when I'm practically run over by another child. What is the deal around here? Does everyone get sugared up before coming to play?

"Ainsley! Oh my gosh, I'm sorry." A blonde woman sees me and stops walking. She begins to smile and that's when I recognize her. "Abel, the trainer, right?"

"Elliott, the interviewee." I watch as a girl I assume is her daughter runs off to play, dropping her coat in the middle of the floor. Turning back, I add, "Looks like the interview went well, after all."

"Much better than I'd expected." Elliot makes quick work of pulling off her gloves and coat to put in the small closet and grabs the child's coat when Dinah hands it to her. "Although, I can't say things are totally secure yet since Ainsley's teacher seems to want to talk to me every afternoon. I'm sorry, Dinah," she calls out.

Dinah replies, "No problem. I gotcha covered."

"At least you weren't getting a talking-to by Ms. Alexander."

Elliott laughs and I notice the tiniest creases around her eyes when she does. "This is true. Anyway, it's good to see you. I need to get this room under control."

She rushes off and Dinah catches my eye. "Half an hour," she mouths, and I nod in response.

I have no idea what Dinah has up her sleeve, but I sure as hell hope she has a solution I can work with.

CHAPTER SIX

ELLIOTT

I don't know how things get out of control so fast. I started working in the childcare center a couple of days ago and things have been running smoothly. When I arrive, everything is calm, and all the kids are playing happily. Then I take a quick break to go pick up Ainsley from school.

I shouldn't be surprised by what I return to. Elementary schoolers have so much pent-up energy already, and when you add winter on top of it, which means no outdoor recess, it's no wonder they're bonkers by the time they get to our facility after school.

Fortunately, my mom-whistle seems to be working a lot like Pavlov's bell—whenever the kids hear it, they come running and sit down in front of me. Even the toddlers have gotten in on the action, because of course whatever the big kids are doing, they want to do, too. Fine with me. It makes it easier to pair up kids with activities.

"Jayden, I know you enjoy reading, and don't you have reading log minutes you have to do for school?"

The second grader nods his head, wide-eyed as he listens. I already know him from volunteering in Ainsley's classroom, so he's one of my more reliable "helpers."

"You know who else likes to read?" He shakes his head. "Rose-

41

mary," I say, gesturing to the dark-haired toddler doing her best to sit crisscross applesauce next to him. "I bet you could let her pick out some books for you to read to her, and when your mom gets here, I'll let her know you finished your reading homework already."

"Okay. Come on, Rosemary." He stands up and then does his best to help her stand as well. "Let's go pick some books, okay? Okay?" he says in his sweetest baby voice, getting right in her face.

She's not concerned, though. Once he has her by the hand, they toddle away to the small corner set up with a few books and pillows for reading.

One by one, I get all the children settled so the adults can finally get back to supervising instead of being referees.

"I love watching you do that."

I giggle at Dinah's comment and turn to respond. "Why?"

"It's like you're a magician. How'd you know he would be willing to read to a toddler?"

"Easy. He wears a Fortnite shirt every time I see him. I'm going off the assumption he won't get any game time until he's done with his homework. We just gave him an extra twenty minutes to build something."

"Is that what they do in Fortnite? Build things?"

"No idea." I grab a wayward shoe someone walked off without and place it on the counter. "Ainsley would rather watch dance videos on YouTube than any form of gaming. I'm gonna walk the room and make sure everyone is still entertained. I'll be back."

I leave her to meander around the two rooms, observing not only the kids but our staff as well. We have a wide age range of workers. Every child's needs are different, and it's nice that we have a variety of staff members to meet those needs, from a grandma whose grand-children live several hours away to a college student working on her child development degree. We even have a part-time male worker who always gets stuck playing basketball with the boys. He loves it though. And it's great for the kids to have a positive male role model. Lord knows even my own child needs to see that.

Everyone appears to be content, happily engaged in whatever

assigned activity I gave them. A few have decided to do something different, but as long as they're burning energy safely, I'm a happy camper. The only kiddo having issues is a fussy baby who's probably hungry, but she is only seconds away from getting a bottle.

So far, I like it here. It's only been a couple of days, and since I'm still technically in training, Dinah is still overseeing me. All that means is she sits at the desk ready to jump in if I need help. There's not much to get stuck on though, except where to find certain supplies and how to fill out particular forms. She's shown me that more than anything as she takes advantage of the overtime to finish all her director duties.

The job itself isn't hard, and I really enjoy the family atmosphere. Moms talk to other moms as they make playdates, staff interact with toddlers they've helped raise from newborns, and Dinah gets updates regarding kids who aged out of the childcare center after attending for years. It's nice to know everyone cares about each other so much. As much as I'd liked my former career, I feel like I must have done something right for the heavens to shine down on me the way they did with this job.

"Everything still running smoothly?" Dinah keeps jotting down notes on her paperwork and doesn't look up at me when I finally stroll back her direction.

I lean against the counter, pleased to be able to answer positively. "Yep. I think we're officially on the downward slope of the madness for the day. Can I ask you a question?"

"Sure."

"What do you think of me adding some 'stations' to the room."

This makes her finally look up. "What kinds of stations?"

"Well, we already have the reading corner and obviously the TV area for cartoons. What if we brought in a small table for the kiddos who want to get their homework done before they get home?"

"You think any of these kids would want to do that?"

I shrug because I honestly don't know for sure. "It's worth a shot. Jayden seemed all too happy to get his reading done. If it doesn't work, we can always take it out."

Dinah leans back and rocks the office chair back and forth. "Fine with me. But I'm making a hard rule—no glitter. I don't care what projects the kids have, do not bring glitter in this room."

I laugh at her insistence, mostly because I get where she's coming from. "Agreed. I am not vacuuming satan's decorations off this floor."

"HA! Satan's decorations. I like that," she says with a smile. "Hey, can I ask you a personal question?"

Weird topic change, but when you're working with the unpredictability of kids, you don't really have the luxury of pussyfooting around topics, I suppose. "I guess it depends on how personal, but sure."

"You're looking to move, right?"

I raise my eyebrows in question. I know I've never mentioned finding a new place to live to Dinah. In fact, the only one who might even have a suspicion about it would be Keely, and that's only because living with my mother came up in the conversation.

"Yeah, Keely told me," Dinah admits before I can answer. She clasps her hands behind her head as she relaxes into this conversation. I'm glad one of us is. "The boss bounces a lot of ideas off me. I think it's because I'm the oldest one here. She thinks I'm trustworthy."

"Are you?"

"No complaint so far. I wouldn't have asked except I might know of a situation that could work for you."

Keely is forgiven.

"You have my attention." I look around the room, making a quick sweep with my eyes to make sure things are still under control while this hopefully-life-changing conversation happens.

"You've met Abel, right?"

"Briefly. Does he own a property or something?"

"Kind of."

Something about her tone makes me take notice, but I'm too busy making sure our two problem kids aren't about to engage in a smackdown for it register.

"He's hoping to rent out his master en suite to help pay the mortgage."

My eyes whip over, looking at her in disbelief. "You want me to move in with him?"

Her head bobbles back and forth briefly. "I guess that's one way of looking at it."

"What other way is there of looking at it? He'll live there, and I'll live there. I'll be cohabitating with a man I've only met in passing twice."

"You won't be living in the same room as him," she says with a laugh. "He'll be down the hall. Besides, he's not just a guy. He's also a single dad with an eight-year-old daughter who goes to the same school as your daughter."

I open my mouth to argue again, but she's not wrong.

"I know it seems a bit unconventional to us old folks, but if Abel was a woman—Hey!" she yells, interrupting herself. "Cooper! Ryder! I've got my eye on you two." She points to her eyes and back at them, the threat written all over her face before continuing her case for my living arrangement. "What was I saying? Oh yeah. If Abel was a woman, you'd be thinking what a great idea this was. Not only would you have a nice place to live that didn't cost you an arm and a leg, but there's also a live-in playmate for Ainsley."

I blink a few times as I process what she's saying. The idea of moving my daughter and myself into a strange man's home is a little weird. But the circumstances make it a little less odd. Don't they?

"Speak of the devil…" I hear Dinah say through the haze of my thoughts. Looking up, I realize Abel has walked in the room.

"Ladies. How's Mabel doing?" He gestures with his chin to the middle of the room where his daughter and my daughter are spotting each other on gymnastics moves. What's that saying about the teacher's kid always being the biggest troublemaker? The proof is doing a cartwheel right next to a baby.

"Ainsley. Come here please."

Little Mary Lou Retton and her sidekick grab hands and run over to me. As soon as Mabel sees her dad, she gasps and clings to Ainsley.

"It's not time to go yet, is it Daddy? I don't want to leave my best friend."

As Ainsley puts together what Mabel is saying, she holds on tighter as well. The two of them look like monkeys hanging on to each other, and they're squeezing so tight their ponytails are about to get tangled together.

"Not quite yet, Squirt."

"Yay!" the girls begin yelling and jumping up and down.

Holding my hands up, I try to get them to calm down. "Okay, okay girls, let's not get out of control again."

They stop with the jumping, but the smiles on their faces aren't going away anytime soon. It's amazing how quickly kids can have a new best friend. I hope they don't catch wind of Dinah's idea or there may be attempted manipulation disguised as tantrums.

"Ainsley." She finally looks up at me. "We're not supposed to do gymnastics here, remember? The babies can get hurt."

Her face falls as the lightbulb turns on and she remembers that whole safety issue I keep having to drill into all their heads. "Yes, ma'am," she says sheepishly, and Mabel rubs her back in support.

Oh boy. If these two end up living together, I can already imagine how they'll work together to take me down.

"You know what would be fun to do?" Both girls turn their attention to me, big eyes waiting for me to make some magnificent statement. "I think you should teach some of the little kids how to dance."

Their faces light up and I can practically see the ideas running through their brains. I need to prepare myself. I'm sure at some point they'll ask for poster board so they can have sign-up sheets and charge by the hour.

"What kind of dance do you want me to teach, Mama? Hip Hop or Contemporary?"

"Surprise me," I say, and they race off to coordinate their new class.

Abel is watching the girls with rapt attention. He has that same look of parental pride we all have when we see our kids' faces light up. "Where does yours take dance?"

"She doesn't." I sigh. As much as she would love it, it's not in the budget right now. I don't tell him that, of course. Nor do I tell him I'm hoping after we move, I can find it in our monthly expenses to get her started. "She trains at this great online place called YouTube."

He chuckles, eyes still on the girls. "You can find some great tips there. I've been known to utilize them a time or two to make sure I've got fresh ideas for my clients."

"That actually makes me feel like a way better mom. So, thanks."

"See? You guys get along already," Dinah interjects. "This is perfect."

I drop my chin to my chest and shake my head slowly. She's pushing this issue hard. I just wish I understood her intentions. Is it because she's a fixer? Or does she think there could be something more here? I don't understand her motivation, but it's too late to stop her now.

She stands up and waves her hands animatedly. "Abel, Elliott is trying to find a new place to live. I'm gonna check on the kids now."

Well done, Dinah. That wasn't obvious at all.

Feeling stupid for being embarrassed by all this, I look up at Abel who seems completely unaffected. It's almost like he knew this was coming, but there's no way. I've worked here for three days and have only spoken to him a couple of times. Unless he has a weird psychic ability, he's probably just better at hiding his shock than I am.

"Dinah said she knew a potential roommate, but I didn't realize it was you."

Or maybe Dinah isn't as trustworthy as Keely thinks.

But there's no reason to split hairs about it now. I don't think Abel has what I'm looking for, but it never hurts to get the information.

"She seems convinced it's a good idea for both of us."

Abel chuckles at my assessment. "I've learned Dinah is usually not wrong. Unless she's trying to sort her own business out, of course."

"Of course," I agree. "I have the same problem."

"Don't we all? That's part of why I asked her to put some feelers out. You weren't here for the fire, but I'm sure you read about it, right?"

I nod, because who didn't? It was all over the news when it happened. It's not everyday people have to be evacuated from the locker rooms because exercise equipment is on fire.

"I lost a lot of clientele, so money is getting really tight and I'm trying to find a way to offset my mortgage a bit. I figured a room-mate, er housemate, might take some of the pressure off. And it's a three-bedroom, two-bath house for Mabel and me. We don't need all those bedrooms."

"But you know I don't come alone, right? You wouldn't be taking on just me. You'd also have..." We look over and see Ainsley incorporating some gymnastics into her dance moves. The other kids have quit trying because they can't keep up. "Tom Holland chan-neling Rihanna over there coming with me."

Abel doesn't answer. Instead, he bursts out laughing. "I knew I saw those moves somewhere. Man, that was the best LipSync episode ever."

"I only saw that part when it went viral, but obviously my daughter found it as well. And memorized it, from the looks of it."

"Good thing I have an unfinished basement I use as Mabel's playroom. She'll have a ton of room to practice all her dance moves." I raise an eyebrow at him and his assumption I'm interested in what he has to offer at all. "Come over and look at the house. This may not be the right fit for either of us, but we won't know until we can walk through and talk about the layout and expectations, right?"

I look at him while I process my thoughts. He doesn't strike me as a creeper, and Dinah has worked with him for a long time. I don't think she'd recommend this kind of thing if she thought she was putting me or my child in harm's way.

And he does have his own daughter. Our kids go to the same

school. We work at the same company. Maybe this could be a good thing. If we got really lucky, maybe we could even help each other out a bit.

No matter what I do, I can't be sure I'm making the right decision if I don't at least go look at the place.

Decision made, I nod my head, eliciting a smile from him. "Yeah. Yeah, you're right. When do you want me to come and see it?"

Behind me, I hear Dinah burst out with "Yes!" but I ignore her. This might not work out, but either way, something tells me things are finally looking up.

CHAPTER SEVEN

ABEL

"How many square feet is it?"

Elliott looks around at the crown molding and seems impressed by the canned lighting. I've put a little bit of work into the house—fresh paint, updated tiles, new mirrors in the bathrooms. All of that stopped when May left and I needed to save every penny for bills, but I'm still proud of what I've done with the place. This is the first home I've ever owned, and I want us to live here for a long, long time, so it's all been a labor of love.

"A little over than fifteen hundred for the living areas."

Elliott's eyebrows lift. "That's it? It feels much bigger."

Her comment makes me smile. "It's the floorplan. Whoever designed it really knew how to use the space." Happy shrieks come floating up from the stairs. "It also helps that there's a basement. I'm sure it would feel smaller if Mabel was kickboxing in the living room."

"No doubt."

We wander in the direction of the large, open living room. Elliott is still assessing. I only had a few hours to get this place clean before she and Ainsley came over. We tossed around waiting until the weekend, but I really want to get someone moved in before I have to make my next mortgage payment. And I get the feeling Elliott wants to get out of her current location sooner rather than later. So, we decided to get together as soon as she got off work tonight.

The girls, who would normally be heading for bath time right now, have made it clear they have no problem with this change of plans. Playing in the basement is the eight-year-old version of going to a club in college, I suppose. As long as they keep any strobe lights and dubstep to a minimum, I don't mind indulging them this one time.

Besides, it gives me time to assess Elliott in more than just the physical sense. Sure, I've noticed she's beautiful. With her shoulder length blonde hair, brown eyes, and full ass, I'm not the only one, I'm sure. It'll be interesting to see if living with her will lead to me having fantasies about her, or if real life will squelch any physical desires I might have. But that's not what I need to be thinking about right now. Tonight I need to focus on whether or not this match up will work.

"You're okay with people moving in and invading your living area and your kitchen? It doesn't feel weird to you?"

I'm not really sure how to answer her question, because it does feel kind of strange. But under the circumstances, I can't really take that into consideration when making these decisions. "A little. But the way I see it, you and I work opposite shifts. We'll overlap for a couple of hours at night, and on weekends, but that's about it. The biggest thing I have to remember is not to sleep naked anymore."

Her jaw drops open, which makes me laugh. That's the reaction I was going for.

"I'm kidding, Elliott. We all wear pajamas in this house. In fact, that probably should be rule number one."

She relaxes a little now that she knows I'm kidding. I may have to go for shock value statements again, though. Her reactions are pretty humorous.

"Speaking of, have you thought about how the sleeping arrangements would work? Who lives in which room?"

I gesture for her to follow me up the front stairs to the second level where all three bedrooms and both bathrooms are, explaining my thoughts as we go.

"Right now, I'm in the master, but I plan on moving into the bedroom across the hall from Mabel's regardless. Those two bedrooms are down this way," I gesture to the right as I step into the hall. "There's a full bath she and I would share right here. It sort of separates these rooms from the master area. Gives it a bit of privacy." Turning toward my current bedroom, I lead her into the large room. "Pardon the mess. I was so busy tidying up downstairs, I completely forgot to make my bed."

"Trust me, an unmade bed is the least of my worries right now," she says while waving me off absentmindedly, too focused on looking around the large room and attached bathroom. It's not a huge master. Nothing fancy. But the double sinks come in handy when more than one person is in there getting ready for the day.

When she opens the walk-in closet door, I quickly push my underwear under the bed and pull the blankets up over the pillows. I'm not a slob, but I guess I was in a rush this morning. Somehow, it feels strangely intimate for someone to see my dirty drawers on the floor.

Closing the door behind her, she keeps her hand on the knob. "When I first thought about moving out, I assumed Ainsley and I would be in separate rooms. But this is so big, I don't think I'd really mind bunking with her while we live here."

"If you don't mind me asking, why are you looking to move? I'm not trying to be nosy. I figure if we're talking about living together, well, why?"

A small smile graces her lips and I'm grateful she doesn't appear offended by my interest. "In a nutshell, I need to get away from my mother before our relationship is ruined."

That wasn't the answer I was expecting at all. "That bad, huh?"

She shrugs her shoulder, but I don't miss the fact that she also looks somewhat defeated. Interesting. "It isn't that it's *bad*, per se."

"Famous last words," I joke, but she's not biting.

"I don't think my mom hears herself talk sometimes and doesn't realize how negative she sounds. Which is weird because she's not a negative person, and I know we've invaded her home, but we live such different lives and can't seem to find out how to gel."

I know Elliott has shifted from explaining to venting, but suddenly, I realize what a good conversation this is to have. Running into issues and misunderstanding with her mother is a reminder that we're going to need some rules in place for sure. But we probably also need an open dialogue about respecting each other's differences. I've been known to leave a dirty dish or two in the sink if I'm too tired to get to it. If that's going to be one of her pet peeves, this may not work out.

I opt to bring that part up later, though. No use mentioning my proclivity to leaving oatmeal bowls soaking in the sink. I'm still trying to make a good impression. "How so?"

Elliott leans back against the wall, her hands behind her. She looks comfortable here already. That's a good sign, I think.

"I think there might be a"—she looks up to the ceiling, considering her words. "A generational gap, if you will."

An image of my grandpa sitting on his porch and yelling at kids to get off his lawn runs through my head. The best part is the kid was Mabel and he still sounded like a grumpy old man.

"You mean the whole 'children should be seen and not heard' thing?"

"You *do* know what I'm talking about," Elliott says with a laugh.

Channeling my Pop's voice, I respond with, "Spare the rod, spoil the child."

Elliott keeps laughing. "Ohmygod, yes. I mean, sort of. My mom isn't one for corporal punishment, but she is much more uptight than I am with parenting. Don't get me wrong, I'm all about teaching Ainsley respect and boundaries and how to be kind. But I also don't want her thinking she is only the sum of her mistakes and has to be the picture of perfection at all costs. I want her to have room to make those mistakes, so I can guide her to be better in a way that doesn't create anxiety." I nod because that all sounds reasonable to me. "My mother, on the other hand, raised me to respect my elders and be obedient no matter what. To a degree, I understand and agree. But I also know that style of parenting created so much anxiety in me and my mother never realized. Growing up, trying desperately to be perfect, was a challenge at times, to say the least. I want to do it differently. I want to hear Ainsley's side of the story when there is a conflict, even if there's an adult involved. If something is wrong, I need to know to protect her. But if Ainsley is in the wrong, it gives me a better ability to help her sort through her mistakes so she can do better next time."

"Wow." I'm impressed with how much she's thought through her role as a mom. I'm lucky if I remember to feed and water Mabel. "I can see how those two styles don't mix."

Elliott blows out a breath. "It's hard, that's for sure. But I love my mom and don't want our relationship to suffer forever over a difference in parenting styles, ya know? I'd rather put a little space between us so we can be close again."

"I think that's actually a really solid plan."

"You do?"

"Sure. I could never live with my parents. They're the total opposite of your mom, which drives me bananas. Super lax. No regard for bedtime or healthy eating or even manners." I can't help but chuckle to myself. "It's a wonder I have the ability to get to work on time, let alone get Mabel there."

Elliott bites her bottom lip, holding back a smile, before it pops out from underneath her teeth. "You do understand my dilemma."

"Oh yeah. I would rather live under a bridge than with my parents. They're amazing people and holidays at their place is unbeatable. But trying to raise a small human there? No way in hell."

Just then, said human screams up the stairs. "Daaaaaaaaaad!"

"Yeeeeees?" I yell back.

"We want some juice!"

"Thanks for telling me!"

Mabel goes silent momentarily until she finally realizes her mistake. Or Ainsley tips her off. Either way, she fixes her verbiage. "I meeeean, can we please have some juice?"

"Juice boxes are in the fridge." Looking at Elliott, I say playfully, "See? Can you imagine how bad that would have been if she had fewer boundaries?"

"You probably wouldn't have any juice in the fridge and not even know it."

"Or Gatorade. Or water bottles. Or milk."

We begin the trek downstairs to where the girls are as we continue to chat about our daughters. Logistically, this could work well for both of us, because they're in the same grade at the same school. I don't want to get ahead of myself, but it's nice knowing there are two of us who'll get the same information and alerts about weather delays and field trips.

They've been here for about an hour and it's getting late, but I also don't want Elliott to leave until I know what she thinks about moving here. It's not that I want to pressure her, but I also don't want to waste time I could spend looking for someone else if she's not interested.

"How soon would we be able to move in?"

Well, there's my answer. I guess Elliott is as ready to move forward as I am.

"It's a matter of me moving my stuff and cleaning the room for you. I could probably have it done by Sunday."

She looks shocked. "That soon? I was expecting you to need two weeks' notice or something."

I chuckle through my nose. "It's only one room to move around. Well, two if you count taking the desk in the current spare room down to the basement. But Joey and I can do that in five minutes, if I can keep him focused that long."

She blows out another breath, this time making her bangs flutter. I give her a moment to gather her thoughts, knowing this is a big decision. While she does, I peek in on the girls in the kitchen.

"They okay in there?" Elliott asks quietly behind me.

I shake my head and chuckle, pulling away from my not very hidden hiding spot. "They're happily blowing air into the juice pouches and seeing how fast the juice squirts in their mouths."

"So, they're making a giant mess we're going to have to get them to clean up later."

"Two kids make triple the work, or so I've heard." Sitting down on the chair in the living room, I gesture for her to take a seat. "Listen, Elliott, I know you need to think about this and probably crunch some numbers. For the most part, I feel like we're on the same page about everything, but I don't want there to be any surprises so I'm gonna lay it all on the line, okay?"

She nods for me to continue.

"I'm not looking to be a landlord or go into the business of owning a bunch of rental properties. I just need a roommate quickly. If I can't offset my mortgage somehow, I'm going to lose the house."

She gasps, but I ignore it and continue.

"It's not as bad as that sounds. I'm nowhere close to foreclosure. I'm just running out of savings while I try to rebuild the clientele I lost in the fire. I'm not a clean freak or anything, but I'm also not a slob. My child is ornery but not mean or aggressive. I don't have a criminal background of any sort, unless you count that time in college when I was detained at the airport for an outstanding parking ticket."

Elliott throws her fingers over her face and giggles. As much as I don't want to, I see the humor in it as well.

"Consequences of that lax parenting style."

"I see that," she says with a laugh.

"I guess my point is, I we could maybe help each other out with our living situation. Not to mention, I kind of like that our lives are sort of already intertwined with the school and all. And the girls getting along is a bonus."

"I agree."

"But I also know this is an unconventional solution, so if you want to give it a three-month trial period and then we can reassess, I'm totally fine with that."

I stop talking and hold my breath. I don't think I realized until this exact moment how anxious I am about everything. I'm normally a pretty even-tempered guy, but if Elliott says no, I genuinely don't know what I'm going to do. Selling the house, finding an apartment close to work, and moving before spring weather rolls around doesn't sound feasible. Not to mention how much harder life will be if I can only afford to live farther away from this neighborhood.

To my delight, though, Elliott starts nodding.

"I think once I thought through the 'weirdness,'" she says, using air quotes to make her point, "it all really boils down to the kids. I had roommates in college. There's always a transition period. And if it was just me, it would be a non-issue."

I wouldn't know since I never went to college, so I'll have to take her word for it.

"The reality is, you parent your way. I parent my way," she continues, "but my way is also a collective 'it takes a village' effort. As long as you aren't raising a hand to my kid or talking down to her, I'm never going to flinch if you call her out on bad behavior and make her stop. But be prepared, I'll do the same with Mabel. It's in my nature to take care of all the kids, not just mine."

"I guess you picked the right job, then."

"Who knew my degree would eventually be worthless. I could have saved so much money on student loans." She grins at me, and I have a feeling we're moving in the right direction. Especially since we're putting it all on the table. Having a roommate is hard. But I think most of us can put up with living with another person. The "make or break" is always with the kids. If we can't agree on how things are handled with them, this won't work.

"And what you were saying..." I say, getting us back on track. The louder the girls get, the more I know we're getting close to all hell breaking loose. It's time to wrap this up. "I'm in total agreement on the kids. If I'm making lunch for one, I'm making it for both. If one is doing homework, they both are. I'm not offering to be Ainsley's father or anything. I just refuse to exclude a child from participating in the world around them because I'm not the parent. I find that to be unfair, cruel, and puts them in a really bad position of being on the outside looking in."

Elliott nods slowly. It appears like she's in total agreement.

"Good. I like that. As long as we agree on how the kids will be handled, everything else is cake."

"Caaaaaaaake!" The girls start squealing from the other room and our time is clearly up. They've now hit the state of exhaustion called delirium.

Elliott quirks one eyebrow at me and smirks. "Thank God for the basement."

I guarantee that isn't the last time she will utter those words.

CHAPTER EIGHT

ELLIOTT

When I got divorced, I was determined to be the bigger person. Regardless of the fact that my ex had put me through hell with his emotional games and narcissistic tendencies, he is still Ainsley's father, and for her sake, it's the right thing to do. Plus, I was just glad to be getting out so I could breathe again.

In the process of moving back home, I made the decision to leave most of our housewares and furniture behind. He was moving into an apartment and would need those things when Ainsley stayed at his place. I, on the other hand, was moving in with my mother who already had it all. It would have been more effort to store them than it would to just let them go.

Of course, within a year, he'd moved into his girlfriend's house and gotten rid of it all. And now that I'm going to my own place, part of me wishes I'd at least kept the bath towels. We're going to need some in our new bathroom.

Everything else though? I'm still kind of glad it's gone. With the exception of carrying out three trash bags of paper and junk from under Ainsley's bed, packing two bedrooms and a bathroom hasn't taken long at all. Although in some ways, it feels like it's taken forever. Mostly because I have "help." And yes, those are air quotes.

"I still can't believe you're taking my grandchild and moving into that man's house," my mother grumbles. But she still pulls the packing tape across the box to seal it shut. I see she's protesting hard. "How do you know he's not a serial killer?"

"I don't," I say honestly. "But I don't really know that about you either and, yet, here we are."

She narrows her eyes at me, obviously displeased at my snark. I sigh in response because I probably shouldn't give my mother crap for being concerned. If it was Ainsley taking her daughter into a similar situation, I'd probably be worried too.

"I'm sorry. That was rude of me." Mom nods once in agreement and begins filling the next box with my summer clothes that have all been thrown on my bed. "I promise I wouldn't put Ainsley in a bad situation, Mom. Abel is a nice man. He's a co-worker and is raising his own daughter all by himself."

And sexy as all get out. I'm not immune to the fact that he's got solid thighs, a really tight ass, and is probably rockin' an amazing six pack. I just can't focus on that since he'll be my roommate.

My mother, however, has no problem focusing on anything and everything that could possibly go wrong.

"But he's a body builder, Elliott. He could go into a 'roid rage at any minute."

I have to give my mom credit. When she goes completely off her rocker, she doesn't hold back.

"He's a *trainer*, Mother," I say, rolling my eyes. Thank goodness my back is turned while I wrap a zip tie around these hangers to hold them in place. I don't want to get grief for my facial expressions. I'm already getting berated enough. "He's not a body builder. He doesn't compete or train for anything. He works out and teaches other people how to work out for health benefits."

He actually might train for something. I don't know for sure. But I'm not opening that can of worms.

"It's weird, Elliott," she continues to rant, making me antsy for when Abel arrives. I need to get out of here for some peace and quiet. The irony of the fact that I'm looking forward to less conversation despite more people living in my new house is not lost on me. In fact, the sooner I can be with those people, the better.

Since I don't have very much and we live close, instead of spending the money on a moving van, Abel elicited the help of his friend and our co-worker, Joey. For whatever reason, Joey has a giant Texas-sized truck. In Chicago. Where there is literally no reason to own a truck. But who am I to judge? I'm just going to take advantage of it today.

"You don't know if his wife left him because he's abusive. Or maybe she didn't leave. Maybe he killed her and buried her body like that guy on Discovery ID. Did you see that one? He wasn't smart enough to bury her somewhere far away. Nope. Asked a contractor to come redo the floor in the basement then threw her body right in the wet cement. He would have gotten away with it if he had made sure her sleeve didn't float to the top and stick out of the floor. Men. I swear they aren't the smartest."

I have no idea what she's rambling about anymore, but I don't care because the doorbell rings and my heart skips a beat from excitement.

"He's here! He's here!" I hear the pitter-patter of little feet running to the door. Actually, no. I hear the thumping steps of an eight-year-old girl who is way more excited to move than I thought she would be. I briefly wonder if that's part of the reason my mother is having a rough time with this. It's not only me moving out; it's Ainsley too. We all know once you give your mother grandchildren, you might as well be chopped liver.

I don't have time to think about it though, as my child has already opened the door.

"Ainsley," I admonish when I make my way down the stairs and find her in the doorway. "You know better than to answer the door without asking me."

"But Mama! I knew it was Abel and we get to go live with Mabel today!"

I should probably push this a little harder to drive the safety issue home, but somehow, I think it'll fall on deaf ears today. So, I cave.

"Fine. But you aren't ready yet, so go finish packing your clothes in your suitcase."

"Okay!" she yells and begins to run off, then thinks better of it. Swiveling around, eyes wide, she asks our new roommate, "Did you bring Mabel with you?"

Abel snaps his fingers like he knew he forgot something. "Darn it, not this time. But don't worry, she'll be home soon to help you unpack all your toys, so you better get a move on."

That does the trick. Ainsley jumps up, throwing her hands in the air in victory, then takes off running to her room, squealing the whole way.

"You know I've been fighting with her to pack all morning."

"What can I say? I have a way with the ladies."

Closing the door behind him, I scoff. "If you never say that again, it would be too soon."

"Yeah, it sounded better in my head," he admits as my mother comes walking down the stairs. Slowly. Assessing Abel as she descends and making sure we know it.

Trying to avoid the inevitable stand-off, I quickly make introductions.

"Mom, this is Abel, my co-worker and new roommate. Abel, this is my mom, Rose Donovan."

Abel immediately smiles and sticks his hand out to shake hers. I assume after our very intense conversation on parenting the other day, he's decided to kill her with kindness. Good plan. "Rose, it's nice to meet you."

She, on the other hand, is already in the process of embarrassing me so much I'm flashing back to middle school. In particular, the time when she came into the living room in her bathrobe while the boy I liked was lying on the floor doing homework with me. I feel that level of mortification when Mom puts her hand out in such a way that it looks like she wants Abel to kiss it and replies with, "You can call me Mrs. Donovan."

"Mother!" I screech.

She immediately drops her hand along with the weird act she's pulling. "Oh relax. I was kidding. You're still way too easily embarrassed. I saw the look on your face. You were remembering when that Tommy boy was here and I wore my robe, weren't you?"

My jaw drops. How does she know? Damn her and her mom voodoo.

Abel chuckles and answers the door when there's another knock. This time, Joey walks in. My mother's eyes widen again, and I know she's wondering exactly how many men I'm going to be living with. I might embellish the truth if she keeps trying to mortify me before I'm all moved out. It would serve her right.

Come to think of it, maybe that's her plan. Rattle me, make Abel think I'm certifiably insane so he changes his mind and I don't leave, giving her free access to compassion-inducing scenarios she can share with her friends for the remainder of her years.

She's a sneaky one, my mother.

"This is my friend Joey." Abel introduces him to my mother before turning to me. "Have you guys met yet?"

"I think we've seen each other in passing but haven't been formally introduced. I'm Elliott. Thanks for helping today."

Joey's smile is full of mischief, and I can already tell why he and Abel are friends. I can envision them being each other's wingmen and getting all the ladies to fall for them and their charming senses of humor. I bet they could get into a lot of trouble with each other if Abel didn't have that whole parenting thing holding him back.

"Yeah, I know I've seen you around, but it's nice to finally put a name to a face. And I never forget a beautiful face," he tacks on, making Abel groan and my mother laugh.

I quirk an eyebrow. "Well Abel isn't really a hard name to forget, and he is quite pretty."

My mother rolls her eyes while the rest of us laugh like a bunch of drunk college co-eds—a little too loud over something that's not all that funny. But at least the ice is broken and the tension melts away.

"You're an idiot," Abel says playfully and gives Joey a man-pat on the back, strong enough to have knocked me over if I were him.

"Let's get this truck loaded so we can get home before it gets colder. Where do you want us to start?"

We trek up the stairs and I point out the rooms we're clearing out. It'll take a couple of trips because of the furniture, but Abel's right. Apparently, there's more snow on the way, and there's nothing worse than tracking that crap into your house where it melts into dirty puddles everywhere.

"Looks like I get to skip my workout tomorrow morning," Joey says with a giant smile as he lifts up his side of the dresser.

"Because you lifted some lady furniture, ya pansy?" Abel shoots back.

They continue tossing barbs back and forth at each other, making me smile. The idea of living with people who laugh and smile and joke excites me. It's not that my mom doesn't do those things, it's that some of the criticisms are so hurtful, it's hard to see past them.

And yet, I'm a little sad about leaving here. This was my child-hood home. It's the place I had my first and last memories of my dad. It's the safe place I've always been able to run to, and it has a wonderful family history.

My parents scrimped and saved to buy this brownstone before I was born so they could start a family. They probably couldn't have afforded it, but somehow, they impressed the previous owner who was ready to unload it and move on with her life. She had been dumped by her husband for a younger model. As scandalous as it would be now, when I think about how it was over forty years ago, I can't imagine how the neighbors must have talked back then. The woman was so bitter from the entire thing she sold the house for well below what it was worth, simply to screw her ex out of his portion of the profits. Or at least that's how the story went.

Since my parents bought it, not much has changed with the exception of the loss of my dad. Ainsley even attends the same elementary school I did. So, for whatever reason, moving this time feels final. It puts a damper on my mood.

Not enough to change my mind, though. Not even close. Instead, I'm tossing some last-minute items in a bag, taking everything I can carry to the bottom of the stairs. The faster I can leave, the less I'll think about it. Like ripping off a Band-Aid. A forty-year-old Band-Aid.

"Are you sure you want to do this?"

I look over and see my mother, a look of anguish on her face. She caught me in a weak moment—staring at my now empty bedroom as I say my goodbye.

"I'm sure, Mom."

Her face changes to one of resignation, and oddly, she smiles. "Then I won't say another word about it."

I grab her in my arms and hug her tight. "I know, Mom. And no matter what, I appreciate you taking us in and giving us a place to start over."

"I love you, Ellie Belly." She pulls me in even tighter, and I breathe in the scent that always reminds me of home—her floral body wash and a hint of cinnamon. Probably from doctoring her coffee. "You are welcome to come back any time."

"I love you. And not on your life."

"Oh, thank God you said that." She pulls away and puts her hands on my cheeks. "I would lay down my life for the two of you, but if I don't get a life of my own soon, I may lose it."

I giggle at her humor and bite my tongue from saying anything about her personal brand of crazy. Instead, I kiss her cheek and pull away, calling for my daughter.

"Okay, Ainsley! It's time to go."

She squeals and comes racing up the stairs, coat half on, pulling up a boot as she stumbles.

"I'm ready! I'm ready!"

Me too, kiddo. Me too.

CHAPTER NINE

ABEL

Living with two virtual strangers has turned out to be pretty easy so far. The girls get along great and spend hours in the basement having dance parties and playing my old-school Wii. I thought about getting rid of it at one point, but then Mabel found it, and it's come in handy to get her energy out in the winter. The old *WipeOut* game is her favorite, and even I have to admit it's funny watching the Mii's go flying off the big balls. That was always the most entertaining part of the watching TV show.

It's also sparked some friendly competition between the girls. As long as it stays friendly and they take regular baths from all the sweat, it's fine by me. But really… the baths. I always assumed girls naturally smelled like flowers and candy. Not so much. An extreme game of Wii tennis leaves them smelling worse than the men's locker room at the gym.

Elliott and I also get along really well. Our humor is the same, as is our taste in music. It's made daily tasks like making lunch and doing laundry much more bearable than it could have been with another roommate. All we do is crank up some tunes and crack jokes while we go about our business.

Of course, the two of them have only lived here for thirty-six hours so far. It could all go downhill at some point.

With that in mind, and because I'm a nice guy in general, I've tried to stay extra quiet this morning. I'm never loud—my goal isn't to wake Mabel up until I have to. And even then, if she can stay asleep until it's time to get ready for school, our day runs much smoother.

But while my child can usually sleep through a nuclear event, I don't know how heavy a sleeper Elliott is. So, I've been hyper aware of how loud the shower water is, the creak in the stairs, the pop when I flip the switch to turn on the lights in the kitchen. I know I'll feel more comfortable the longer I do this, but today, I've grimaced at least half a dozen times, especially when ole Betsy gave me problems. It's been rough staying quiet, and Marv won't be here for another ten minutes.

So far, so good, though. I haven't heard a peep from anyone.

Quickly, I throw yesterday's leftovers in my lunch kit and begin the process of gathering all my things.

My gym bag.

Mabel's school bag.

Mabel's clothing bag.

Lunches for everyone.

I think I have it all. The only thing left to get is the child in question.

Turning for the stairs, I stop quickly when I almost run over Elliott who is sporting the wildest bedhead I've ever seen, and yet, I still haven't heard a peep. How did she miss that squeaky stair?

That's actually the least of my concerns right now. More importantly, a quick assessment has me wondering if her eyes are open and how much comprehension she has. Is Elliott sleepwalking? She didn't tell me she wandered around unconscious in the middle of the night. This is going to present some problems if she wanders out the door. I'm not prepared to chase her down the street in this weather. Chicago PD doesn't play around, and it would look awfully suspicious for me to be chasing her around in the middle of the night. I have no desire to get a face full of snow when I'm tackled and handcuffed.

"Why are you looking at me that way?" Elliott's groggy voice cuts through the silence of the house.

Huh. I guess she's awake.

"Because I thought you were sleepwalking."

"Why would you think that?"

Gesturing to the small mirror hanging behind her, she turns to look. I watch in the reflection to see her reaction to her current state. All she does is blink a couple times. At least I think she's blinking. It's hard to tell since her eyes are barely open to begin with. That's the only reaction she has. Even her mouth doesn't move, only stays slightly ajar.

"Huh," she finally responds. "I see why you came to that conclusion." She licks her lips and scratches the back of her head, making the rat's nest called her hair bob up and down. "What time is it anyway?"

Patting down my pockets, I'm glad for an excuse to check for my phone anyway. "Uhh..." I click on the screen. "About 4:40."

Elliott's eyes have suddenly gone from slits to wide open. Or at least wider. Or not as narrow. Regardless, she's definitely alert now. "Why are you up so early?"

Sliding my phone back in my pocket, I peek out the window to see if my Uber is here yet. "My first client shows up at five."

"That's horrible," she declares and then immediately yawns, as if the effort of this conversation is exhausting her.

"Why are you up, anyway? You don't have to be there until ten."

She plops down on the couch, curling her legs up under her until she's in a ball, resting her head on the arm rest. "I thought you were a burglar."

"Seriously?"

She shrugs. "New house. New noises. I'll get used to it."

Lights shine through the blinds and fade away as my ride pulls up, right on time.

"Well, it'll be quieter now. My carriage awaits, so I'm going to grab Mabel and leave." I only get one foot on the stairs before Elliott stops me.

"Wait, you're taking Mabel?"

I look at her quizzically. "Can't leave her here. I can't trust she'd actually go to school. She'll use any excuse to get out of it."

One more foot up the stairs, and I'm thwarted by Elliott's words again.

"That was before. I'm here now."

I put myself in reverse and take back the two steps of progress I've made. Seems like a metaphor for my life, but I don't want to focus on that part now. I've got a cab to catch.

"I can't ask you to do that, Elliott."

"Why not? The girls go to the same school."

She's right, but this isn't something we've discussed before. It feels unnecessary to rely on her for help when I've been single parenting just fine. It's not always easy, but taking care of my child isn't a sacrifice. "Because it feels like an imposition, and I don't want to put you out."

"Abel, I have to get Ainsley up at seven anyway. And make her breakfast. And make her lunch. What's it gonna hurt?"

I laugh through my nose. "Double the kids means triple the workload for you, remember?"

If she wasn't back to having slits for eyes, I'd swear she rolled them at me.

"Oh yeah. Because it's hard to scramble an extra egg and throw a second juice box in a bag." She makes a valid point, but I'm still not sure if this is crossing a line. We've discussed how we'd treat the kids, but we've never talked about a situation like this. "Come on, Abel," she pushes. "Let Mabel sleep. You know she'll feel better if she gets an extra two hours."

I look up the stairs as I consider her proposal. As much as I want to argue, Elliott is right. It would be so much better for Mabel if she didn't have to be disturbed in the quasi-middle of the night. Not to mention I could add an extra client every day if I didn't have to stop and get Mabel to school every morning. I could use the extra money.

"Fine. But if you're going to take her to school, let me pick both girls up this afternoon."

"You don't have to do that—" Elliott insists, but I put up my hand to stop her.

"It's only fair. Let's try it this week. You do morning drop-offs. I do afternoon pickups. I can either keep Ainsley until you get home and feed her dinner, or I can drop her at the gym on my way home."

"And you'll have to let me know how Ms. Alexander takes the new arrangements."

I see her wits are still about her, despite the massive yawn that just came out of her again. I smirk. "Oh yes. I'll be sure to let you know how that goes."

"And if any PTA moms hit on you."

I groan. "You know about that?"

"Up until two weeks ago, I only knew you as 'Hot Single Dad'," she says with a snicker. "Imagine my surprise when I realized who they were referring to."

"You do realize we are about to be the latest gossip of the volunteer copy room, right?"

It's her turn to groan. "Great. Now I have to come up with a meet-cute to keep them entertained. If you come up with a stellar story about how we met, let me know."

Snickering, I grab my bags off the floor before realizing I only need one of them today and dropping the others. "Go big or go home, huh?"

"You vastly underestimate how much I like it at home."

"As long as you make me sound awesome, I'll let you decide how and where it was love at first sight." A small beep of a horn reminds me Marv is already here. "I gotta run. Mabel's clothes are in this bag and this is her school bag. Don't let her trick you into believing she has food allergies because she doesn't. And if you need anything, you know how to reach me."

"I refuse to interrupt Gina pre-three cups of coffee. I've been warned multiple times to leave her be, even in an emergency. We'll be fine."

"I trust you." And I do. I don't know why, but with the exception of the whole imposition issue, I have zero concerns about Elliott being in charge of Mabel. Maybe it's dad-intuition. Maybe it's because Dinah recommended her. Maybe it's that criminal background check she had to do for employment. Regardless, if these living arrangements last longer than our trial period, Elliott and I really might be able to help each other out.

Jogging out the door and down the steps, I hear Elliott lock the door behind me. Within seconds, I'm in the backseat of my favorite Ford Escort. Even better, I'm not trying to cram everything on the small seat next to me without dropping a child in the process.

Very quickly, I'm situated, and yet the car isn't moving. "Uh... Marv? You okay?"

"I'm waiting for you to realize you forgot your kid. Not sure how I remember and you don't, but I'm not here to judge. I just drive."

"I appreciate you looking out for me, but I didn't forget her. I've got a new roommate who is going to take her to school."

He harrumphs and hands me my lukewarm cup of coffee before putting the car into drive and easing away from the curb. "You gonna trust some hooligan with your daughter? You can't be too careful these days."

A dozen sentences. That's all we've ever spoken to each other, yet Marv is still so protective of my daughter. I know I'm trying to save money, but there is no way I'm going to stop using him every morning even if I can jog to work again. He's never said it, but I get the feeling Marv needs the money as much as I do. Plus, I get a cup of coffee out of it. It's not as good as my Betsy's, but the company is better.

"Elliott is actually a single mom, so she knows what she's doing. And her daughter goes to the same school as Mabel. Same grade and everything."

He harrumphs again. "Living with a woman? In my day, that was considered bad form. She'd get herself a reputation."

"Then it's a good thing we live in a new millennium, right?" I pat his shoulder as he pulls up in front of the gym. Handing him back the mug, I add, "Let the wife know this morning's coffee hit the spot as always. I'll see you tomorrow."

"Wait... you still want me to pick you up?" Marv looks genuinely curious as to why.

"Of course!" I say with a smile as I swing the door open. "How else am I gonna get my first cup of joe in the morning?"

I flash him a grin and race from one door to the next, chasing the heat. The wind is blowing extra hard this morning and the chill cuts right through my clothes and into my bones.

"Good morning, Gina."

She grunts her response, staring at the monitor in front of her. I'm not sure if she's waiting for the computer to boot up, or merely pretending so she doesn't have to talk to anyone. Again, I'm left to wonder why the hell she doesn't change her shift.

I smile and wave at the few co-workers who are in the building as I pass, most of them giving me quizzical looks. I never realized how weird it would look for me to come to work without lugging my child-sized burrito with me. Even Morgan seems shocked when I get to the desk and only have one bag to put down.

"Uh... did you forget something this morning?" She swivels back and forth on the chair.

"Elliott is going to take her to school."

"Elliott? Who's Elliott?"

Furrowing my brow, I glance at her briefly while clocking in. "You don't know Elliott? She works in childcare. She's new."

Morgan's eyes light up like the lightbulb went off in her brain. "Oh yeah, I know her. She's cute. But wait. Why is she watching Mabel? I didn't know you guys were friends."

"She moved in this weekend, so it's just easier for her to take the girls to school in the morning and me to pick them up in the afternoon. We'll see how well it works. It might not. But today I'm enjoying not having to worry about my eight-year-old sleeping under the desk when my first client gets here."

Morgan stops swiveling and holds her hand up. "Back up. You

and Elliott live together? Didn't you just meet a couple weeks ago at the staff meeting?"

And here we go. I'm sure this isn't the first time I'll be having this conversation. Thank God Joey was there to help with moving so I don't have to try and explain it to him in front of people. The jokes were bad enough over the phone.

"I needed to offset my mortgage. She needed a place to live. Win-win." I suspect that answer isn't going to cut it, but it's the easiest one I've got.

"Sounds like it's more than just a win if you already have her taking care of your kid."

Morgan rolls the chair over so I can grab my binder of client logs out from the drawer. "It's not like that. Our girls are in the same grade at the same school, so we're going to try and help each other out. We could all use a little relief every now and then."

"You mean like at 4:30 in the morning when you have to work."

"That's exactly what I mean. I'm not getting all my hopes up, but we're going to try and see how things go."

"I'm glad for you." Morgan stands up and stretches. The day is about to begin. No use in sitting around. "You've needed the help for a while. It helps that she's your type."

I scoff. "Let's not get ahead of ourselves."

"She's not your type?"

"I didn't say that. But I don't need you scaring her off. She just moved in and so far, she's the most considerate roommate I've ever had. If she leaves, I'll get stuck living with someone like Joey."

Morgan grimaces. I see we understand each other now. "Point made. Now if you'll excuse me, I need to go walk a little bit to get my energy up."

"Still caffeine free?"

"I could kill you for convincing me to eat clean. I've dropped those few pounds, but I'm not sure the sacrifice of my beloved coffee is worth it."

"And yet, here we are."

"Yeah, yeah. Make yourself useful and put the yoga mat we have stored under the table away, would ya?" She turns and walks away, me chuckling at her snarky attitude. She's not wrong. It's absolutely my fault she's clean eating. I recommend it to all my clients and harp on them until they finally follow through, if only to get me to shut up. Being that Morgan is my former client and a new employee, I simply reminded her she needed to walk the walk if she was going to talk the talk.

I blame the string of curse words she gave me after my comment on the caffeine headache she was sporting.

Flipping through my file, I make mental notes on what I'll be doing today.

"Beeeeeeast!" The voice booms through the room in greeting as the man attached to it heads my way. Time to get this day rolling.

CHAPTER TEN

ELLIOTT

"It's very late, so as soon as we get inside, I want you to run upstairs and brush your hair. Your dad is going to be here in a few minutes, and I don't want him to have to wait."

I don't tell my daughter that my instructions have less to do with making him wait and more to do with not wanting to interact with him for longer than necessary. Derrick may be a jerk, but he's still Ainsley's dad. She can make her own determination about him when she's older.

Ainsley nods as she skips, her breath coming out in little puffs of white because of the chilly air. It's dark out but fortunately, because it's still early by adult-standards, the streets are full of activity. We're not the only ones just getting home for the day, I see.

Racing up the steps to get out of the chill, I put my new key in the lock and turn.

My new key. I love that. There is a feeling of freedom being on my own again.

As the door opens, though, I face the fact that I'm not totally on my own. However small it is, I still have a bit of help in my life. And currently, that help is making dinner. The smell of something fantastic invades my senses.

"I'm hungry, Mommy." Ainsley's mouth is probably watering from the aroma like mine. Lucky for her, her dad usually caters to whatever she wants for dinner. Too bad for me, I was going to have a grilled cheese sandwich. It's not going to come close to comparing to whatever Abel is making.

"Me too, baby. Hurry up and take your shoes off." She complies and bounds up the stairs with me calling after her, "Don't forget to hang up your backpack on the hook."

I have no idea if she has her selective hearing turned on or not, but by the thud I hear on the floor above me, I'm pretty sure it is not. I'd fight with her about it, but frankly, I'm too tired from disciplining other people's children today. I'd rather choose my battles right now.

Removing my coat and gloves, I hang them in the closet and remove my shoes. I love snow when it falls. I hate slush when it melts. I hate it even worse when it gets tracked it all over the house.

Padding my way into the kitchen in my fuzzy socks, I see Abel and quip, "Hi honey, I'm home."

His face lights up as he glances up at me from the pot on the stove. "Hey, how was your day?"

Wow. That's the nicest greeting I think I've ever had when coming home. A girl could get used to this. I find myself wondering for the umpteenth time why his wife would ever leave a catch like him.

Leaning against the doorjamb, I cross my arms, the sounds of another Wii game softly wafting up the stairs in the background. "Let's see, I would say it went well, except I think my stations are working better than I had hoped."

"That's good news, right?" Abel dumps some seasonings into the mixture and stirs carefully so he doesn't slop any over the side and onto the stovetop.

"Normally, I'd say yes. What I didn't plan on is a third grader using the homework station to do her math homework. Nor did I expect her to need my help. Whoever came up with common core should be shot."

"Sounds awful." Holding out a spoonful of the soup he's cooking, he offers it to me. "Here. Try this. It'll make everything better."

Who am I to argue when the house smells this amazing?

Opening my mouth, my eyes lock on Abel's as I take the spoon. Immediately, the flavors explode in my mouth. Chicken and spices, some basil, and a little something else, but I'm not sure what. A moan of appreciation comes from my chest, and I realize what an intimate moment this really could be, especially when he smiles at me. But it doesn't feel weird. It feels carefree and normal.

It's Abel. He's just easy to be around him. Easy to talk to. Even easy to take a bite of soup with him holding the spoon. In the couple of weeks we've lived here, none of our interactions have ever turned creepy. Not for the first time, I thank my lucky stars I ended up with a really good roommate. Dare I say, an almost-friend. If he lets me keep sampling his cooking, we might end up more than friends.

"That is amazing. What is it?" I ask, as I finish swallowing.

He's obviously delighted at my reaction. "Chicken and quinoa soup."

Quinoa? What the hell is quinoa?

"I'm sorry, what?"

He chuckles as he takes his own taste, using the same spoon he fed me with. I'm a little more flattered at that realization than I should be. "Quinoa is a pseudo-cereal grain that I use in the place of rice. It is extremely good for you, and I always buy the fresh brand that hasn't been processed and bagged, so it has extra health benefits. In fact," he continues as he opens a cabinet and pulls out some bowls, "every ingredient in this soup is organic, additive-free, preservative-free, gluten-free, and pesticide-free." Handing me a steaming bowl of yummy goodness, he tacks on, "Enjoy your very first clean eating meal."

I have a hard time tamping down my excitement. I wasn't kidding when I said it was amazing, and with as hungry as I am, this is the best surprise I could have come home to. "And here I was going to have a grilled cheese sandwich. You didn't have to cook for me."

"In the words of a certain sleepwalker, it's not hard to add one more serving if I'm already cooking."

I should have known my words would be used against me at some point. "That's not exactly what I said, but I'm so hungry, I'm not going to argue at this point."

I lift the spoon to my mouth, but before I can shovel any in, a short, blonde terror runs right past me, nearly knocking me off balance.

"Ainsley!" I call out, just as she yells, "Sorry, Mom. I'm coming Mabel!" and stomps down the stairs to the basement.

Abel looks highly amused at what was almost a terrible food tragedy. "You better be glad that didn't fall," I remark as I try again. "I don't know where the mop is around here, so clean up would have been all on you."

"I never questioned your ability to hold on to your food for one second."

"Smart man." I begin eating, although scarfing might be a more appropriate term. If this man cooks like this regularly, I'll be the first to say I lucked out on who gets which shift with the girls. I might need to step up my game and bring him a smoothie or protein shake or whatever trainers eat in the morning, so he never stops making dinner.

"Is everyone eating?" Abel continues to dish out servings. I should probably quit shoveling it in like a pig and help him set a table or something. Eh. I'll do that before my second serving.

Shaking my head, I pause to answer him. "My ex is coming to pick up Ainsley any minute."

"What time was he supposed to be here?"

"Half an hour ago." Abel turns to me, an incredulous look on his face. I just shrug. "He likes to see how far he can push me. He's too wrapped up in himself to realize I don't care that much if he's late. He still has to have her home by eight, so who is really missing out?"

"Ainsley."

Bang on. "Yep. But she's gotten used to it and thinks he's flakey. The amount of grace she gives him is off the charts, but what are you gonna do? Their relationship doesn't have anything to do with me, as long as she's not being hurt by it."

"Smart thinking." He carries two bowls to the small table across the way. I follow with my almost empty bowl, trying to decide how long I need to wait to get more so I don't come across as desperate. "I wish I could say that about Mabel."

"She doesn't see her mom?" Genuine curiosity takes over. I never thought to ask why Abel has custody. Maybe because he's not the only man I know raising a child. By the huff he responds with though, it doesn't sound good.

Abel takes a big bite from his own bowl before continuing our conversation. "May only shows up when she wants something or wants to use Mabel for something."

"Like what?"

"Like when her manager, also known as her boyfriend, wanted to promote her as a doting single mother. I guess he was trying to drum up interest in her modeling career or whatever. She called and asked to take Mabel for the day, and since she lives in New York, who am I to say no when my kid's mom comes into town, ya know?" I nod, because that's what any reasonable parent would do. "I didn't find out until later they spent the day getting hair and makeup done, and doing an 'impromptu,'"—and yes, he uses air quotes—"photo shoot that was suddenly all over her social media."

I crinkle my nose. Nothing is worse than a parent who tries to use their kids as trophies. "Well, that's wildly inappropriate."

"Tell me about it," he says between bites. "I wasn't even mad she shared the pictures. They were really pretty. It just rubbed me the wrong way. I guess it showed her intentions, and I have an issue with that."

We go back to our food, each in our own thoughts. Him, probably thinking about those pictures. Me, oddly grateful that at least my ex shows up. Late, yes. But at least he's around.

Speak of the devil. A knock at the door indicates Derrick is finally here.

Popping up from my chair, I begin to make my way to the kitchen to call for Ainsley when Abel stops me.

"I'm going to get more anyway. Want me to call her while you answer the door?"

No. I'd rather not talk to Derrick for that long. But I don't say that. Instead, I take advantage of the moment. "Sure. And would you mind getting me a little more soup too?"

"You like clean eating," he jokes, a huge smile on his face.

"I like eating when someone else makes it," I joke back. "Cook every night, and you'll have me detoxed in no time."

"Don't tempt me. I'm always up for a challenge."

Derrick knocks again, because despite making us wait on him for over thirty minutes, he seems to have no patience of his own. Abel's eyebrow rises, and I know he's thinking the exact same thing.

With a sigh, we go our separate ways and I prepare myself to hold my tongue and play nice. "Ainsley's best interest, Ainsley's best interest..." I mutter to myself before pulling the door open.

Derrick pushes his way past me and into the warmth of the house, shivering. Granted, he's covered in snow flurries, but I still have very little care that he's cold.

"Brrrr." He rubs his hands together and pulls the cashmere scarf from his face. No hat for Derrick. Couldn't let those five-thousand-dollar hair plugs go to waste by covering them up. "I didn't realize it was going to snow tonight."

"Yeah, the forecast has been calling for it for days."

"Huh. Who knew?"

I bite my tongue to stop myself from answering with, "Everyone in the greater Chicago area who pays attention to the weather." That would be counter-productive to the civility I work hard to have with him.

Derrick looks around the room while pulling off his gloves. "So, this is the new place. I'm impressed. I didn't know you could afford a place this nice."

I ignore the dig and keep my hand on the doorknob, knowing if I step farther into the living area, he'll take himself on a tour. Better to keep myself next to the front door so he doesn't misunderstand my desire to have him run free.

"What can I say? I was in a better position than I thought, and the right opportunity dropped in my lap."

At that exact moment, Abel walks out of the kitchen, two bowls in his hands. He places them on the table and approaches.

In a matter of milliseconds, my brain registers that this could go any number of ways.

1. Both men play nice and all goes well.
2. Neither man plays nice, and I have to figure out how to clean blood off the floor and look for bandages.
3. Only one of these men play nice and the other pitches a huge hissy fit with me later.

Abel shoots a smile at a scowling Derrick and holds out his hand in greeting.

Number three it is.

"Hey, I'm Abel. I've heard a lot about you, Derrick."

I almost choke on my own spit at his ability to lie like that. He's heard very little about my ex and none of it has been good.

I watch as Derrick literally stands up taller and juts his chin out before taking Abel's hand. He is obviously unhappy about there being a man in my house, and I wouldn't be surprised if he's squeezing Abel's hand as hard as he can right now.

"Unfortunately, I've heard nothing about you." I roll my eyes at his attempt to make things weird. Abel, on the other hand, just rolls with the punches. I'm finding that to be true of him most of the time.

"Well, our living arrangements are pretty new, so I'm sure it wasn't intentional on Elliott's part."

If eyeballs could pop out of a person's head simply from widening your lids too fast, Derrick's would be rolling across the floor right now. He whips his head to look at me so quickly, I'm also surprised he doesn't snap his neck. This is going to be a really fun conversation later.

"Anyway," Abel continues, as if he didn't just poke the bear, "I'll call Ainsley again. I think they were playing Wii boxing, and you know how that goes. Good to meet you, Derrick." He turns and saunters off, and I swear he puffs out his chest more than normal.

What is happening here? Neither one of these men want me in a romantic sense, so why are they suddenly peeing on my leg?

As soon as Abel is out of sight, the inquisition begins.

"You're living with *him*?" Derrick hisses. "Our court order specifically states you can't live with someone of the opposite sex without my permission."

I cross my arms, trying not to speak with as much anger as I feel.

"That court order also states those parameters are null and void if you do it first. Which you did. Without telling me."

He gapes at me. "That was only for a couple of months."

"I guess you should have thought about that before moving in with Muffy or whatever. Her name alone should have been your first indicator it wouldn't work out long-term."

"That's beside the point."

"No, it's exactly the point, Derrick. Abel isn't even technically my roommate. If you want to get nitpicky, he's my *housemate*. Not my boyfriend. Not my lover. Not the man I'm living with. He's a single dad with a girl in Ainsley's class who had part of his house to rent out. He's also my co-worker. This isn't a cohabitating situation. There is no sex happening here. It's a living arrangement. That's all."

"Well, I don't like it. You don't know he's not a serial killer."

I squeeze the bridge of my nose. "Now you sound like my mother."

His gasp sounds more like that of a little girl than a grown man. But considering he's being a big baby now, I guess that's about right. "I resent that. I am nothing like your overbearing, condescending..."

"Daddy!"

A little voice cuts off all conversation and Derrick and I both paint smiles on our faces as Ainsley comes racing into the room, wrapping her arms around her father's middle.

"I'm hungry. Where are we going to eat?"

"Wherever you want, baby girl." He kisses her on the top of the head and pulls away. "Where are your shoes and coat? We need to go."

"Right here." Ainsley practically bounces to the closet and pulls out everything she needs to go out into the cold. Unlike her father, she's discerning enough to put on a hat as well.

In a matter of seconds, she is bounding out the door and down the steps, Derrick pulling up the rear. As I get ready to close the door, he turns to me. "This conversation isn't over."

"We're not married anymore," I say quietly. "You don't get to decide that." And I shut the door in his face.

Leaning my forehead against the cool wood, I take a series of deep breaths. I made it. One more argument down with my child being none the wiser. Well, she might know. Kids aren't stupid. But at least we argue respectfully. That's a positive, right?

"Let me guess," I deep voice says behind me. "He doesn't like that you live with some guy he doesn't know."

I push off the door and head back to the table and my second serving. Fighting with Derrick makes me hungry. Or maybe I'm emotional-eating. Or maybe it's just that good. Regardless, I have no issue stomaching more soup.

"Yeah, well, it didn't help that you did the whole male challenge thingy and led him to believe there is something beyond a living arrangement here."

Abel shrugs but there is no remorse in his body language or facial expressions. "He was going to be pissy about it either way. I wanted to make sure he knew he wasn't going to come into my house and act like an ass. And if he did, he'd know who he'd be up against."

"Fair point," I say around my bite. "But I'm going to hear about this for weeks."

"Be glad you don't have to deal with May. The second she finds out I'm living with a woman, I guarantee she'll start sending me nude texts."

I crinkle my nose in disgust. "If she wants you back, she needs to get back here. Not do stuff like that."

"She doesn't want us back. She just doesn't want anyone else to have us either."

"They never do, do they?"

He shakes his head with a "Nope."

Gesturing to the bowl next to his, I ask, "Is Mabel coming to eat?"

"She will. She asked for two minutes to finish her match. She's never beaten the opponent before, so I didn't have the heart to tell her to quit now."

"Understandable."

"Hey." He puts his spoon down and steeples his fingers together. "How did it go this morning anyway? With Mabel?"

I bob my head back and forth like it was so-so, to buy me some time to sort out how to explain it to him. It was actually worse than so-so. Way worse, but I don't want Abel to worry. Little girls can be difficult. It's nothing I haven't dealt with before.

Still, he deserves to know the truth. "It was a little rough at first," I confess. "I think it threw her off that you left without telling her, but once she realized Ainsley was here, she hopped out of bed quickly."

That's downplaying it. Truth be told, Mabel pitched a huge fit about me not being her mom and not making her do things. I was on the verge of calling Abel when Ainsley came in and started jumping up and down on the bed. That made Mabel laugh and change her mood. From that point forward, the excitement of going to school together trumped the trauma of my rules. If it weren't for Ainsley, though, I'm not sure she ever would have gotten up.

"Oh yeah. She hates mornings."

I don't bother correcting him, but Abel only seems to realize the half of it. Mabel doesn't only hate mornings. She seems to hate rules and anyone in authority. When she declined the scrambled eggs I'd offered her, since that's what we were having for breakfast, she got mad that I wouldn't make her anything else. Instead, she slammed her cup of milk down on the table, spilling it everywhere. Then she told me this is her house and if she wants something else, she gets it. Sure enough, Ainsley and I ate eggs. Mabel poured herself a giant bowl of cereal, ate half of it, and didn't bother cleaning up her dishes.

Frankly, it was way more stressful than I anticipated.

"I'm sure we'll find a groove. Transition is hard for everyone." I opt to leave it at that. There could be any number of reasons why Mabel was difficult this morning, so I need to give her a little bit of grace. I'm sure tomorrow will be easier.

"I'll make sure she knows what to expect for tomorrow."

"I'd appreciate that, thanks."

A few minutes later, Mabel slinks up to the table, quiet as a mouse. It's odd coming from a child like her, who was just trying to win a heavyweight belt two minutes ago.

"What's wrong?" Abel asks her before I can.

"Nothing." Her sullen face and the fact that she's spinning her spoon around in her dinner indicates there is actually something wrong.

Abel puts his arm around her. "I made your favorite. It's chicken and quinoa."

"I know."

She still doesn't look up.

"Then why aren't you eating?" Abel asks, concern written on his face. "Are you sick?" He immediately puts his hand to her forehead which she bats away.

"No, Dad. I just don't want to."

"Why not?"

"Because I don't want to eat at home with you. I want to eat at a restaurant with my mommy, like Ainsley is right now."

I close my eyes, guilt setting in for my thoughts about this little girl and her lack of respect for authority. Of course, she's bucking me. She's still grieving over the loss of her mother and here I come with my kiddo, into her house and shoving it in her face that Ainsley has a mom and she doesn't.

I wish there was a way I could fix this, but there's not. And if I tried to, it would only make it worse because Mabel doesn't know me that well yet.

Abel puts his arm around her and kisses the top of her head. "I know, baby. But if you want, we can try video messaging her right now. Maybe she's eating dinner too."

Mabel's face lights up at the prospect and she nods her head vigorously. That's all the response Abel needs to take his phone out, press a few buttons, and get the call started.

It rings four times and as Mabel's face starts to fall again, a voice comes through the phone.

"Hi, baby! What are you up to?"

The phone is faced away from me, thank goodness. Not that I would be included on this call. It's really none of my business. But I also can't guarantee if I saw her face I would stay as in-control as Abel did when Derrick was here. Nothing angers me more than a parent who has no regard for hurting their child. Nothing.

Mabel begins bouncing in her chair, face lit up with excitement. "Guess what, Mom? I beat Crazy Craigen on level four! He didn't stand a chance!" She stands up and begins throwing jabs in the air. "It was awesome. And now I get to start level five tomorrow."

"Wow," the voice says, not sounding enthusiastic at all. "Did you try that nail polish kit I sent you? Ombre nails are the latest thing."

Mabel stops bouncing, looking a little dejected. I glance up over my bowl at Abel, who is holding eye contact with me. By how tight his jaw is, I know he's concentrating on me so he doesn't say something inappropriate—regardless of how truthful it might be.

"I didn't know how to do it," Mabel finally says quietly.

"Mabel, we talked about this," the voice chides. "If you can't figure out the instructions, YouTube is your friend."

Abel squeezes his eyes shut and shakes his head.

"See how pretty Mommy is?" she continues. "It took lots of practice to be this beautiful. You can do it, too. You just have to try."

"Okay, Mommy."

I watch as Mabel's face falls and my heart aches for her. I know

Mabel loves her mother, and I would never fault her for that. But the more I listen, the more I understand the depth of selfishness this child had to deal with, and still does.

"Anyway, I have to run. I'm going to a gala tonight with a lot of potential networking connections. But we'll talk again soon, okay?"

Mabel nods, tears clearly welling up in her eyes.

"I love you, Mabel. Big kisses!" The sound of a big smooch comes through the speakers and then it goes silent, not just over the phone but in the room too.

After a few seconds, Abel sighs. "Mabel, why don't you sit down and finish your dinner? When we're done with your bath, we can play some Uno. What do you say?"

She shrugs but sits, not picking up her spoon. I can't imagine how she must feel right now but my own maternal instinct kicks in, wanting to do something to make things better.

"Mabel, if you'd like, I know a thing or two about doing nail polish. Maybe we could work on the ombre look together."

She looks up through her eyelashes, tears all dried up. "You are not my mother." Then she pushes her chair from the table, stomps up the stairs, and slams the door to her bedroom.

Well, that didn't go well. And I can only hope it isn't foreshadowing for our future as housemates.

CHAPTER ELEVEN

ABEL

I rarely work Saturdays. It's one of the perks of having seniority. It probably has more to do with my willingness to be at the gym at five in the morning during the week, but I like to pretend I have some sort of clout.

Regardless, around the holidays, it all goes out the window. One would think all that is needed to keep customers happy at a gym is maintained equipment, fun classes, and good customer service. Tabitha's smoothie bar is a giant perk with all the therapy she doles out along with the drinks.

But no. Management believes we need to cater to families more. I don't disagree, necessarily. I just don't care to spend my off day back at work being a bouncer to pint-sized patrons when Jolly Old St. Nick shows up today.

"Are you girls excited to see Santa?" I ask, as I stir the oatmeal on the stovetop. It's going to taste great with the local honey I've been saving since summer.

"Oh yeah, Daddy!" Mabel calls from the table. "I can't wait to tell him what I want for Christmas." Ainsley breaks out into a fit of giggles, and Mabel whispers loudly, "I have to say that. He still believes in Santa. I don't want to ruin it for him."

I shake my head in amusement and then my face falls almost immediately. *Oh shit. I hope Mabel didn't ruin it for Ainsley.*

Fortunately, Ainsley whisper-yells back. "My mom still does too. I have to hide her present until Christmas Eve."

I fight back a chuckle at these two. I'm not sure who they think is bringing their presents if their parents are snuggled in their beds dreaming of Kris Kringle's arrival, but I'm too entertained to ask. Besides, who am I to ruin the fun they're having by keeping this secret from us?

As they continue giggling and being less-than-quiet with their discussion, I finish breakfast and dish it out.

Serving the girls, I look up from where they're sitting to see Elliott making her way toward the kitchen with pigtails in her hair and wearing a tight red sweater dress with white trim hugging tightly to her body. The green stockings are a nice touch, and they match quite well with the scowl on her face.

"Well, good morning. Don't you look precious," I chide to see if I can get a rise out of her.

She doesn't slow her steps as she complains, "I was tricked."

"What?" I laugh out the word, knowing full well what's she's mad about.

"This wasn't part of my job description."

"But you look so cute with the pigtails, and the red outfit, and the painted on... what are those? Freckles?"

She bats my hand away when I gently swipe at her hair. "There's nothing cute about a forty-something wearing pigtails to work so she can dress like an elf."

That stops me in my tracks. "Wait. You're how old?"

"Forty-two." Holy shit. I had no idea she was that old. I thought late thirties at the absolute most. Not that her age matters. She just seems so much more youthful than I would have expected of a forty-something. "What's it to you, Beast?" she challenges, hands on her hips.

Crinkling my nose, I grimace at the nickname. "You heard about that, huh?"

"Now that my home away from home isn't a mecca of mass hysteria, you'd be surprised what kinds of shouts I can hear. I can even hear... "Her eyes go wide as if she's telling me something amazing. "Actual conversations!"

"No!" I joke, throwing my hand over my heart.

"Yes! It's amazing."

"I bet. Since being able to hear is no longer a problem, are you gonna sit on Santa's lap today and whisper all your secrets in his ear?"

She turns and grabs a bowl, dishing out her own serving of oatmeal. "That depends on who is playing Santa, I suppose. If he's the smelly guy that used to do it at the mall, I'm out."

"Well, you're in luck. Turns out the suit fits me!"

Elliott stops what she's doing to look me up and down. Not sure if she's being flirty or getting ready to lob a verbal zinger my direction. "Oh, well then, I'm for sure not sitting on his lap. You may not smell like booze and cigarettes, but that protein shake with double greens is no picnic."

Verbal zinger it is.

Wait. Was that a zinger or did she take advantage of the moment to tell me the truth?

I go for discretion as I cup my hand over my mouth and blow, trying to smell my breath. By the look on her face when she catches me, I'd say I'm not very stealth.

Eh. May as well get down to the bottom of it, then. "Seriously?"

She finishes her bite, shaking her head as she does. "No. You're minty fresh."

I narrow my eyes. "Really? You aren't backpedaling, are you?"

Her only answer is to roll her eyes and breeze past me to sit with the girls who are no longer giggling but shoveling food in their mouths as fast as possible.

"Good morning, girls," Elliott greets, as she gets comfortable with a single foot wedged underneath her.

"Mmmnnnnn", they mumble around their food. I knew my oatmeal was good, but I didn't realize it was *that* good.

Dropping her spoon in her bowl, Ainsley licks her lips and says, "Done. Is it time to go yet?"

Quirking an eyebrow, I pretend to not know the magic is already gone for these two. "Are you girls excited about meeting Santa or something?"

They flash each other a conspiratorial look before Mabel answers.

"Dad. You know it's not the real Santa coming to the gym, right?"

"Do *you* know it's not the real Santa?" Elliott asks, having missed the entire whisper-yell conversation a few minutes ago. I'll have to enlighten her later.

The girls look at each other again. This time Ainsley is the bearer of the bad news. "Yes, Mom. We know. The real Santa would never show his face in public. So, you don't have to be nervous about talking to him today."

Elliott blinks a couple of times and looks up at me. I can only smirk and shrug as I wait for her response. "Oh. Well then, I guess the pressure is off. What's the rush?"

"Dad is dressing up in the Santa suit," Mabel replies quickly, dropping her own spoon in her now empty bowl. "He's gonna look so funny."

"Hold on." I raise my hand, as if I have something hugely important to say and need their undivided attention. It works. "You're only excited to go so you can make fun of me for wearing a smelly suit and an itchy beard?"

I would hope my daughter would have a least a little bit of guilt over her own intentions. But apparently, I'm expecting too much. The only response I get is a shrug of her little shoulders and a "Well, yeah."

Awesome. My child has turned against me. So, I do the only thing I can—try to deflect.

"How come you aren't making fun of Elliott, then?"

"Hey!" the woman in question says around her food. "What did I do to you?"

"Tell me I have protein-shake breath."

She opens her mouth to respond, then thinks better of it. "Point made."

I nod once and turn back to the girls. "Seriously. She's a forty-two-year-old woman in pigtails. Surely there is a joke in there."

Ainsley rolls her eyes at me. How in the hell did I end up outnumbered here? Oh yeah. I let two more women move in. "My mom is thirty-five, Abel."

"Yes. Yes, I am," Elliott responds quickly. "Why don't you girls take your bowls to the sink and put on your Christmas shirts while you wait for us slowpokes."

The girls race off as commanded, chanting, "Slowpokes! Slowpokes!" as they go. I, on the other hand, don't take my eyes off Elliott, one eyebrow quirked in question.

Catching my gaze, she looks around like there's no way I could be staring at her. Finally, she asks, "What?"

"Thirty-five, huh?"

She drops her spoon and wipes her mouth with a napkin. "I don't feel as old as my birthdate says I am."

"You lied to your daughter?" I say with a snicker.

"I let her do the math. Who am I to say she's wrong? It would break her heart to know she subtracted wrong." Elliott jumps up from the table, grabbing my breakfast dish on her way past me. "Girrrrls! Are you almost ready to go?"

A small chorus of cheers and squeals come wafting down the stairs. If I didn't know better, I'd think there was a group of young girls upstairs, not just two of them. Who knew girls were so loud?

Between hats and coats and boots and gloves, it takes a few minutes to get everyone out the door. Fortunately for us, its late enough in the day that while cold, the sun keeps the chill from being bone deep. Or maybe it's my distraction at Elliott's figure in that elf dress. Who knows?

Soon enough, the girls have skipped the entire way to Weight Expectations, and we're all headed through the door, girls still squealing. For kids who claim to not believe in Santa, they're awfully excited to tell him what they want. Then again, if they know it's me, they also know it's a guaranteed way to give me their lists.

"Thank God you're here." Dinah races towards us before we're all the way in the childcare center and de-winterized. "We've had more RSVPs than expected, so we need to get you suited up and ready to go."

"I thought I was going to bouncer first and Joey was going to Santa." I grab a hanger, so my coat doesn't end up on the floor with the melting slush.

"Joey bailed."

I drop my coat. Forget the slush. There are worse things. Like getting stuck in fifteen pounds of padding for two shifts instead of one.

"What do you mean he bailed?"

"Claims he got sick. Keely is pissed." That tidbit is not only not surprising, it makes me feel a teensy bit better. "Not that any of us have time to do anything about it," Dinah continues. "People are going to start lining up any minute, and we've got to get you dressed. Ooh, Elliott you look amazing. Like a sexy elf."

Elliott's face flames in embarrassment at the compliment. Dinah's not wrong though. I've been trying very hard not to think the same thing about my roommate.

"Not the look I was going for," she responds. "But thanks anyway, I guess. Where do you want me?"

Elliott and Dinah chat about the logistics of the event and how line control needs to be run while I grab the giant wardrobe bag out of the coat closet and lock myself in the bathroom. Thank goodness I remembered to relieve myself before we left the house. The toilet in here is only inches off the floor for all the potty-training kids. Last thing Santa needs is to pee on his own shoe.

Pulling out my phone, I quickly send a text to Joey.

Me: You better be really sick, asshole.

Joey: I feel like I'm dying.

Me: Serves you right since you're dead to me.

His middle finger emoji response is almost immediate. I chuckle at the text but don't have time to keep poking at him. I have a giant, itchy suit to put on while I pray it doesn't give me lice or bedbugs.

Yuck.

"Do it for the kids, Abel. Do it for the kids."

After about ten minutes of untangling buckles and tying hidden elastic so the pants don't fall down, I'm finally channeling Father Christmas.

Quietly, I open the door and peek out.

Holy shit. In the few minutes I've been hidden in the bathroom, a line all the way out of the door and around the corner has formed. Dinah wasn't kidding when she said it would take hours to get through this. No wonder she wanted to split this into two shifts.

Joey really better being dying now, or he will be next time I see him.

"Santa!"

I don't know where the scream came from, but suddenly the cheers are deafening, the line surging forward. Well, surging as much as a bunch of polite parents will allow while there are children every-where. I'll give our members this much—they know Dinah doesn't play. If there are issues, she'll be the first to shut this whole shindig down.

Welp, there's only one thing to do in a situation like this.

I emerge from the bathroom and make sure to keep the door closed enough that no one can see what's behind me. I raise one hand in the air and wave. "Ho, ho ho! Ho, ho, whoa! What the—?"

"I gotta go potty!" a small child yells as he pushes past me into the room I just came out of, holding himself. So much for pretending that was Santa's workshop.

Looking around, I catch Elliott's eye. Mostly because she's trying really hard not to laugh at me. Not *with* me. Oh no. She's definitely laughing *at* me. I cock my head, letting her know I know full well she finds this whole situation hilarious. That's when she loses it, her laughter joining the other joyous sounds in the room.

Making my way to the decorated chair Dinah has reserved for me, er, Santa, I take my place.

"Thanks for joining us, Santa!" Dinah says with an exaggerated smile. "You look great."

"My suit jingles all the way," I say sardonically.

"I know. It's fantastic." And then she lifts her phone up and very obviously takes my picture. "That one's going on our social media page."

"If you tag me," I say with sarcastic sweetness, "you're getting coal in your stocking."

"Good thing Santa isn't a mind reader, or it would be something worse than coal." Turning away from me, Dinah addresses the crowd loudly. "Okay everyone! Are you excited to meet Santa?"

The crowd goes wild again, so I give them a few more obligatory *Ho-ho-ho*s and try my best not to scratch my cheeks to rid myself of the itch from the synthetic beard. Dinah goes over the instructions and, all too soon, is leading a bouncing kid my direction. Immediately, the girl jumps up on my lap, barely missing kneeing me in the junk.

This is going to be long day.

CHAPTER TWELVE

ELLIOTT

"I'm just saying…" I continue as I rinse the dinner dishes and hand them to Abel to put in the dishwasher. This is the second time we've loaded the dishwasher. Apparently, they weren't actually clean when I put them away earlier. Oops. "You could have asked to take a break instead of sitting there the whole four hours."

Yep. Four hours. It took two hundred forty minutes for every single child in line to sit on Abel's lap, tell him what they want for Christmas, and take a picture. Part of the reason it took so long is because of how many parents wanted their own selfies with Jolly Old St. Nick. At first, Dinah tried to stop them, but eventually she gave up.

For as long as they had to hang out and wait for us to finish "working," the girls did remarkably well. Although, they could barely keep from bouncing around during dinner, and we haven't seen them since they raced downstairs to play their favorite Wii games. There is a possibility we may never see them again with all the pent-up energy they're releasing.

"Hell, no." Abel takes the last dish from me and jams it into the packed machine. "I was not going to stay there a minute longer than I had to."

"I understand, but if you had to pee, you could have said something. It would have given you time to get to a big-people-sized toilet instead of the baby one that splashed toilet water all over your foot." I neglect to say what we both know—that splatter wasn't water.

He shuts the dishwasher and grabs a towel to wipe off his hands. "I admit that was not my finest moment, but it was a small price to pay to get that suit off. I'll probably have ringworm now. In fact, my back feels itchy. Do you see a rash?" He turns around and lifts his shirt up, showing me nothing but beautiful, toned back muscles.

If he only knew I was a sucker for a man's back and shoulders, he'd be less likely to flash my favorite muscle group at me. I can't be held responsible for my womanly reactions when they're right in my face.

Fortunately for both of us, I have unusually good self-control and am old enough to be his very beautiful older sister. Or so I tell myself.

"You don't have a rash, Abel. But you do have some ir-*rash*-ional fears. Get it?"

I laugh out loud at my own joke, while he huffs and pulls his shirt back down. "Sure. Laugh at all the diseases I'm going to come down with. It's easy to do since you didn't have to wear a rental suit," he grumbles and turns back around. "I don't even wanna think about it anymore. It's over and done with. Let's go get a Christmas tree."

The sudden topic change startles me. "What? What are you talking about now? How did we go from that to this?"

"Santa. Christmas. A Christmas tree," he explains. "I've fallen so far behind I haven't decorated at all. I feel terrible about it. Mabel and I love the holidays, but I feel like I've been pulling double duty, so it fell by the wayside. Let's take the girls and go get a tree. It'll be fun."

He's not the only one who can't seem to keep up with the rapidly approaching season. With the move and my new job, I hadn't thought much about shopping for gifts, let alone decorating. Part of me also didn't want to overstep my boundaries. It's one thing to put up some lights in our bedroom, but another thing completely to hang stockings on the mantel of someone else's home. As much as I feel comfortable living here, and as great as Abel and I get along, I'm still very aware that this is his house I pay to live in. And it would be weird to have all our stuff combined since we're nothing more than roommates and coworkers. Right? Maybe? I don't even know at this point.

But since he's offering, I might as well push aside my concerns in the interest of giving the kids happy childhood memories.

"Sure." I rinse out the sink quickly and grab the towel he hands me to dry my hands. "Maybe we can get some hot chocolate at that little stand around the corner on our way."

"Do they use real chocolate or chocolate flavoring?"

"Does it matter? It's Christmastime."

Mr. Nutrition considers my words momentarily, and I know he's weighing the pros and cons of keeping his body a temple or giving his daughter a little Christmas joy.

"Fine."

"Christmas joy, it is," I exclaim.

"What?" he asks, eyebrows furrowed.

I wave him off. "Nothing. Let's grab the girls and go before it gets too late."

The initial call down the stairs is met with groans and resistance. Until Abel follows up with the words "Christmas tree" and "hot chocolate." I barely have time to move out of the way before a couple of elementary schoolers knock me out of the way on their way to the coat closet.

Ten minutes, two potty breaks, four coats, and eight snow boots later, we all head out the door.

Walking down the neighborhood street, it hits me exactly how neglected our house really is. All the streetlights have a giant snowflake attached and lit up. Every home has a Christmas tree in the window. Those that don't have beautiful menorahs. Even the few trees lining the streets have oversized Christmas bulbs in various colors hanging from the branches.

I'm glad Abel thought of this. My failure at Christmastime will be one less thing for Ainsley to talk about with her future therapist. The trauma of sharing a room with her mother might still be on that list. Although, the fact that she's skipping down the street is a good indicator I might not come up at all.

"Four please."

In my desire to take it all in and enjoy this moment, I didn't realize Abel was already ordering our drinks from the small takeout window.

Toffee Coffee is a tiny little shop that is only open a few hours during the day but is highly loved in this neighborhood. The owners of the building renovated one room of their home to allow for a walk-up window for customers long before the city required building permits for that kind of thing. As the story goes, Toffee, the woman who started the business, needed a way to provide for her family after her husband was killed in the war, so she would sell lunch out the window to construction crews or other passersby. It was extremely popular among the locals and accomplished exactly what she needed for her family.

When Toffee remarried, the business was no longer needed and closed down. But when one of her children inherited the building upon her death, the idea sprung up again. Permits were filed, a business plan was put in place, and Toffee Coffee was born.

To this day, there's no entrance, no place to sit, no free WiFi. Just really good coffee, hot chocolate, and tea. I like to think Toffee would be pleased to know she left a legacy behind. Isn't that what all of us want to some degree?

Handing me a steaming cup, I thank Abel and take a quick sip. "Thank you for buying. I was so busy enjoying the lights, I didn't realize you'd already ordered. I'll make sure to spring for our drinks next time."

Abel takes his own sip while collecting his change from the employee in the window. "There's going to be a next time?"

I gesture to the girls who are happily playing one of those hand slapping games with rhymes that boarder on inappropriate. "If they have anything to say about it, I'm guessing yes."

"I know it wasn't the goal," Abel says as we each grab a cup for the girls, "but having a live-in playmate has made getting things accomplished so much easier."

I nod in agreement. "I know. Although I'm not convinced it'll last forever. The honeymoon period is bound to wear off at some point."

"I hope not. I don't think I've ever been able to look over my client plans without interruption unless I'm at work."

"You shouldn't be looking at them at home anyway. Haven't you heard that all work and no play makes Abel a cranky boy?"

He chuckles in response. "If Abel ever becomes a cranky boy, remind me of that."

We round up the girls, who are more than happy to sip on some liquid sugar, and meander the two blocks to the parking lot turned Christmas tree lot for the season.

Lights are strung up around the perimeter, giving it the illusion of decoration instead of just a clever way to keep people from taking off with the trees. That, along with the scent of pine, the snow on the trees, and giggles of two excited little girls, makes my spirit soar. There is nothing like watching the holidays through the eyes of children. Life events can get mundane when you are an adult. It can turn into yet another responsibility that has to be dealt with. But seeing the wonder on their faces is like reliving my own childhood—when everything about this time of year is extraordinary—well, I can't help feeling my own sense of fascination.

"Welp, what kind of tree should we get?" Abel tosses his now empty cup in a nearby trash can. I'm still sipping on mine, despite the fact that it's now cold chocolate.

"What are our choices?"

He gently runs his fingers over some delicate branches as we peruse. "I'm sure they have the normal ones—Fraser fir, Douglas fir, maybe a Blue Spruce if we're lucky. Those are always fat and happy. What kind was your favorite as a kid?"

I shrug with a lack of knowledge on the topic. "We always had a fake tree."

Abel, open-mouthed, stops in his tracks and stares at me. "You had a *fake tree*?"

I quirk my lips, fighting a smile at his over-the-top reaction. "Yes?"

He shakes his head, like he's shaking off bad memories. "What kind of monster would do that to you?"

And now that laugh comes. Not at what he is saying, but the ridiculous look on his face. He looks truly heartbroken over my unfortunate childhood.

"You've met my mother," I finally say.

He thinks for a second, hands on his hips. "I'm not sure what to say without sounding like a total jerk."

That starts my giggles up again. This conversation isn't funny, but somehow, I find it hilarious. I may need to find out what Toffee Coffee is putting in their drinks. Even the girls seem a little more amped up than normal.

"Then don't say anything. Let's just find a tree. Girls!" I call out as they chase each other in a totally inappropriate game of tag inside a place of business. "Slow down! And find a tree! Oh my god, they're going to knock something over."

"Probably. But I'm too shaken up by your lack of real tree knowledge to notice at this point."

I smack him on the arm lightly as we continue to stroll around the lot, debating the merits of each potential winner. Some are too tall to fit in the house. Those are also known as "pricey." Others are too skinny. The girls finally come down off their sugar high long enough to join us. Of course, that's a relative term. At least they're within talking distance now, even if they aren't paying attention.

"Is there anything I can help you find?" A tall man with a bushy beard and a flannel shirt approaches. His name tag says "Nate" and his beanie screams "logger." It doesn't really, but he fits the exact stereotype I see in my mind of a guy who cuts down trees for a living.

"We're still looking around." I'm beginning to feel overwhelmed by the vast number of options. This is probably why my mother always had a fake tree. It came out of a box, no questions asked, and you made do with what you had.

"If you're looking for something specific, let me know." His eyes smile along with his mouth, and I can almost feel his excitement. Looks like the girls aren't the only ones delighted for the holidays. "And by the way, you have a beautiful family. Twins?"

It takes me a minute to figure what he means, but when it hits me, I start laughing. Abel has clearly beaten me to it because he's the first to answer.

"Irish twins," he says with a glint in his eye, making me laugh harder.

The salesman gives me a quizzical look. Frankly, I don't blame him. Basically, I'm laughing in the face of his kind words. Not on purpose, but he threw me off guard.

"Well, they're lovely. They were pointing out a bird's nest in one of the trees. Although, they were disappointed there weren't any eggs in it."

"I have no doubt," Abel responds, still keeping up the ruse rather than explain our situation. "They're a handful, that's for sure."

"Girls always are." Nate heads off to another group of customers. As soon as he's out of ear shot, I smack Abel again.

"I can't believe you let him believe we're together," I hiss through my laugh.

Abel waggles his eyes making me roll mine. "Why not? It was funny."

"Well, sure. But how would he come to that conclusion?" I mutter, still baffled.

Abel leans in closer so I can hear him despite lowering his voice. "It's not a far stretch. You're hot. I'm hot. We came here with our kids. Who wouldn't think we're together?"

His words stun me. Is he being serious with his flirting right now or playing around after too much hot chocolate? I honestly can't tell. Even worse, I don't know what I think about it. He's right that he's good looking. But I'm in my forties. He's practically a baby. In another life, maybe. But now? Under these circumstances?

I don't have time to ponder anymore because he suddenly cries out, "OH MY GOD! They have one!"

The girls and I all turn simultaneously to see what has turned Abel into a child in a candy shop. I should have known.

Abel has a giant, oversized grin on his face, and I swear if this was a cheesy Christmas flick, there would be a light beaming down from the sky right over the Blue Spruce he's standing in front of.

Mabel begins jumping up and down, clapping excitedly. "Oh, it's so pretty, Daddy! It's so fat!"

"Fat and happy. Just the way I like my trees."

The four of us begin circling his find, looking for any potential issues.

"Needles aren't too stiff," he says, pulling a few off to inspect them. "Trunk looks solid." Mabel is watching her father intently, pulling on branches in imitation. It makes me nervous, but not really my place to step in.

"Wait." I hate to be the bearer of bad news, but while he has been inspecting the front, I've been looking at the back. "This entire side is... well... I don't know the rules about live trees but this one seems to be dead back here."

"What?" He makes his way around to me, inspecting what I'm seeing and leaving Mabel alone.

I finally cave, my nerves getting the best of me. "Mabel, honey. Can you stop pulling on the branches? We don't want to have a bald spot there."

She responds with a glare and another yank. The tree moves slightly, and I sigh because what else can I do? She's not my child. If Abel doesn't see an issue, and no one is getting hurt, it's not my problem.

Abel stands up, disappointment written all over his face. "Well, damn. It's like the whole back side just shriveled up and died. Now this half price sign makes sense." He sighs deeply. "But the front is so perfect. I guess we could put it in the corner of the room to hide all this, but I really wanted to put it in the window."

"Maybe they have another one," I say cheerfully, trying to offset the discouragement he's feeling. "I bet Nate would know. And since he thinks our family is precious…"

Abel smirks at me, clearly more amused than he was a few seconds ago. "That's a good idea. I'll go ask…"

Before Abel can finish his statement, there's another jerk, a loud crack, and the tree suddenly falls to the ground. Behind it, sporting her own stunned look, is Mabel with a small branch of needles held in her hand.

No words even need to be said as he and I glance over at the giant sign reading "You break it, you buy it." The trunk is clearly split in two, rotten and practically hollow on the inside. Regardless, we're about to come home with a half-dead tree. I know it. Abel knows it. Mabel knows it.

Apparently, Nate knows it, too, as he ambles forward, the same kind smile affixed to his face. "Looks like you guys just wiped out my clearance rack. Blue spruce it is!"

And the alligator tears promptly begin sliding down Mabel's face.

So much for Abel's dream of having a Christmas tree in the front window. This one is going in the corner to hide the dead branches. Once we figure out how to rig the trunk, that is.

CHAPTER THIRTEEN

ABEL

W ork has my body's clock so jacked up I can't seem to sleep in anymore. Not even on Christmas morning. So here I am, at five a.m., wide awake and brewing a pot of coffee, while I wait for Mabel to get up. Well, trying to make coffee. Betsy has decided to take the day off again.

"Come on, Betsy," I grumble, while I smack her in the sweet spot, grateful I have time to deal with her this morning. "Show me some love."

I need all the caffeine I can get since it could be a while until Mabel gets up. My girl loves her sleep almost as much as she loves her Wii.

Speaking of which, I can't wait to see the look on her face when she sees "Santa" brought her a new one, complete with all the upgraded games. Finding it wasn't easy or cheap, considering the gaming system is practically obsolete at this point, but nothing is too good for my girl. Especially since part of me feels like I'm having to do the Christmas of two parents. Running up a credit card I don't need is a small price to pay to give her some joy on Christmas morning.

I think.

Presents aren't going to take the place of her mother, but it is so wrong to want to give her as many distractions as I can on one day out of the year?

Now that I look around the room at the giant pile of gifts, I'm second-guessing this thought process. I'm not sure blowing my careful spending habits is going to lead to a good time, or if all will be forgotten under a sea of wrapping paper.

Maybe I didn't think this through enough. Honestly, I don't think she needs everything I got her. And maybe having everything her little heart desires won't do much more than give her a false sense of entitlement.

Ouch. That's a harsh realization to my parenting skills. But I suppose it's not the first time I've been aware that I cave a little too quickly and spoil a little too much. The last two parent-teacher conferences hinted at such. Not to mention the Christmas tree is in the corner hiding the damage to the back.

In my defense, a significant chunk of these gifts are from my parents and siblings. Still, we may have gone a bit overboard, which is how I ended up standing here, bleary-eyed, banging on the side of my coffee maker, and having daddy-guilt.

The obvious answer to this dilemma, and I'm not talking about the appliance I fight with every morning, is talking to Elliott about this. Not that it really has anything to do with her. Unless Ainsley only gets a couple of things while Mabel is spoiled rotten. That'll make me feel bad.

Sighing, I rub my hand down my face and thank my lucky stars that at least my liquid energy is finally dripping into the pot, but the promise of a caffeine boost isn't helping me forget the issue at hand. The real issue. Well, one of the real issues. Somehow, the lines are becoming blurred with Elliott and moving beyond the basic woman/man attraction. I'm not sure why. When she moved in, I assumed we'd be roommates and would cross paths every once in a while. It never occurred to me that our lives would become inter-twined, and I'm a bit perplexed as to how it happened.

Actually, I know the answer. We need each other. Parenting is hard. You wouldn't think it would be, but keeping a tiny human alive and healthy, and growing them into a functioning adult, is the hardest job out there. It's exponentially more difficult when you are doing it by yourself and don't have a co-parent who is equally responsible. Even if they aren't physically in the house, a parent's job never stops. Falling into our little "it takes a village" situation has relieved the pressure on both Elliott and me, which is why it works.

It's also probably why I'm conflicted. Part of me is worried this fantastic situation I've gotten us into will all fall apart.

The other part of me doesn't care about the consequences. That part wants to push this friendship even further.

There. I admitted it to myself. I want to date Elliott. I think I already knew it, but the night at the tree lot brought it to the forefront of my mind. When that Nate guy pointed out we had a nice-looking family, I could see it plain as day. Us, as a family, with Elliott by my side, holding my hand.

The image shocked me for about half a second, and then suddenly had merit. Elliott is kind and beautiful and a great mom. She has a fantastic sense of humor and is witty. She's smart and motivated but prioritizes her family over everything else. She's a little bit unsure of herself, but it translates as being humble.

And I like her. I like her a lot.

And that could cause problems for all of us if we aren't careful.

Pushing my opposing thoughts out of my mind, I settle onto the couch and flip on the television.

The benefit of being up this early is I get to enjoy a cup of coffee while indulging in one of twelve back-to-back showings of *A Christmas Story*. Man, I love this movie. It reminds me of my own family. The cranky dad who lovingly yells at everyone. The sweet mother who always keeps a gentle temperament and dotes on the younger brother.

Oh, look at that. He won't eat unless he's a piggy. Gross.

Yeah, that kid definitely reminds me of my brother Eugene all right. He was the whiniest little shit and always refused to eat. I've never figured out how he grew up to be a beat cop in Chicago. I didn't know they had a need for officers who scream like Mabel when they see a spider.

I chuckle at my own joke, knowing full well Eugene has actually grown up to be a pretty tough son of a bitch and the force is lucky to have him. I'd never tell him that to his face, though. Nor will I ever call my mother sweet and gentle to her face. Technically, she's both of those things, but with a large Italian flare. If this movie only added in two older sisters and more hand gestures, it could be the family I grew up in.

Speaking of which, I need to make sure Mabel and I are out the door by two. My mother will be livid if we don't make it to Christmas dinner on time. And by *on time*, I mean early enough to peel potatoes, set the table, and yell that the kids are a bunch of hooligans and ask: "Who's raising these monkeys?" It's tradition.

Staring at the boob tube, my thoughts once again wander to Elliott, wondering what she and Ainsley are doing now. Are they awake yet? Are they watching the same movie I am? They spent last night with her mom and won't be back until tomorrow, which is understandable. Yet, it's strange to not have them here. In the short amount of time they've lived here, they've integrated themselves into our lives in such a big way that it doesn't feel right for us all not to be together.

"It's Christmas!" a boisterous voice shouts from the top of the stairs, and Mabel comes barreling down, an exaggerated thump with every step. I smile at her exuberance. Now, this is what Christmas is all about. "Are these my presents, Daddy? Is this all for me? Can I open them?"

Okay, maybe it's not supposed to be all about gifts. We'll work on it.

"Whoa, whoa, whoa," I say with a laugh, placing my coffee cup far back on the table so it doesn't get knocked over as she bounces around. Any day could be the day my beloved Betsy gives out. I can't risk losing any liquid gold. "Hold on a second. Maybe you can start with 'Merry Christmas, Dad.'"

"Merry Christmas, Dad," Mabel says with a monotone voice

usually reserved for hormonal pre-teens. When did eight become the new twelve? "Can I open my presents now?"

"You don't wanna watch this movie with me?"

Immediately, upon looking at the screen, her cute little nose wrinkles up in disgust. "I hate this movie. The next-door neighbors' dogs are the worst. I'd have to file a complaint with animal control."

I'm not sure if I'm offended that she hates my favorite movie, impressed at her problem-solving skills, or disappointed that I likely won't get the chance to see how it ends anywhere other than in my mind.

Shrugging to myself, I decided holly-jolly is the way to go. "Okay. One at a time, though," I yell over the sound of her shriek as she runs to the tree and begins ripping things open.

Forget it, I think to myself, settling back onto the couch and grabbing my mug again. Who cares if she rips through four million gifts in two minutes as long as she's happy, right? I'm perfectly content being an observer.

"New boxing gloves!" she yells, looking at them for a hot second before throwing them over her shoulder and grabbing another gift.

"A Harry Potter shirt!" Again, over the shoulder it goes.

"A box of chocolate-covered cherries!" These are placed carefully on the table. Of course. She's growing up to be a foodie already. Not that it distracts her from the task at hand.

Another rip of paper. Another yell.

"A... coffee maker?"

I furrow my brow, wondering who would have gotten an eight-year-old the ability to binge drink caffeine and if it's Eugene's idea of a joke.

"Let me see." I scoot forward on the couch and take the appliance out of Mabel's hands. Fortunately, she only ripped the top of the paper off. The rest is still intact, with a card affixed to the side. The envelope clearly has "Abel" written on it.

Pulling it off, I hold up the card for Mabel to see.

"Oh, thank goodness," she spouts off. "I thought Santa was

losing his touch." Then, she turns on her heel and continues the whole rip/yell/toss pattern.

I've lost all sense of parenting focus, too interested in the mystery machine, as it will now be referred to. Who would send it to me, and why? The adults in my family don't exchange gifts anymore, too interested in spending our hard-earned money on the children. And Joey has never given me a gift.

As I open the card, I have my answer—Elliott.

My breath hitches at the shock of her thoughtfulness. I know she's struggling financially as much as I am, maybe more so, so for her to sacrifice like this makes me like her all the more.

Abel –

Merry Christmas to the best roommate I could have ever dreamed up. You have no idea how much I appreciate you taking us in and giving me a sense of independence again. I know, I know. We rely on each other a lot to get through the days, but it's nice having my own space again. Even if we're invading yours.

I hope you enjoy this new coffee maker so you can put poor Betsy out of her misery. I know you love her, but Abel, it's time to let her go peacefully. She doesn't want any more lifesaving measures. Pull the plug, already!

I throw back my head and laugh because she's not wrong. I should have replaced poor Betsy a long time ago. Only using her a couple times a week though didn't make it seem worth it.

Have a wonderful day with Mabel and we'll see you sometime tomorrow. Or late morning if my mother doesn't quit bitching about what a waste wrapping paper is.

Elliott.

"Who's it from, Daddy?" Mabel asks, interrupting my thoughts. "Did *Santa* bring it?" Even her emphasizing the word Santa with obvious disgust doesn't detract from the odd sense of excitement I feel about this gift.

It's not that it's a coffee maker. You can get any number of cheap ones at just about any store. It's that Elliott was thinking of me. That she made me a priority and went out of her way to find me the perfect thing.

And it is *absolutely* perfect. Now that the wrapping paper is all off, I can see it's a Bonavita BV1900 TS with heat control to guarantee the perfect temperature. I've seen them before, and they're on the lower price scale of the best brands on the market. Which means they aren't cheap. It also makes me feel bad about the rinky-dink gift I snuck over to her house through her daughter.

"Um," I have to clear my throat of the strange lump that suddenly developed. "It's from Elliott."

"Elliott?"

Sensing distain in her voice, my excitement fizzles. "Yes, Elliott. Is that a problem?"

Mabel shrugs and turns away, pretending to be scouting for another present. I know she's avoiding answering my question. But what can I do? This is a weird transition for her. As much as I want her to get along with Elliott, it's going to take some time. Maybe I should schedule a fun outing for all of us. Or a spa day for just the girls. Or maybe I should ignore the pissy attitude until Mabel gets over it. I don't even know.

Why don't they give you a preteen-of-a-divorced-family-with-an-absent-mom book when you have a kid? That's harder than parenting a baby. All they need is to be fed, burped, and changed. These hormones are way more work to figure out.

Moving my head to crack my neck in the hopes it rids me of the sudden tension in my shoulders, I try to level with her. "Mabel, Elliott isn't trying to be your mom. She's trying to be Ainsley's mom, and we're helping each other out."

She grumbles something under her breath I don't catch.

"Say that again, please. Only this time make sure I can hear it."

Mabel's head whips around so fast it's a wonder it doesn't spin right off her head. "Then why is she waking me up in the morning? And making a breakfast I don't like? And taking me to school?"

"So, you don't have to wake up at four in the morning. And so, I can take an extra client before school. She's helping me out like I help her out. It's no different than me picking Ainsley up after school."

"It's very different." She stomps her foot to emphasize her point, which I'm not getting.

"How?"

That makes her stop and think. Considering how long it takes her to answer, I think she's starting to see my point.

"Because you're hot. All the moms say so. She's helping cause she thinks you're hot."

Maybe she's not seeing my point at all. Or maybe she's stubborn like her mother. Either way, she turns her back on me, a sure-fire indicator she's done with this conversation and would rather open presents.

I'm not sure who learned the lesson here. Her, that Elliott is our friend. Or me, that presents won't ever serve as a distraction for heartache in the form of parental neglect, no matter how many there are.

CHAPTER FOURTEEN

ELLIOTT

C hristmas has always been my favorite time in the Donovan
household. The house is decorated with multiple trees, lights
everywhere, and celebratory knick-knacks from all different parts of
the world. The effort my mother puts in to make this place a winter
wonderland is truly astonishing.

Tucking my legs underneath me, I watch Ainsley open her next
present while sipping on my cup of coffee.

Speaking of coffee, I wonder if Abel opened his present yet and
if he likes it. I know he's attached to his Betsy, but she's going to
give out any day now. With as much as he loves his morning brew, it
could be bad news for those of us caught in the crossfire of an un-
caffeinated Abel.

That's probably an exaggeration. Abel is such a naturally happy
person; I could switch him to decaf, and no one would ever notice.

Still, he loves it. Besides, I got the new fancy coffee maker for
half off when one of our members mentioned trying to unload it. She
was telling Tabitha at the smoothie bar that she got duplicates for her
wedding. Unfortunately, without a gift receipt, the store wouldn't
take it back. Since Tabitha didn't want it, I swooped in and got it for
myself.

That's not completely accurate on how it went down. At first, the member was hesitant, being she didn't know who I was. But the second I mentioned it was for Abel, her eyes lit up like the wreath on my mom's porch, and she gushed all over me about how "If anyone deserves it, he does. Make sure you tell him it's from me!" Then, she giggled and bounced away. And I do mean bounced. Every part of her. I could have probably bounced a quarter off the abs on her. I, on the other hand, have lost actual quarters in my fat roll.

Regardless, I thought it was the perfect present, and I really hope he likes it.

"A Hatchimal!" Ainsley exclaims, excitedly holding up her new, uh, toy? I don't even know what to classify the thing as, but it was on her list, so here it is.

"Do you like it?" Well, that was a dumb question for me to ask. It's not as if her giant smile means she's sad.

"I do, Mommy! What kind is it?"

"Uhhhh…" There are different kinds? I snatched that sucker up on sale at Target. I didn't know I was looking for a specific… creature… or whatever it is. "It's a surprise!" I finally say, making Ainsley delighted all over again and my mother giggle. She knows I have no idea.

"Elliott, it's your turn," my mother finally says. Because in this house, Christmas morning is controlled chaos. One person passes out all the gifts—usually Ainsley because she's small enough to reach the ones that have to be pulled out from behind the tree. Lord knows no one wants to see my butt sticking out from underneath the decorations, nor do we want said butt to knock anything breakable off the branches—then, we each take turns opening. It helps us see what everyone gets so we can all "ooh" and "ah" over everything. But I like it because it makes Christmas morning last for hours, instead of being over in minutes. The holidays are such a blur anyway. Being forced to slow down for the morning isn't a hardship.

If only my mother would let us throw the wrapping paper on the floor, instead of it immediately putting it into a giant trash bag before its completely off the gift it's attached to…

"Which one are you going to open, Mommy?"

Looking at my small stack, I opt for the letter-sized envelope sitting on top. My name is written in rough handwriting, and I immediately recognize it as Abel's.

Taking my time, because that's what a Donovan does on Christmas morning, I slide my finger underneath the lip and slowly pull it open. I pull the paper out and a small square drops onto my lap.

Picking it up and turning it over, I immediately throw my head back in laughter. It's a magnet and it says "Clean." Turn it upside down and it says "Dirty."

"What is it?" Ainsley asks, so I show her. She obviously doesn't understand the significance, so I let my mother explain what a dishwasher magnet is while I read Abel's note.

Elliott –

I figured the best gift I could give you is the gift of not having to redo the dishes again. Three times for one load is enough. You're welcome.

Although, triple-sanitized silverware isn't something I'll ever turn down.

Thanks for always helping out with Mabel. And always helping out with me.

Abel

My heart swells at his words, despite how nonchalant and clearly "friends only" they are. I think it's less about what he wrote and more about his thoughtfulness. Leave it to Abel to find the perfect thing for me, knowing I don't have space to store "stuff." And knowing my brain goes in a million directions at once.

It makes me miss him. Miss them. I miss waking up to the sound of him banging on Betsy and miss hearing the girls race down to the basement for the daily Wii battle. I miss doing dishes side-by-side with Abel and talking about random things. I miss his cooking, and I miss the way he smells when he walks by.

Don't misunderstand, it's nice spending Christmas morning, just the three of us. But it would be nice to spend this holiday at home.

Maybe next year we can do it that way. We can invite my mother to spend the night and...

Wait. No. That's not how this works. Abel and I are roommates, nothing more. Right?

All these thoughts confuse me. Not just because we've only been gone for a day, if that, but because I can't have a crush on Abel. I *can't*.

A crush could lead to kissing, and kissing could lead to sex, and sex leads to a relationship, and then it's all downhill from there. I like living there too much. I like my independence too much to screw it all up over a crush on a man half my age.

Sixty percent of my age?

Seventy percent of my age?

How the hell old is he anyway?

Regardless of the percentages, dating is not on the table for a myriad of other reasons, so I need to stop thinking about this very thoughtful gift and the strange way it makes my stomach flip-flop.

Any time now.

No more flip-flopping.

Just a normal stomach.

Why is it still flopping around like a fish out of water?

And why can't I come up with a metaphor that doesn't involve fish?

"Your turn, Gigi!" My mother allows Ainsley to pick out the next gift she's going to open, and I try really hard to keep my focus on the woman who raised me, not the man who raises me up on a regular basis.

Oh geez. This is out of control. I don't know what my problem is. Or maybe I do. Maybe I need the attention of a man my own age to keep me occupied. Derrick never filled my emotional bucket, so to speak. Clearly, it needs a little pouring in of compliments, so I can get over myself and these irrational thoughts.

"Oh Ainsley! I love it!" my mother gushes, as she pulls a deep purple sweater out of the box. "Did you pick this out?"

My daughter nods excitedly. "I picked purple! Mom said you'd like blue better, but I knew purple was your favorite color like me."

My phone buzzes an alert. The matriarch and the baby of the family don't seem to notice, too engaged in the discussion of all the clothes we considered giving as gifts, which gives me the opportunity to check the message. I know who I'm hoping it's from, and I'm a little disappointed in myself for those thoughts.

Until I see that it is, in fact, Abel texting.

Abel: Thank you for my gift. You spent way too much money on this!

Me: You don't know this about me, but I'm actually a bargain hunter. You'd be surprised how little I actually shelled out.

Abel: I'm not sure if I'm hurt to not be worth very much money or thrilled to know you found a good deal! Either way, Betsy has been retired and the Mystery Machine has officially taken over her spot.

Me: Mystery Machine? That's what you named it?

Abel: For now. I'm not opposed to renaming, but it was a mystery figuring out who sent it to me, especially since Mabel got to it before I did in her attempt at breaking the world record for fastest present opening.

Me: Oh no! Lol. I'm glad you figured it out.

And I'm glad we open presents in an orderly fashion to avoid issues like that. I don't say that to Abel, though. Everyone does the holidays different, and as long as everyone is happy, there's no right or wrong way.

Me: I'm also proud of you for letting Betsy go. And my condolences.

Abel: Lol. Thanks. It's a hard time for everyone.

Abel: What time will you guys be back tomorrow?

Me: Probably a little after lunch. Will you be there?

Abel: We'll be here. Probably still finding bits and pieces of wrapping paper on the floor.

Me: I'll be sure to pull out the vacuum. ;)

Putting my phone down, I don't wait for a response. Instead, I turn my attention back to my child, who is back in her little spot, slowly unwrapping her next gift, completely oblivious to her mother's internal conflict. I have to keep reminding myself that Abel is my roommate. A fantastic, kindhearted, generous roommate, but nothing more. That's the way it has to be.

CHAPTER FIFTEEN

ABEL

"Okay, I've got popcorn, chips, miniature brownies, and caramel M&Ms for the cutie," I joke, as I hand the bowl to Elliott, who shoots me an annoyed glare that quickly turns into wide-eyed delight. "And some leftover peanut brittle." Placing the rest of our goodies on the table in the living room, I pick up a piece of the brittle and hold it up to the light to inspect it. "Although, I'd be careful with this stuff. I'm not sure if it's from this year or last year, so it might actually pull one of your teeth out, depending on how sticky it is."

Elliott laughs around one of her M&M's. "It's from Dinah, and since I haven't known her that long, I guarantee it's from this year."

"Aaaah. Except I knew her last year, so I knew peanut brittle was coming. You don't know if I combined our collective leftovers," I joke and plop down next to her on the couch.

Her eyebrows rise. "Wow. You're taking this 'what's mine is yours' thing seriously, aren't you?" she amuses and pops another piece of candy in her mouth.

I squeeze the sides of her knee in response, making her squeal from the unexpected tickle.

I win.

"It's called space-saving," I admonish. "No reason to have duplicate tins hanging around, clogging up the kitchen."

Elliott shakes her head and rolls her eyes.

So far, tonight has been pretty fun. It's New Year's Eve and neither of us had plans, so we opted to hang out at the house with the girls. It worked out well since Ainsley was supposed to be with her dad tonight. I don't know the whole story, but somehow, she ended up being brought home early, and not shockingly, on the biggest party night of the year.

None of us were disappointed.

Quite the contrary. Mabel was so excited by her friend's unexpected return, she decided we should have a huge New Year's Eve party. And by huge, she meant lots of snacks I had to prepare, and she and Ainsley would dance around the living room to whatever "Rockin' New Year's Eve" special is on this year.

With such short notice, I had to scramble to find the appropriate snacks. We don't typically keep junk food in the house. Or, at least, I don't. Turns out, Elliott has been hiding a few things here and there. Not that I'm mad about it on tonight of all nights. It meant I was able to find appropriate party food with a couple of hours to spare before the new year, when we'll probably all resolve to eat healthy again. It happens. Nothing spurs on the desire to eat better like completely overdoing it while celebrating the "New Year, New You."

"Oh! I almost forgot!" Elliott uses my thigh to push herself up off the couch. The contact sends a warm feeling from my leg straight through the rest of my body. What would it be like if that was our normal way of touching? How would it feel if I could put my arm around her when she sits back down and hold her close? Would her body melt into mine? Would she rub her hands down my chest? Would I rub my hands down hers?

A man can dream, right?

Almost as quickly as she left, Elliott bounces back in the room, more party supplies in hand. "I can't believe I forgot these! Look, girls, I've got party hats, some noisemakers, and a few sparklers left from the Fourth of July." She stops and looks out the window.

126

"Although, I don't know how well those will work when it's snowing."

"Again?" I turn to look out the picture window. Sure enough, giant flakes are falling. I don't mind snow, but I wouldn't mind a reprieve from almost-daily accumulations.

The girls, on the other hand, are too excited with the new party supplies to notice. I am not nearly as enthusiastic, too busy rubbing the buzzing out of my eardrum after my wild child purposely blew the horn in close range.

Elliott says something else I don't catch.

"What?" I bang the side of my head in an overexaggerated gesture. "I've suddenly gone deaf in the last thirty seconds from those horns blowing in my ear. Good thinking, by the way." I give her a sarcastic thumbs up.

"Girls, let's save the horns until midnight, so we can get really loud."

Ainsley complies. Mabel, not so much. She continues her attempt at making music by adding some sort of rhythm to the single note.

Wait. Is that supposed to be "Wrecking Ball" by Miley Cyrus? Huh. That's not half bad.

"Mabel, please," Elliott pleads. "Your dad is old enough without him needing hearing aids prematurely."

"Right," I say and immediately register what she just said. "Wait. It's not very nice for the pot to call the kettle black."

Elliott shrugs with an ornery smile. "And yet, you agreed."

"Only because I couldn't hear you," I grumble like a petulant child who wants to always be right. I'm pretty sure the incessant horn blowing is making this conversation about a thousand times harder to have. "Mabel!" I finally yell loud enough to be louder than her horn. "Stop with the horn, baby."

Mabel smiles and drops the horn on the couch and grabs a shiny, pointy hat that has fringe all around it. Putting in on her forehead, she bounces back over to Ainsley, laughing about being a unicorn.

Ah, it must be nice to be eight. Old enough to be relatively self-sufficient, still young enough to enjoy imaginative play.

"I wish I could get her to listen to me like that," Elliott cracks as she sits back down.

Her quip piques my interest. Putting my arm on the couch behind her, I turn to face her. "Does she give you lip in the mornings before school?"

Elliott refuses to look at me, but if I'm not mistaken, her face is getting a little flushed. That's not a good sign.

"If she is, I need to know."

Still no response.

"Seriously, Elliott, I need you to tell me if Mabel is giving you grief in the mornings. I've been working with her on respecting authority better, but if I need to talk to her again, I need you to tell me."

Elliott sighs, but at least she finally looks at me. "That's the thing. I don't know if it's lack of respect, or just trouble transitioning to us moving in."

"What's the difference?"

"Motivation, I guess." Elliott's gaze drifts back to the girls, and a smile immediately graces her lips. "It's tough to lose a parent. I did it as an adult, and it sucked. I can't imagine being a child and not simply losing a parent, but it being the parent's choice. I'm trying really hard to be sensitive to how she's probably feels every time 'Ainsley's mom' tells her to do something."

If I wasn't sure how I felt about Elliott, I'm pretty sure I'm half in love with her now. Not many people would take a child's feelings into consideration during a major life change. Nor do many people take motivation into consideration when thinking about someone else's bad behavior. I like that about her. I like it a lot. Probably more than I should.

"Hey." I nudge her with my knee, so she'll look at me again. "I think you are an amazing person in general. But for you to see beyond the things Mabel says and does to the why of it, that bumps you up to the extraordinary category in my book."

Embarrassed, she rolls her eyes and tries to turn away. "Whatever, Abel."

I nudge her again. She's not getting away from this so easily. "I'm serious. I know Mabel can be—" I look over and find my child playing a strange game of tag, now with two hats over her eyes. "A little weird sometimes." Elliott huffs a laugh. "And she's full of energy and as sassy as they come. I want you to know how much I appreciate that you're taking the time to look beyond that, to see the person beneath. She's my whole world, ya know?" Of course, Mabel takes this opportunity to run right into the wall, smooshing both hats and possibly blinding herself. It remains to be seen. "And that'll never change. Even if she pokes both her eyes out from some ridiculous accident that could have been prevented."

"Oh yeah." Elliott responds with a laugh of her own, as she keeps her eyes on the girls. "Amazing how we can love them despite things like that."

She points at Ainsley who has a hat on her rear and is yelling, "I'm gonna catch all my farts and light the whole hat on fire! It'll be a giant fireball!" Mabel is rolling on the floor, howling with laughter.

I'm only half-kidding when I ask, "You think peanut brittle ferments into some sort of stimulant?"

"I have no idea. But they definitely need to be cut off from the sugar."

Simultaneously, we lean forward and grab all the treats with sugar in them off the table. The girls immediately protest until we promise to turn on a movie of their choice. Bad move on my part. They choose some Disney kids musical about a dancer turned boxer. Bonus points that it covers each of their favorite activities. Negative points for it being a musical.

Yay, me.

But it at least keeps them somewhat entertained while we wait for the main event. And by "somewhat," I mean they have to dance and sing through every musical number, and when it's solely dialogue, they're glued to the TV. Still in the standing position, of course. No need to waste precious time sitting down and standing back up with this many songs to enjoy.

"Dad!" Mabel shakes my shoulder, rousing me from my relaxed state. "Dad, did you sleep through the movie?"

I suck in a big breath. "Nope. Just resting my eyes."

"Was that your eyes snoring during their rest?" Elliott quips. I shoot her a dirty look.

Mabel nudges me again, so I return my attention to her. "Why did you sleep through the movie? It's my favorite."

With some quick thinking on my part, I blurt out, "Well I couldn't see the screen because you ladies were dancing in front of the TV. I was listening really hard and imagining everything that was happening."

Elliott does a terrible job of stifling a giggle, until I squeeze her knee again. Mabel just glares at me.

"That is a terrible excuse, Daddy. But I'll forgive you."

"You will? That's sweet of you, baby."

"Yep. Because we can watch it again tomorrow, and we'll dance *behind* the couch so you can see."

The smile on my face is frozen. "Amazing idea."

Mabel nods once, like she's putting a period on the end of the conversation.

"Well, that backfired on you, didn't it?" I hate it when Elliott's right.

"Not quite." Pushing up off the couch, I begin to grab the now empty bowls of popcorn to clean up. "If they're dancing behind the couch, they can't see that my eyes are closed."

"Oh, I can't wait to see you try to sleep sitting up."

"Please," I retort. "I mastered that move in my high school chemistry class. Mr. Berik would drone on and on about reactions. Man, he was boring. And blind as a bat. As long as we were upright, he never knew we were sleeping."

She hands me a few dishes I begin rinsing before putting them in the dishwasher. "It's good to know you got so much out of your public education."

"Those are life skills, Cutie."

"Stop trying to make that a nickname, Beast."

"Mom! Abel! It's time!" Ainsley races out of the room as quickly as she raced in. A glance at the clock indicates she's right. The ball is about to drop.

I slap the magnet on the dishwasher and quickly wipe my hands before following Elliott into the living room where girls are already counting down.

"Fifteen! Fourteen! Thirteen!"

I watch the three women of the house as they count backward, giant smiles on all their faces. As hard as the first part of the past year was, I'm grateful it ended on such a high note. I find myself looking forward to the coming year and where it's going to take us all.

"Three! Two! One! Happy New Year!"

The crowd in Times Square goes wild, probably for the second time tonight, since we're an hour behind, and people begin hugging. The camera zooms in on couples who can't keep their hands off each other, giant confetti falls from the sky, and "Auld Lang Syne" begins playing in the background.

In our living room, however, the girls are jumping up and down, hugging each other tightly.

"Happy New Year, Abel," Elliott says, and comes in for a hug.

"Happy New Year, Elliott." We begin to pull away, and I look into her eyes. Suddenly, the air in the room completely shifts. The tension palpable. I watch in what seems like slow motion as Elliott licks her bottom lip, practically in invitation. It's all the encouragement I need.

Tilting my head down, I press my lips to hers, slowly. When she doesn't pull away, when she kisses me back, I shift my body to face her fully and bring my hand to her face. Cupping her cheek, I open my mouth a tiny bit to lock our lips more intimately. She reciprocates, so I slowly press my tongue forward, seeking entrance into her mouth.

"Eww..." The sound of giggles snaps me back to reality. Apparently, Elliott has the same issue since she practically jumps away from me.

I look over at the kids, who are still giggling, hands over their mouths as the combination of excitement, shock, and probably residual sugar make them deliriously giddy. I chance a glance back at Elliott who has the same look on her face I'm sure I have on mine: total and utter shock.

Her fingers are pressed against her lips, the same lips I was just gently kissing, and I want so badly to know if she is regretting what happened. Personally, I'm not sure what to think. In three seconds flat, this roommate situation got so much more complicated.

How did that happen? Where do we go from here? And why do I want to do it again so badly?

CHAPTER SIXTEEN

ELLIOTT

Plodding down the stairs to make some coffee, I realize I'm going to need an extra cup this morning. I was up all night, thinking. More specifically, I was thinking about that kiss at midnight.

I would be a big, fat liar if I said I wasn't attracted to Abel. What's not to lust after? The chiseled jaw? The lush brown hair? Those abs or rock-hard thighs? Yeah. He's a real ogre, all right.

I guess I'd never expected a man as amazing as Abel would be attracted to *me*. And to be perfectly honest, I'm not completely sure this attraction isn't one-sided, and he was just caught up in the moment.

That's probably more accurate. It happens all the time. Like when someone is in a plane crash with a stranger, and they're the only survivors, and they end up falling in love on a deserted island while they wait to be found.

Except not at all like that, and I need to lay off the nighttime dramas for a while. It's messing with my sense of reality.

But still, Abel's never made a move on me. He doesn't flirt with me any differently than he flirts with everyone, and I know for a fact he's not really hitting on Tabitha. It's the way Abel is. It's his form of "communication," if you will. Things just got a little out of hand last night. That's all. No reason to freak out. No reason to worry. Just ignore it, and it'll go away.

I triple check the magnet because I have no interest in doing double the dishes again, then satisfied with what is says, pull open the dishwasher while I wait for the coffee to brew and begin the act of putting away all the clean silverware. That'll keep my mind off of things.

Except these are the bowls we used for our snacks last night. When we put them in the sink to clean up and the countdown began. When we hugged in the New Year and Abel kissed me. On the lips. His tongue snaking out from between his lips, wanting to tangle with mine...

"Good morning, Cutie."

"Ah!" I yell and lose my grip on one of the spoons, caught totally off guard in my inappropriate daydream.

Abel, being as agile as he is, catches it before it hits the floor. "Whoa! Did I scare you or something?"

Heart racing, I decide to go with his option. "I haven't had any coffee," I say, still clutching my hand over my heart. "So, I don't think my awareness levels are up to par quite yet. But I'm okay." I wave a hand like my breathing is going to go back to normal at any time, even though with him in the room, I'm lying to myself. *Deflect, Elliott. Deflect.* "And why are you still trying to make *Cutie* a thing?"

His lips curl up in amusement, and he grabs a handful of silverware to put away. "Not trying, Cutie. Succeeding. It's our thing."

I roll my eyes, knowing I'm never going to win this battle. I might as well join him. "Whatever, Beast. What's up?"

"We should talk about what happened."

And here we go. The brush-off conversation that starts with "We got caught up in the moment," and ends with "Let's forget it ever happened." I'm not thrilled about having to kick my fantasy to the curb so quickly, but I do appreciate he's facing this head-on instead of stringing me along.

Not that I think there's really a chance we would date anyway, so it's not really any kind of stringing.

Regardless, it's probably best to get this conversation over with. I discreetly take a deep breath, steeling my emotions for the letdown while maintaining my status as a functioning adult. "Yes, we should."

"We should date."

"I agree—wait, *what*?"

"We should try dating."

I blink once.

Twice.

Three times.

Shake my head, because surely, I heard the right words but put them into the wrong sentence in my head.

No. No, the words keep putting themselves together the same way. But... what?

"I think my brain isn't, like, wording correctly right now." I move my hand around about my head, like it's a jumbled mess. "Did you say you think we should date?"

Abel grabs my hand from the air and pulls it down, wrapping my fingers around a mug. I'm not sure if he wants me to put it away or fill it with coffee. "Your brain is wording fine. Interesting phrase, by the way. And yes, that's exactly what I suggested."

Let's pause for an After-School Special real-life moment. A thirty-something god of the gym, for some unknown reason, has decided this forty-something divorced mom, who refuses to lift anything more than a pound of ground beef, is the best the dating pool has to offer. There are only two explanations for it:

1. On-line dating truly has hit rock bottom.
2. Abel is taking steroids just as my mother predicted.

His voice is remarkably low for someone who could break into a 'roid rage at any moment, so I'm going to have to go with option number one. And what a sad day in the life of singlehood, am I right?

Regardless, I can't tell Abel my thoughts because that would be weird. This whole situation is weird. Dating the guy I'm living with and working with would be weird, wouldn't it? "Don't you think that would be weird?"

There. Maybe Abel has the answer for me.

Instead, he shocks the crap out of me by saying, "Why? You aren't attracted to me?"

My mouth drops open. "What? Why would you ask that?" If he could read my mind, he would know that isn't the slightest bit true. Hell, if my daughter wasn't sleeping in the same room as me, I might have indulged myself with a few of my attraction fantasies and had some "me time," as my seventh-grade health teacher used to call it. That was a traumatizing story in itself.

"So, you aren't attracted to me."

Well, now he's just being ridiculous. "I didn't say that." I give him an eye roll for good measure. "I mean, I'm not *un*attracted to you."

Especially when he gives me that smile. You know, the one he flashes right before he says something ornery. It's kind of my favorite. "So, you aren't repulsed by me. That's step one of every solid relationship."

My mouth opens and closes like a fish out of water. Again with the damn fish references. I haven't had enough caffeine to figure out how to twist the conversation into a more neutral territory. And I certainly can't tell Abel the truth—that I think he's mature beyond his years and will be an amazing boyfriend to someone. I just don't see how that can possibly be me. The problems it would cause the girls alone don't make it worth it.

"Think about it," he finally says when I don't respond, and hands me the last clean mug before turning to walk away.

Oh, don't worry, Abel, I think to myself. *This is the only thing I'm going to be thinking about for days. I can already feel it.*

CHAPTER SEVENTEEN

ABEL

She doesn't think I noticed, but I saw the surprise and confusion in Elliott's eyes when I told her I wanted to see her on a more intimate level. I wasn't trying to screw with her, but she acted surprised and then gave me that deer in the headlights look; I couldn't help but keep going. She's fun to mess with. Realistically, she likes to joke around with me too, so I don't feel bad about it.

But I also recognized she needed time to process the idea of taking our relationship to the next level. So, I left her alone about it and acted normal. Slowly but surely, her guard has come back down.

At this point, I know she thinks we aren't going to have this conversation, but we absolutely are. She is a hot-blooded woman, and I'm a hot-blooded man. My divorce is final, so there is no piece of paper standing in my way. The only thing I need to do is convince her that we're good together and can be even better if we take this next step.

I'm not worried. I can be a convincing guy. I just have to find the way to prove I'm right, and doing so means I'm going to have to take this really slow.

"I still think we should date," I announce as I storm into the dining room like a man on a mission.

Well, not *that* slow. I need to make progress forward.

Elliott's fork stops, halfway to her mouth. Lowering it slowly, she licks her lips. She's not fooling me. She's buying time to come up with her next argument. "Didn't you call me your best friend the other day when you were talking to your mom on the phone?"

I was hoping she'd overheard that.

"Yeah. So?"

Leaning forward on her elbows, I already know which direction she's going with this one, and she's wrong.

"Dating your best friend is a terrible idea."

I lean forward as well. "It's a great idea. Aren't the best relationships founded on friendship?"

She purses her lips, and backs up, picking up her fork again to continue eating her Sunday breakfast. "I'm not having this conversation."

I back off as well, but only temporarily. She can't hide her smirk from me.

Two weeks later, while cooking dinner:

"You know, dating is just friends who are committed to having benefits with only each other." I chance a glance at her as I slice the zucchini for the "noodles" I'm making for dinner.

Elliott snickers while stirring the alfredo sauce she's making from scratch. "So, what you're saying is you could see yourself having sex with me?"

"I don't know. Let me think about it." I close my eyes and realize I am way better at imagery than I knew. Seriously. And if I thought Elliott was beautiful with clothes on, when she's naked in my mind, she's practically a goddess. I better open my eyes before she sees the physical effects of my lust. "Just thought about it," I say, going back to my chopping. "Not bad. Definitely worth doing again."

Her shocked face makes her eyes and mouth the same size before she blurts out, "Ohmygod, I don't want to talk about this."

Liar. She's smiling again.

Ten days later:

"You know I'm eight years older than you, right?"

I look over at Elliott, who is sitting next to me on a park bench. It's still cold outside, but for January, "cold" is a huge step up from "bone-chilling, breath freezes on contact with the air." When the girls asked to play outside, we decided to take advantage of the weather before we're stuck inside again.

But that's not the part that's important right now. What I'm excited to focus on is how I knew I was right. I haven't brought up one conversation in close to two weeks about dating, but Elliott's been thinking about it. I knew my plan would work.

"Yeah. So?" I don't say anything else. I want Elliott to do the talking this time. If I'm going to ease her fears, I need to know what they are.

"If relationships are just friends committed to benefits, you should know an additional eight years of life and a child means I come with saggy boobs."

That's all she's worried about? Her boobs?

I furrow my brow and shake my head. "So what? I have a beer gut."

She rolls her eyes, which I have learned is her go-to response to most of my humorous antidotes. "You have no gut. You have washboard abs."

"Give me eight years. I'm aging too, ya know."

"Ohmygod, I'm not talking to you."

You don't need to, Cutie. Just keep thinking.

Eight days later, while sharing a bowl of popcorn in front of the TV:

"They're not just saggy. These boobs are small too."

I pause briefly from my chewing as an image of a topless Elliott rolls through my brain. It's not my fault—I didn't bring up her boobs. I'm just a guy having a normal response to the topic at hand.

Obviously, the look on my face gives me away because she smacks my arm, snapping me out of my daze.

"I don't think your boobs are small, Elliott. I think they're perfect because they're yours. Besides, my penis isn't ginormous like the men in your books."

She opens her mouth to argue, but suddenly processes my last sentence. "Are you saying you have a micropeen?"

Taking a page out of her book, I roll my eyes. "No. I'm average in length and girth. And even if I wasn't, I'm not opposed to letting my fingers do the walking."

Her jaw drops momentarily before she turns back to the TV, grumbling, "I don't want to talk about this."

Yes, you do.

A week later:

"I'm not the girl who initiates sex," Elliott announces, as she comes barreling into the kitchen while I'm doing dishes. She's wild and animated, talking with her hands. I have to work really hard to not look up from the soapy pot I'm scrubbing. I don't want to scare her off. "I mean, sometimes. But, most of the time, it has to be the guy."

"No problem," I say nonchalantly. *Don't spook her, Abel.*

"No, really. I'm game for it if you get me going. But you have to start it. It's not even a libido thing." She keeps trying to convince me, but actually, I'm pretty sure she's trying to convince herself. "It's a personality thing."

"Okay."

"I feel like you aren't taking this seriously."

I finally look up and meet her eye. "I'm not."

"But I thought you wanted to have sex with me."

"Who says I have to take sex seriously? It can be fun too. Just wait until you find out the things I can do with some whipped cream." I waggle my eyebrows, hoping to make her laugh.

She doesn't. But she does blink rapidly a few times, frozen in place, before storming out of the room muttering, "We're not talking about this."

Maybe not. But I'm starting to think we don't have to. It's only a matter of Elliott wrapping her brain around the inevitable. And that makes me excited.

Three days later:

"What do you think of oral?"

140

I choke on my bite of ice cream, completely caught off guard by Elliot's candor. "What kind of question is that?"

She looks at me innocently, but I'm not fooled. She's trying to set me up. "You want to date. It's an honest question. We need to be on the same page."

She forgets two can play this game. And I am very, very good at games.

Turning back to the TV, pretending not to be affected, I say, "Make sure to eat some pineapple."

"Are you kidding me?" she sneers. "That's so sexist."

"You're right. I'm kidding. Want a bite of my ice cream?" I grab a small scoop and hold it out to her, knowing she can't resist sweets. "It's this new healthy kind I found at the store."

"Sure. What kind is it?" Elliott opens her mouth wide and closes her lips around the spoon.

"Pineapple. So I taste good for you too."

Elliott immediately starts choking.

Mission accomplished, I think, as I pat her on the back.

The next day:

"I don't understand."

The look on Elliott's face tells me she's finally ready to talk about this for real. No more games. No more dancing around the topic. A real, adult conversation about the state of our relationship.

Wiping my hand on a dish towel, I toss it to the side and lean back against the sink. "What's there to understand?"

"It's just..." She looks up at the ceiling and bites her lip. "You could have anyone in the world. Anyone. But for some reason, you're propositioning me. An average, everyday woman who is old enough to be..."

"Watch it," I warn. "That's my best friend you're talking about."

"...your aunt." She quirks her eyebrow in challenge, which makes me smile. But we've got to get back on track, and she needs to know how I really feel.

"Look. Everyone chases the whole head-over-heels feeling with all the lusting and can't-be-apart-for-three-minutes. Been there. Done that. How long did it last?"

Elliott shrugs. "I don't know. A couple years, I guess."

"Exactly. I already love you." Her eyes widen. "Yeah, I said it. You're one of my best friends, so that love is already there. And you probably feel the same, right?"

She pauses, and I can tell she's really processing my words. "Well, yeah."

"We live together well. We work together well. We could stay roommates and we'd be perfectly happy. The only thing we're talking about is adding sex and the possibility of sleeping in the same bed to our future. That's it."

She bites her lip and looks down. "But what if someone comes along that you fall in love with?"

The vulnerability on her face speaks volumes about how scared she is. I realize I did the right thing by planting the seeds of dating and letting her come to her own conclusions on her own time.

Walking toward her, I grab her by the arms and rub up and down. "You can only fall in love with someone if you're looking to find it. I'm hoping to find it with you. Once I'm committed, that's it for me. That means not flirting with any other women. Not going on dates with other women. That means being committed to my very best friend in the whole world. And maybe taking her in the ass at some point."

Elliott's laugh is loud and boisterous, and I know her fear is being overshadowed by her love of the unexpected twist in conversation. "Pig." She slaps me lightly on the arm.

"Maybe. But I'd like to try being your pig. What do you say?"

She sighs. "I'm so much older than you."

"I know that's a sticking point for you, but think of it this way: statistically, men die before women, so we're basically the same age."

"Statistically men mature slower, so I'm basically your grandma," she deadpans.

"Did you just call yourself my grandma?"

Elliott cringes. "It was a poor choice of words. I didn't realize it would sound bad until it was too late. But it also proves my point."

I chuckle. "You've never seen my grandma. You are nowhere close to looking like her. You are sexy and sweet and funny. You're a great mom and a great manager. You make running a daycare look like the easiest thing in the world, and you make being a mom look like cake too."

"Are you trying to butter me up?"

"Is it working?"

"Maybe a little."

I smile and do something I've only dreamed of for the past six weeks—I lean down and kiss her. She tastes like coffee and chocolate and a hint of pineapple, which makes me laugh against her lips.

"What's so funny, Beast?" she whispers, never breaking contact with me, instead tangling her hands in my hair.

"Pineapple," I murmur and wrap my arms around her waist, pulling her closer.

"A girl can't be too prepared."

And then we stop talking, communicating our excitement and even our fears about this new venture, with only our mouths. It's exactly how I thought it would be.

Perfect.

CHAPTER EIGHTEEN

ELLIOTT

"I wanna take you on a date."

I look up at him from unloading the dishwasher and stare at him like he's lost his mind. We've been officially "dating" for a couple weeks now, and as much as I hate to admit it, Abel was right. Nothing much has changed. Our morning and afternoon routines are the same. We still have witty, fun conversations. He's still bright-eyed and perky first thing in the morning. I'm still like one of the extras from *The Walking Dead*.

The biggest change is the kisses we sneak when the girls aren't looking, which is much of the time, considering they're downstairs. Playing Wii. Again. Although Wii boxing is still banned.

Not that I should be surprised by any of this. Living with Abel wasn't ever a hardship, and I've learned quickly dating him isn't a hardship either. I should have known. He doesn't bring me flowers or chocolate, but my love language has never been gifts anyway. I couldn't care less about roses and jewelry. But a man who pitches in and pulls his own weight, as well as some for others? Now that's the love language I can appreciate.

"And what, exactly, are we going to tell the girls since they don't know we're dating?"

"That's easy." He slings his arm over my shoulder and leans down for a quick peck. "We're going to tell them we have to go to a work event."

"Okay. That's doable. But are we gonna leave the girls at home on their own?"

"There is such a thing as a babysitter," he deadpans.

I tap my finger to my lips. "Your parents don't know we're dating. My mother doesn't know we're dating. Basically, no one knows we're dating, so exactly where do you want to find one of these illusive babysitter things?"

"Another easy one," he exclaims, throwing his arms out victoriously. "Joey."

"Joey? Are you kidding me?" The Joey I know would love nothing more than to give me grief about my private life, so cluing him into this new relationship is a negative. The short time I've known him from living here, he seems to think making me blush is a good life goal. It doesn't bother me, necessarily; I would just prefer not to hand him ammunition.

Abel's arms and face fall. "What's wrong with Joey?"

"First, he would spend the entire time in the basement with two young girls sparring with him. That's weird."

Crossing his arms, Abel huffs. "Only if you make it weird. I call it teaching little girls how to defend themselves."

I point my finger at him. "You just made it a million times creepier."

"Yeah, that sounded better in my head."

I huff a small laugh and continue. "Second, if Joey comes over to babysit, he'll know there is no work event and, therefore, figure out you're taking me on a date. So will the girls. And the cat will be out of the bag."

"Hmm. You bring up an interesting problem." Abel thinks for a minute before his eyes light up. "I've got it. We'll tell them we have to go to a PTA meeting."

"We're not on the PTA."

"Joey doesn't know that."

"But the girls will as soon as we don't show up to volunteer for anything."

"Eh. We can tell them we had irreconcilable differences at the meeting and quit." Moving closer, Abel places his hands on my hips and pulls me closer. He's always doing that. Touching me in little ways and sneaking in small kisses when no one is looking. I like it. I like that he's affectionate and makes it a point to let me know he's attracted to me. It can get a little dicey when keeping a new relationship under wraps. But Abel knows exactly what to do to make me feel confident that this is truly a good thing.

"But really," he says, his tone changing from Playful Abel to Sensual Abel. "Go on a date with me, Elliott. I know we're hiding from the girls because this is a little too insta-family. But let's go somewhere to be just Abel and Elliott. Not Mom and Dad, or coworkers or employees. Just us."

Well, when he puts it like that...

"Fine." I look at up him and smile, feeling some nervous excitement over our first night out. "When?"

"Hold that thought." Without letting me go, Abel pulls his phone from his back pocket and presses a couple of buttons. I'm not sure which ones since he's taller than I am, but soon enough, the phone is pressed to his ear and I find out. "Hey, Joey. What's up? Yeah?" Abel grimaces. "Ew. Joey. No. Joe... seriously... That's gross! I'm not interested in your sex life. Stop!" I press my face into Abel's chest, unable to stop my giggle. He pinches my side, tickling me and making me squeak. "I didn't call to hear this stuff, so stop talking for two minutes. You done? Thank you. I need a babysitter tonight. You free? Uh huh. Yeah, it's a PTA meeting so Elliott has to go too. Is that okay? Ainsley's pretty mellow compared to Mabel, but it's still double the kids. Yeah. Cool. See you in a bit."

Shutting down his phone, Abel quirks an eyebrow as if he's won some invisible contest I didn't know we were playing. "He'll be here in two hours."

"Sounds like a plan. So where are you taking me? It better be somewhere fancy," I joke, secretly hoping I can wear jeans, no matter where we go.

He bobbles his head back and forth momentarily. "Fancier than work. Not as fancy as a wedding."

Now he has my interest piqued. "So, dress like I'm actually going to a PTA meeting?"

He stares at me blankly. "I have no idea. I've never been to one."

"You're missing out, Beast. That's where you can find all those hard-up single moms who spend all day at our gym." I pat him on the shoulder, a grimace set firmly on his face, and go back to putting the dishes away.

"That's exactly why I don't go to those things." An honest to goodness shudder runs through his body. Who knew men could have such a strong reaction to women hitting on them? It's practically visceral.

"But seriously, Abel. Where are you taking me?"

Abel's face lights up but he remains tight-lipped. "Just be ready for anything, Cutie."

Famous last words, I'm sure.

* * *

"Doesn't the aquarium close at six?"

Abel's gloved hand squeezes mine as we walk quickly up the steps to Shedd Aquarium, one of the largest aquariums in the world and a popular tourist spot when people visit in the summer. Because who in the world would purposely come to Chicago in the winter? Crazy people, that's who.

But no one ever accused us of being sane. We're the ones who lied through our teeth to our coworker about why he is currently in our basement playing referee to two eight-year-old maniacs. Every part of that statement proves how insane we actually are.

"Normally it's closed now," Abel says. "So, we're going to Shedd After Dark."

"What's that?"

Abel stops, forcing me to do the same, and stares down at me. "You've never been to Shedd After Dark?"

Confused, I ask, "No?"

Chuckling lightly, he resumes his walk, pulling me along beside him. "You're in for a surprise tonight, then. It's basically cocktail hour with marine animals and with*out* anyone under the age of twenty-one hanging around."

Sure enough, when we make our way through the front to get tickets and check all our winter gear in the coatroom, it's like the aquarium has been transformed. I've been here during the day before, but I've never seen it like this. The lights are dim, there's a bar set up, and live music is being played in the open area in the front. Abel was right; this is going to be fun.

"I wasn't sure what to get you, so it's white wine." Abel hands me a good-sized glass filled almost to the top. "I hope I guessed right."

"You did," I say with a smile. "Thank you."

Taking my hand in his, Abel smiles. "Ready to explore?"

"Let's go."

We follow the crowd wandering around the aquarium, unaware of people trying to get by as they drink and chat with friends. It's clear everyone is content to just relax and enjoy whatever display they end up in front of. Who can blame them? The Amazon Rising exhibit isn't only full of soothing water sounds from the habitats, it's also warm and humid. It's only the beginning of March. Winter is far from over in this part of the country, so the climate in here is a nice change.

"I haven't been here in years," I marvel as we pass a particularly rambunctious crowd and make our way to the Great Lakes exhibit to hang out with the "locals" for a bit. "I've always loved the aquarium. There's something peaceful about it."

"Probably a combination of the sounds of the water and the silence of the animals gliding by."

"Don't forget the colors. I love all of it."

"So, you haven't brought Ainsley here?" He points out a giant sturgeon we can apparently touch. I shake my head, partially to answer his question and partially putting the kibosh on any plans he has for me to touch a fish tonight.

"I always have good intentions but never seem to follow through." It's a fact that makes me feel guilty if I dwell on it too long. So, I try to avoid thinking about it at all costs. "I'm pretty sure the girls are supposed to come on a field trip here next year. Maybe I'll sign up to chaperone."

"You're a really good mom, you know that?"

My eyes cut away from the fish they were looking at and focus on him instead. Abel has no idea how good it feels to hear him say that. My ex loves to point out any flaws in my parenting he can find, I'm sure to make himself feel better about his own shortcomings. And my mother, well, living with her didn't exactly build me up. So, these little moments are important, which scares me a bit. How can one man so quickly become my very best friend and so much more?

"Thank you. How do you always know what I need to hear?" I half-joke, hoping to hide how genuinely grateful I am. I don't want to bring this date down with my deepest, most insecure emotions.

Abel shrugs and takes a sip of his low-calorie beer, which looks completely unappealing. "I'm of the mindset it's less about knowing what someone needs to hear than being truthful in my opinions."

"And yet, somehow that opinion happened at the exact time I was feeling bad for never bringing Ainsley here." I raise an eyebrow at his chuckle.

"You're not hard to read, Elliott."

He has a valid point. "I guess I don't really try to hide my feel-ings, do I?"

"It's one of the things I like about you." Leaning in, he whispers, "You're real."

I'm not sure how to respond. It's not like most people try to be fake, in my experience. Then again, I never lived with Abel's ex, so I could be completely off base. Still, knowing that this part of me I don't particularly care for is something he likes makes me bite my lip as I try not to blush and giggle. Too many times, "real" has been perceived as "oversensitive," which makes me feel sensitive. I know —vicious cycle.

Before I can respond beyond my initial schoolgirl reaction, Abel takes my hand again. "Come on. I wanna show you something."

Winding our way through the crowd, he leads me down some stairs to another display, losing our drinks somewhere along the way. The Wild Reef is dark, lit up only by the lights in the water tunnel all around us.

"Wow," I breathe while watching dozens of different colored fish in all shapes and sizes lazily swim by. The colors are striking, and I can't help but put my hand on the glass, wishing I could get closer.

"Beautiful, isn't it?"

I can't tear my eyes away from the sights in front of me. Not even to answer my date. "I've never seen anything like it."

"It's my favorite part," he admits, standing so close to me the heat from his body radiates to mine. "It always reminds me of how small I am compared to the rest of the world. How small my problems are. Is that weird?"

"Not at all. There's something very centering about watching them. They're so at peace with their surroundings. I wish I could feel like that sometimes."

"Don't you?"

I shrug because that's a hard question to answer. "Maybe sometimes. I worry a lot. About finances and if I'm raising Ainsley the right way. About how much the divorce negatively affected her. I guess I can't really hide what I feel, because I feel too much."

"That's not a bad thing, Elliott."

"Not always. I think..." A piece of coral moves, distracting me from my thoughts. Especially when I realize it's not a piece of coral at all, but a fish disguising himself in the rocks. "Holy cow, do you see that?" I ask excitedly, unable to contain my smile. "It's amazing!"

"Absolutely stunning."

Something in Abel's tone has me turning my gaze to him. He's not paying attention to the sea life in front of us at all. No, he's staring at *me*.

Suddenly, I'm very aware we're the only ones down here. Either this area is off limits and we didn't realize it, or no one besides us has ventured this far from the bar. As an added bonus, we're not in danger of any children interrupting this moment in time.

As we continue to hold eye contact, the tension in the room cranks up several notches. My heart begins beating rapidly and my breathing is suddenly heavier. Abel moves closer but too slowly for me. It's as if some dormant part of me has woken up and I can't keep my hands to myself a moment longer.

Grabbing him by the lapel, I pull him into a dark corner. It won't completely hide us, but it's dark enough we'll have plenty of time to pull apart if we're interrupted.

"What are you doing, Elliott?" His playful tone tells me he knows exactly what I'm doing.

So quietly he has to lean in closer, I say, "You said you wanted to date a cougar. Maybe it's time for me to pounce."

For a moment, we stare into each other's eyes before our brains finally process what I just said, and we burst out laughing.

"I was going for sexy, but I think that came out cheesy instead, didn't it?"

Abel nods, still laughing. "So, so cheesy." Then, his laughter abruptly stops. "Good thing it's my favorite thing to eat."

I only have time to gasp before his lips are on mine and we become oblivious to everything around us. Gone are the brightly colored fish and magnificent lights. Instead, we are a sea of tongues and breath and hands grabbing at any part we can find. His thumbs graze my nipples causing me to gasp, which immediately elicits a groan from him.

I've never had this before—this kind of animalistic attraction. Well, maybe I've had this kind of attraction before, but never had an outlet for it. But Abel is matching me nip for nip, suck for suck. My womanly desires aren't just turning him on, they're urging him on. Begging him to take this to a new level of connection.

But we can't. Because we're in a public place. And even when we go home, there are two girls there. Two precious, sensitive children who don't need to wonder what "those noises from Daddy's room" are.

Slowly and reluctantly, I pull away. It takes a few minutes for us to calm down enough to stop. It takes even longer to get our breathing under control.

Abel leans his forehead against mine, our hands clasped tightly together between us. "You're amazing, you know that?"

"You're not so bad yourself, Beast."

A comical sound bursts out of him briefly before he separates us completely. "Come on. Let's go see the penguins." I wipe the lipstick off his mouth so it's not obvious what we've been up to. "I need to cool off a bit."

Glancing down at his crotch, I realize a little lipstick is probably the least of Abel's worries right now.

And me? I've never been more disappointed in my living arrangements in my life. There won't be any hanky-panky as long as my daughter shares a room with me. And doesn't that thought just start the mommy guilt cycle all over again.

CHAPTER NINETEEN

ABEL

"You know you're not a cougar, right?"

Elliott looks at me quizzically as we walk hand in hand along the lakefront trail. It's a cold night, of course, being that it's only March. Still cold enough for Elliott to be bundled up in a gray scarf and matching beanie with a red-tinged nose. But a little cool air will do us some good. Well, me anyway. While the penguin habitat was chilly, it did nothing to shrink a certain part of my body that was wound up from our kiss.

And, holy shit, was that a kiss. I've locked lips with many women in my life, and no one has ever elicited the same kind of response Elliott did. Then again, no one has ever been like Elliott either.

I've never thought of myself as being shallow, but I'm starting to wonder if part of me from long ago saw my ex-wife as more of a trophy wife than a nurturing partner to build a life with. I can't figure out any other reason why twenty-something Abel was attracted to May. She's not a bad person, per se. Although abandoning your kid for a less than mediocre modeling career might make that debatable. It wasn't until she was gone that I realized she was vainer and more self-centered than I'd thought. .

Granted, when we were married, I didn't spend my days picking apart my then-wife to focus on her flaws. That's not a good way to maintain a healthy relationship. But in hindsight, I see it clearly, and I'm no longer sure which head was making all the decisions back then.

I'm sure now, though. Elliott is everything that matters. She's kind and generous, and the epitome of cute in a sexy way only a woman can pull off. And yet, she is practically the opposite of vain. I've known her long enough now and seen how her ex treats her to recognize her lack of ego can sometimes bleed into dangerous emotional territory, which is why I feel the need to reassure her now.

"Back there, when you were attacking me with your lips…" She smacks me playfully in protest. "You said you were a cougar. I want you to know, just because you're older than I am doesn't make you a cougar."

It's painfully obvious she doesn't believe me, and this age gap causes her some stress. "I'm pretty sure that's the exact definition of a cougar."

I scoff. "No way. I'm almost positive a cougar isn't just older. She's also looking to get laid by younger men only."

"You don't think I'm trying to get in your pants?"

I stumble and stop walking to regain my ability not to trip on my own feet, as visual images of me taking her up against the wall in my kitchen assault me. No idea why we're next to the fridge in this random fantasy, but it doesn't make it any less hot. Blowing out a breath, I work hard to keep my voice from squeaking with sexual excitement. "After tonight, I'm not too sure anymore."

"Hey! You wanted that kiss as much as I did."

"Oh yeah, I did." I nod exaggeratedly. "I have no complaints, nor am I trying to discourage you. I'm merely telling you there is a difference between an older woman who wants sex from a younger man, and a woman who happens to be older than the man she's dating."

Elliott's nose crinkles, which makes her even more sexy/cute. "It feels weird. Me being older."

"How come?"

"I don't know. I guess I was raised in a generation where the norm was for a man to be older than his girlfriend. Maybe it has something to do with his ability to take care of her."

I scoff playfully. "You don't think I can take care of you?"

"Oh, I have no doubt you could." She reaches over and squeezes my arm. Of course, I immediately flex. It's practically an involuntary reflex for single me. "I've seen these biceps before."

We laugh at the good-natured twist in this conversation, but I don't let it go on for too long. I need Elliott to really understand where I'm coming from. I'm not risking this great roommate situation for a fling or a few dates while we both keep an eye out for our one and only. I really, really like Elliott. I already love her as my friend. The rest is just a matter of time and circumstance.

"I'm serious, Elliott. I have a stable career and am a homeowner. I have a daughter in school. I've been married and divorced. I'm not twenty-one with *Sports Illustrated* posters hanging on the walls of my bachelor pad."

"And thank goodness for that. I'm not sure how any of them could compete when you have the real deal right here." She gestures up and down her body, and I'm assaulted with yet another visual image, only this time I'm eating breakfast. While she's lying on the table. Because she's breakfast.

I'm eating her for breakfast.

This cold is doing nothing to help the situation I've got going on down below. If only the temperature would drop about a hundred degrees...

But Elliott is shivering, so abandoning the topic and heading home might be the best option right now anyway.

"This conversation isn't over," I say and put my arm around her shoulder, pulling her close to me.

She snuggles in closer and clasps her hand in mine. "I'll get used to it eventually. I'm well within the cougar guidelines anyway."

"Cougar guidelines?"

"Half your age plus seven is how young you can date without it looking weird." She pulls away and looks up at me while we walk. "You've never heard that before?"

"No. So that gives you anyone above the age of, what...twenty-eight?"

"Supposedly."

"So, you could date Joey."

"Guess so."

"That is *so* not happening."

She giggles while I guide us toward home.

* * *

If the look on her face is any indication, she is *definitely* not dating Joey now.

"What in the world happened here?" Hands on her hips, Elliott looks less than amused at the disaster we walked into. Maybe even less than less than amused. So much less. Actually, she looks downright angry.

"The girls know better than to leave dishes on the table and... Oh my god Abel, what happened to the kitchen?"

Dirty pots and pans are scattered all over the counter as if Joey cooked a seven-course meal. But judging by the splatter on the ceiling, it was only spaghetti. The handful of noodles stuck to the wall by the sink is also a good indication of what he attempted to cook. Doesn't explain why it took more than two small pots to make noodles for two small girls, but I've known Joey for years. This is honestly pretty clean compared to some of the disasters I've walked in on before.

Grabbing the step stool, I place it near the stove and wet a dishtowel.

"What are you doing?" Elliott asks, still seemingly stunned by what we've come home to and not sure where to begin to get things back to normal.

"First thing to know about when Joey babysits—always be prepared for a clean-up job. Second thing to know," pointing up, I add, "anything red gets wiped up first before it stains."

"Oh, for shit's sake," Elliott cusses—which she never does— before yelling, "Girls! We're home!"

A squeal and an overexaggerated "Oh my god they're home" that most likely came from Joey can be heard from down the basement stairs, right before the thunder of them all barreling our way begins.

The girls immediately throw arms around us, hugging in greeting. Fortunately, we've done this enough times Mabel waits until I climb down the ladder for hers instead of knocking me over. I wasn't kidding when I said this isn't the worst state I've seen my kitchen in after leaving Mabel in Joey's semi-capable hands.

"I don't know what happened, man," Joey starts, and I know exactly where this is going. "I was making them some spaghetti and the sauce exploded everywhere."

"How in the world does spaghetti sauce explode?" Elliott still looks miffed, but thankfully, she isn't one to go apeshit. At least, I hope she doesn't. We may need Joey for more "PTA meetings" and personally, I think deep cleaning the stove is worth it if Elliott and I get to make out like that again.

Joey rubs the back of his neck, looking completely stumped. "I don't know. I turned the stove on and then put the sauce in. I went downstairs to check on the girls and, suddenly, there was this 'poof' sound, and when I came back up it was everywhere."

Elliott shakes her head. "And the noodles over the sink?"

He shrugs. "I was making sure they were done. I don't eat a lot of heavy carbs, so I wanted to make sure they were nice and cooked for the girls. Oh and Elliott, you've got a good one here. Ainsley kicked some serious ass on those big balls. Am I right, girl?"

Elliott and I look at each other and smirk like twelve-year-old boys trying not to laugh over how creepy Joey sounds, knowing full well he's talking about the *WipeOut* game again. But we don't miss that both his and Ainsley's smiles are huge as they fist bump and bond over her win that round. And that's when Elliott's anger seems to fizzle out completely.

All I can do is shrug at her realization, because it's one I came to long ago. As long as he builds up my kid when I'm gone, destroying my kitchen isn't all that important. I'm pretty sure Elliott just came to the exact same conclusion.

"Okay, girls," I jump in as Mabel tries to defend why she kept bouncing straight into the water. "You are up way later than normal, and you have school tomorrow. Both of you—jammies."

"But I didn't shower yet," Mabel protests, while Ainsley turns to argue with Elliott, who is shaking her head at her daughter's blatant attempts to stay up later.

"No time for showers. You'll have to slap on some deodorant because I have to work in the morning too, and you don't want me to be grumpy tomorrow afternoon, do you?"

Mabel rolls her eyes. "You're never grumpy, Dad."

"And you don't want me to start now. Seriously. Jammies." I smack her on the bottom as she caves and drags her feet across the floor into the living room, shoulders slumped melodramatically. Ainsley looks just as defeated.

"How did it go, really? Other than," Elliott gestures around the room, "this."

Joey crosses his arms and legs and leans against the counter, not even attempting to clean up. No shocker there. But he's still smiling, which is a good sign at his evening. "It was really great. When Abel said there would be two of them, I expected double the trouble. But they keep each other entertained, don't they?"

"Oh yeah." I rinse out the washcloth and climb back up the step stool to reach a few spots I missed. "It's been a huge help to me that I'm not the only one for Mabel to talk to."

"Bet you didn't see that one coming when you moved Elliott in, huh?"

"Nope. It's been great. Mabel has a live-in playmate, and I feel like I'm doing only half the work around here."

"Half?" Elliott jumps in. "I'm thinking you do forty percent."

"Only because you have to rerun the dishwasher all the time."

She gapes at me. "I do not. I have a handy dandy little magnet to help me out now."

"Which cuts down half your workload," I banter. "Hell, I think I should get extra credit for it."

Elliott rolls her eyes then her sleeves, and gets to work on the dishes in the sink.

"Y'all are weird," Joey says matter-of-factly. "If I didn't know any better, I'd say you've turned into an old married couple already."

Out of the corner of my eye, I see Elliott has the same reaction I'm having—frozen to the spot. Because that's not obvious at all.

"Whaa..." she clears her throat. "What do you mean?"

"About being an old married couple?"

Elliott nods and I watch as a blush starts to creep up from her neck. If this continues, she's going to be beet red in a matter of seconds. Another dead giveaway.

"Just that you're so comfortable around each other, joking around. People don't usually act like that unless they've been together for a while."

I'm not sure how to respond without putting my foot in my mouth, so I say nothing. Elliott appears to be doing the same, which combined, makes us look suspicious. I know that. I'm pretty sure Elliott knows that. I just hope Joey doesn't figure out it.

He looks back and forth at us, and I watch as his expression morphs from one of relaxation to sudden realization.

And then the jaw drops open.

Yep. He knows.

"You!" He points at me and then back at Elliott and then back at me. "You!"

"Shhh!" Elliott hisses and pushes his finger out of the air. "The girls will hear you."

He holds his hands up in defense. "The girls that are upstairs putting their jammies on? Not likely. But you!"

"Me, nothing!" Elliott insists. "You know nothing! There is nothing to know!"

She turns away from him, which means Joey now turns to me. "Yoooooooooou!"

Joey has definitely been hanging out with my kid too long if he can turn on the dramatics as much as a pre-teen girl.

I calmly step down from the stool, fold it up, and slide it next to the fridge. "Me, nothing, Joe. Quit freaking out about this."

"Abel!" Elliott yells in reaction to my lack of denial, at the exact same time Joey yells, "So you admit it?!"

"He's already figured it out, Elliott. Might as well quit denying it." And I'm not actually sad about this. I would never intentionally "out" us until Elliott and I had talked about it first. Regardless of being adults and living in the same house, we're still co-workers too. Workplace dynamics can get sticky if you don't tread lightly. Not that Joey treads lightly on anything, which is why I didn't tell him before.

She huffs a sigh. "I mean, yeah, okay."

"You admitted it too!"

Elliott pushes his finger down again, since he can't seem to control it in all his excitement.

"Keep your voice down," she hisses in his face. "Fine. Yes. We're dating."

Joey gasps, but Elliott continues before he can start freaking out again.

"But the girls don't know, and we'd prefer to keep it that way— so keep your voice down."

"But..."

"No! Joey, listen to me." Elliott's tone softens as she explains our thought process. The concerns we have over the girls getting too attached if this doesn't work out, the jealousy Mabel already has over Ainsley having two parents, the desire we have to remain friends and roommates no matter what. I'm honestly not sure if he agrees with everything we say, but at least he understands and respects it. Sort of.

Pausing to think, Joey purses his lips and looks back and forth at us before making me wonder why I keep him around. "So, you're banging your roommate."

"No," Elliott immediately says.

I just laugh. Man, he's funny sometimes. "It's not like that, and you know it," I admit with a smile on my face.

He shrugs. "What I know is I am a hot-blooded American man, and I'm pretty ticked you got to this one first. She's pretty hot."

"That's really nice, Joey," Elliott says sweetly, but I know her well enough to know she's not finished yet. "But with this kind of mess from making the easiest dish in the world, there is no way in hell you will ever get in my pants. Hot-blooded American man or not."

Joey has the wherewithal to look sheepish. "Yeah, I'm not exactly the best cook."

"How about next time we leave money for pizza instead?" I offer up. "And you start wiping the stove off."

I throw the washcloth at him, and he catches it just before it smacks him in the face.

"There's gonna be a next time, huh?" Joey waggles his eyebrows up and down. "Things are that serious?"

I'm not sure how to answer him. "Serious" is a relative term. I'm not just screwing around with Elliott. Actually, I'm not screwing around with her at all at this point. But I would hardly say our relationship is serious. Is it real? Absolutely. Is it for the long-haul? Hopefully. But we have way too much fun being together to call this serious. I know that's not quite what Joey means, but it still seems like the wrong way to label what's happening here.

"Yes, this is a genuine attempt to see where things go." There. That seems like a more appropriate way to answer his question. "This is not a fling or a roommates-with-benefits situation."

"Well, I approve. Not that my opinion matters at all," he adds with a shrug, as he puts half-ass effort into getting the sauce off the stove. I'd worry about the cleanliness of his own place if I didn't know for a fact that he orders pre-cooked healthy meals for this very reason. The only time he tries to cook is when he's trying to be a good babysitter. Lord help his future wife when they have a kid. "But that cougar things makes it even more hot."

Elliott drops something in the sink making a loud "clang."

"Yeah, we don't need to talk about that part," I say with a chuckle. "Elliott's having a hard time with our age difference."

Joey reels back in surprise. I think he's actually looking for an excuse to quit cleaning and he's going with "so surprised he forgot what he was doing." "What's wrong with having an age difference?"

Elliott doesn't look away from the dishes. "It's a weird feeling being older than the guy I'm dating. I'm old school. I'll wrap my brain around it eventually."

Joey looks at me quizzically and then back at her. "You're not much older than Abel. Wait, are you?"

"I'm forty-two, Joey."

His jaw drops open again. Seriously, I need to stop having Joey babysit if he's going to start channeling a pre-pubescent girl when anything surprised him. "Jeez, woman, you look amazing for your age."

That gets Elliott's attention enough that she turns to shoot him a glare. "Just what every woman wants to hear. That she looks much better than how elderly she actually is."

"Seriously, Elliott. That's why you think this is a big deal? You know how old you actually are. The rest of us assume you're in your thirties, so it doesn't cross our minds there's an age gap."

Elliott's face softens, and I can't help but feel thankful he's having an easier time getting through to her than I have been. Irritated he thought of this angle first, but mostly thankful.

"Besides," he continues, putting me on high alert. There's no telling which direction this will go. "When you're old, like for real old, he'll still be young enough to cater to your every whim."

Elliott's eyebrows shoot up, and I can tell she's visualizing all the ways her future self could benefit from this. "I've always wanted to have a cabana boy fanning me and feeding me grapes."

"There ya go!" Joey exclaims. "He can even wear a speedo!"

Elliott's eyes flash over to mine and she gives me a flirty shrug. "Make sure you keep those abs in shape."

I shake my head because this conversation has turned ridiculous.

Not that I should be surprised, considering who is involved. But at least Joey is working for my benefit.

Now that his work here is done, Joey lets out a huge yawn. "Well, kids, on that note, I need to head home. Work comes early, you know."

"You're going to leave us with this mess to clean up?"

"Trust me, Elliott," I answer for him. "You don't want Joey to help. He'll make it worse."

"Hey!" Joey protests and thinks before nodding. "Okay yeah, he's right. I'm a terrible cook. I'm an even worse at housekeeping. Which is why I hire a maid once a week."

Elliott shakes her head and laughs. "And that's strike three. No way I'd date you now."

"No worries," he answers and tosses the dishrag in empty side of the sink. "I don't feel like getting a beat down from the Beast anyway. I'll catch you guys tomorrow."

He saunters out of the room, yelling an "I'm out, ladies!" up the stairs to the girls who immediately race back down to hug him goodbye as well. Elliott and I continue to clean in silence, listening to the sounds of our kids and their favorite babysitter, just enjoying the moment. Like I said, "serious" doesn't describe us. Nothing about our lives is serious. But it is easy. Exactly as it should be right now.

CHAPTER TWENTY

ELLIOTT

W e're late. Of course. But that's what happens when you go out on a date during the week and your babysitter lets the kids stay up. Not that I'm complaining. It was a fantastic date. The cleanup when we got home sucked, though. Okay, maybe I'm complaining a little.

Or maybe I'm just tired of fighting with two eight-year-old girls who think their time is more important than the school's start time.

"Ainsley! Mabel!" I yell for the umpteenth time as I stomp up the stairs. "Girls, we have to leave in ten minutes, and you still have to eat breakfast!"

"Almost ready, Mama!" Sure enough, Ainsley is finally standing in the bathroom brushing her hair. She looks tired, but at least she's dressed and almost ready to go. It was a rough start, but once her feet hit the floor, she finally started making progress.

Mabel, on the other hand, is nowhere to be found.

"Mabel." No answer. "Mabel, are you almost ready?" Still no answer. "Mabel, do you need help with anything?"

I round the corner into her room and there she is. Not only ignoring me, but tucked in her bed, blankets up to her chin, sleeping.

Rolling my eyes to the ceiling, I pray for patience because this is not going to help us get out the door any faster, and she is already on my last nerve with the way she backtalks every morning. I try to give her grace because I'm fully aware she's struggling with the loss of her mother, and I represent everything she doesn't have. But that still doesn't make it okay for her to be a little brat to me. And it certainly doesn't make it okay for her to make us all late.

I really need to address it with Abel. At first, I assumed the attitude would taper off, but it keeps getting worse. I hate the idea of the potential confrontation, but if things keep going the way they are, he'll have to start taking her to the gym again. I don't think anyone wants that. Not even me.

Right now, though, I don't have time to worry about a conversation that hasn't happened yet or pussyfoot around Mabel's issues. I have errands to run before work and taking the time to walk into the school, sign both girls in, and discuss with the principal why they are tardy is not on my list.

So, I do what anyone in charge of a defiant child would do—I grab the blankets and pull.

"Hey!" Mabel yells as she's uncovered. "Those blankets were warm." She's remarkably coherent and non-groggy sounding for someone who was "sleeping" a few second ago.

"So is your winter coat," I say flippantly. "Which you need to have on in nine minutes so we can get to school on time."

She paws at her blankets which I refuse to let her have. "That means I can sleep for a little longer."

"No. You can't. Get up and get dressed. You're already going to miss breakfast."

"What?" she screeches, suddenly sitting upright. "You can't do that!"

"I didn't do anything, Mabel. This is the third time I've woken you up. When you choose not to follow instructions, you lose out. Now, get up." I pull the sheet and blankets all the way off the bed and toss them into the corner. I can fix that later. What I'm not going to do is make it easy for her to go back to pretend sleep.

Turning to walk out of the room, I hear a sniffle behind me. I'm not about to fall for it, but I need to at least be a good person and address it on the off chance something is actually bothering her.

"Mabel, I'm not angry. You just need to get a move on."

A lone alligator tear runs down her cheek. "I'm tired because Joey let us stay up so late."

"We're all tired from last night. But everyone else is up and at 'em. Like you need to be."

Aaaaand the tears dry up faster than they came, a scowl re-emerges, and Defiant Mabel rears her ugly head once again. It's a sad day when that's considered normal in the morning.

"Fine!" she yells, jumping out of bed and stomping her feet on the floor, hands in tight fists. "I'm up! Are you happy now?"

"Very. You've got eight minutes."

As I walk out, Mabel yells after me, "I hate you! I hate you so much!"

"I'm not here to be liked, Mabel," I say calmly, refusing to lose eye contact. I won't back down from an eight-year-old, no matter how in control she thinks she should be. "I'm here to keep you safe and on time. That's it."

Now that the hard part of the morning is finally over, I check on my slow-as-molasses child again, who needs a bit of help with her hair. Then we head downstairs for Ainsley to grab a banana for breakfast and for me to gather our things.

Backpacks – Check.

Lunch boxes – Check.

Purse with keys and work badge – Check.

"Two minutes, ladies! We have to go!" I yell, as I begin pulling coats out of the closet and slipping my own on.

"Coming, Mom!" Ainsley grabs her coat from the back of the couch, and I'm thankful at least one of these girls is working with me this morning, however slow-going she's been.

"Mabel! Let's go!"

The words are no more than out of my mouth when the devil child comes sauntering down the stairs, still in her Vampirina jammies. Her eyes are trained on mine, and I know she wants to get into yet another power struggle with me. Little does she know I've done this before with Ainsley. It didn't work out so well with her, which is why, for the most part, she doesn't test me anymore. Still, I have to address it before walking out the door. I may need to refer back to this conversation if things go badly with her father when he finds out about this.

"Why aren't you dressed?" I ask, as Mabel quietly puts on her shoes.

"I am."

"You're still in your jammies."

"I'm wearing them to school," she says calmly and stands up to reach for her coat.

Just as I suspected. Thankfully, her hair is done, and I thought I heard her brushing her teeth, so really, there's no reason to fight about the rest. I'm not interested in having another control battle with her and, frankly, I'm not going to be the one who is embarrassed by wearing jammies all day, anyway. At this point, natural consequences might do a better job of getting through to her than I am.

"Okay. Well, let's go."

Mabel pauses momentarily, and I catch the look of surprise on her face. I admit, she's good at schooling it quickly; no doubt a trick she learned from her mother.

Okay, fine. That was very judgmental of me. But I refuse to believe the devil side of this child came from her father. I'm not sure he has a mean bone in his body. Ornery bones, sure. He's practically built from those.

We walk out the door, Mabel still eyeing me every so often like she's waiting for me to say "I'm kidding! Go change." But I don't. I hand everyone their stuff, shuffle us onto the small porch, and lock the door behind us, as if she hasn't fazed me at all. That's the only real way to win with kids, right?

"Let's go friends. I think we're going to make it on time."

The girls fall into their normal morning routine, skipping ahead of me, backpacks bopping up and down as they giggle with each other. Except for the purple cartoon character on Mabel's pants, we give the appearance it's been just like any other morning. Until Mabel turns around and starts walking backward.

"I need a donut."

"Sorry, Charlie. We've got places to go and people to see." I make sure my tone sounds friendly and fun. Not that I'm feeling affectionate toward her right now. But my patience is returning now that we're back on track and she'll still only eight. It's my job to be the bigger person.

"But the donut shop is right there." She points across the street to one of my favorite haunts. Really, I'd love to stop in. But that would be admitting defeat.

"It is. But we don't have even a minute to spare, so let's get a move on, ladies."

I keep my voice light, assuming it will diffuse things before they escalate again. My first indication that it's a mistake to give her the benefit of the doubt sometimes is when she stops walking. Second indication? When her hands go to her hips.

Lord, here we go again. Give me strength...

"But I haven't eaten breakfast."

"That's what happens when you refuse to get up."

She cocks her head slightly, like her highness doesn't appreciate my answer.

Well, I don't appreciate her attitude, so I guess we're even.

"But I'm gonna be hungry."

I shrug and refuse to acknowledge that she is really starting to irritate me. "You should have thought of that earlier. You were warned several times and told you had ten minutes to get dressed and eat. You took all ten minutes piddling around your room."

Mabel's face turns red as she stomps her foot, a shriek coming out of her mouth that is so loud, random passersby turn to see what all the commotion is about. Ainsley's so shocked at this behavior her eyes get wide.

"But I'm hungry!" Mabel screams, still stomping. "It's your job to feed me! Feed me! Feed me!"

I cross my arms and roll my eyes. "I tried. You refused. Tell your teacher. Maybe she'll care."

It's a low blow for me, but it does the trick. Mabel turns on her heel and stomps the entire rest of the way to school. It's painfully obvious to anyone walking down the street she isn't just angry; she is *livid*. But she's also quiet, so I can't find it in me to care.

I am a horrible person sometimes.

Ah, well. That's motherhood in a nutshell.

By the time we get to the school grounds, Mabel is at least fifty yards ahead of us. Ainsley opted to fall back with me, because apparently, anger fuels Mabel's ability to move faster than turtle speed. No telling what else it fuels, but with her love of kickboxing, my kid probably has the right idea.

Mabel rounds the corner first and is halfway up the stairs when Ainsley and I stop.

"She'll be fine," I try to reassure her. "Once she focuses on something else, she'll stop being mad at me and her mood will change."

"I don't know, Mom." Ainsley shakes her head in disbelief. "She's really mad at you."

"She's always mad at me, hon. It has nothing to do with me, so you don't need to worry about it, okay? Just have a good day at school, learn something new, and make good choices. Sound good?"

Ainsley nods and gives me a small smile, her cute little nose bright red from the cold.

I hug her goodbye and wave as she speed-walks up the steps into the large brick building. Before she's even inside, Ms. Alexander is already approaching. How she made it out of her nice warm office, down the steps, and to me in that short amount of time is baffling.

"Ms. Donovan." Uh oh. She already sounds pissed. We haven't been here long enough to get in trouble, so I'm not sure what she's already cranky about. "You probably don't know this, but Mabel is wearing pajama pants."

I feign shock and throw my hand over my heart. "What? Really? The girls told me they were the latest in children's fashion." Yes, it's snotty of me to act like this, but I'm tired enough of conflict today that I can't help myself.

I must be a better actress than I realized because Ms. Alexander continues as if my words weren't dripping in sarcasm. "Be that as it may, it's against school policy for children to wear nightclothes during school hours."

I furrow my brow. "Are you sure? Because every year we have Polar Express day and kids are encouraged to wear their jammies. The memo comes home in Ainsley's backpack, and I get an email reminder."

Ms. Alexander startles. She probably wasn't expecting me to fight back. If dealing with Mabel gave me nothing else this morning, it put me at the edge of my limit for other people's crap. And I can smell this turd of a policy from a mile away.

"Well, there are exceptions to the rule."

"Oh. Good. Well then, thank you for making an exception for Mabel this morning. I'll make sure she doesn't try to dupe me again."

Ms. Alexander's mouth opens and closes and opens and closes again. Clearly, I've stumped her on how to respond. Has it always been this easy or am I truly on fire today?

Finally, she finishes our conversation with "Well. I will hold you to that."

She turns around quickly, obviously determined to keep the upper hand. Unfortunately for her, I'm feeling feisty today and refuse to let her win.

"Thank you, Ms. Alexander. Have a great day!" I call after her cheerily. She doesn't even bother to acknowledge me.

Sighing, I run through my mental list of what I need to do now.

- Go to the bank.
- Swing by the post office for stamps.
- Hit the grocery store for a quick lunch since I didn't have time to make one this morning.

- Share a morning lunch with Abel so I can tell him about Mabel's behavior.

Oh, how I wish going to the dentist was the fourth thing on my list. I have a feeling it would be way less painful than what I have in store.

CHAPTER TWENTY-ONE

ABEL

I don't bother trying to stifle my yawn as I make my way to the smoothie bar. It's been a rough morning.

After our date last night, I had to peel myself out of my bed to make it here on time. It was worth it, of course, but still not fun to power through at four-something in the morning. Didn't help that I was right in the middle of a fantastically erotic dream where Elliott was bouncing on my big balls—and I don't mean on the Wii.

To make things worse, my five-fifteen client was extra motivated today and challenged me to see who could run a mile faster. Never one to back down from a challenge, I took Trevor up on it. I kicked his ass, of course, but at the cost of depleting my energy.

My six-thirty class was relatively mild, although the snow-bird ladies—which is what I lovingly refer to them as, even though none of them have ever been to Florida—were more chatty than normal and wanted my input into why a beautiful woman like their grand-daughter—yes, *all* their granddaughters. Amazing how they all seem to have the most beautiful one—is still single and would I be interested in their phone numbers.

I wasn't, of course. And it has nothing to do with the four babies by four baby daddies. Swear.

Okay, fine. Even if Elliott wasn't in the picture, I have no interest in instability. Even if the woman in question is a sure thing. Model-esque physique only goes so far. I learned that lesson the hard way.

Sliding onto a stool at the counter, I drop my head onto my arms. Not terribly professional of me, but I don't care at this point. I'm more interested in how Elliott's morning went. Hopefully, it was better than mine.

"Long night?"

I open my eyes and look up at the voice across the counter. Tabitha.

"You have no idea."

She bobs her head back and forth and hands me a cup of coffee. Good ole Tabitha always knows what her customers need.

"I have more idea than you think."

"What does that mean?" I wince as I burn my lip on the freshly brewed cup of joe. It doesn't deter me from blowing on it and trying again.

"I hear you and the roomie are becoming chummy."

My eyes flick up to hers. *Fucking Joey.* "I should have known that asshole couldn't keep a secret."

Tabitha shrugs. "Give him a break. It's the most exciting thing to happen here since the place burned down."

She's not wrong. And I should be upset Joey spilled the beans when we specifically asked him not to, but truth be told, I'm actually okay with people knowing. It's my other half that's still having the issues. "Yeah, well, Elliott is still wrapping her brain around the age difference, so do me a favor and keep it to yourself, will you?"

To keep herself busy, since Tabitha can't seem to stay idle for long, she grabs a rag and begins wiping down the already clean counter. "Why? Most women would kill for a younger man. Less chance of needing a Viagra prescription."

I take another sip, praying the caffeine gets to my blood stream quickly. I don't know why Elliott thinks I'm so much younger than she is. Clearly my body feels way older than my physiological age today. "You make a valid point. But I think it has less to do with age and more to do with nerves about a new relationship. Like she doesn't want to get too relaxed too soon. It's fine. I'm trying not to push her. She's my friend, ya know? Whatever she needs."

Tabitha "awws" which makes me roll my eyes.

"I always knew you were a sweetie, Abel. I just want to squeeze your cheeks now." She reaches over the counter to grab my face, but I back away, scowling at her.

"Hey." The woman in question sidles onto the stool next to me and hands me a grocery sack.

"Aw!" Tabitha says again and puts her hand to her heart. If I didn't know better, I'd swear she has happy tears in her eyes. "Young love is precious."

Elliott's jaw drops open and she whips her head around to look at me. I hold my hands up defensively.

"Don't look at me." Then, I start digging in the bag to see what's for lunch today.

"Freaking Joey," Elliott grumbles in her non-cussing cussing way. "That man can't keep a secret for anything."

"Why do you think I never tell him anything of importance?" I respond without much thought and pull a pre-made meal out of the bag. "What's with the fancy food today? Did we run out of leftovers?"

Elliott grabs the second meal and takes the two plastic forks out of Tabitha's hand. "I didn't have time pull any together. It was a rough morning."

Immediately, my interest is piqued. I have a bad feeling she's referring to my kid. "What does that mean?"

Elliott sighs and avoids eye contact. Tabitha, on the other hand, looks bored. "Okay kids. I'll leave you to it. I was hoping this newfound relationship would give me hours of entertainment, but clearly you've jumped over the honeymoon phase and right into the boring shit."

I snort a laugh and lick the sauce off my thumb from the lid of the container. "Sorry to disappoint you."

"Call me if a customer comes." Tabitha disappears to the back room, no doubt to take full advantage of the lull to work on some inventory. She's always complaining about it being hard to count jars of supplies when she has to stop and make someone food. Eventually, management will get its head out of its ass and get her some help with that. Maybe.

Turning my attention back to my girlfriend, I bring us back to the topic at hand. "So, what happened this morning?"

Still avoiding my gaze, Elliott plays with her food. Finally, she drops her fork and turns to face me. "Mabel went to school in her jammies."

I nod, having already gotten the call from the school about it. "I know."

"And you're not mad?"

"I figured there was a story behind it, and I'm bound to believe your version over Ms. Alexander's."

"Ms. Alexander is convinced the girl's duped me into thinking it's the latest fashion trend."

"You're not that gullible."

Elliott picks up her fork and begins playing with her food again. "You know that. I know that. Ms. Alexander doesn't know that. I'm not sure if Mabel knows that."

Ah. This *is* about my kid. "You gonna tell me what happened or are you gonna keep pussyfooting around it."

She peeks up at me through her lashes and crinkles her nose. "That obvious, huh?"

"Painfully." I put my own fork down and swivel to face her. I only have a limited time to eat before my next client, but this is too important. "Level with me."

Elliott mimics my movement and turns to face me. I can already tell this is hard for her, which means it must be really bad. I can't help but wonder, though, if our versions of "really bad" are the same. "We were almost late today. Again. I woke Mabel up three times, and she refused to get out of bed."

"Sounds about right. She hates mornings."

"As do the rest of us. But I shouldn't have to pull her blankets all the way off the bed for her to finally get up."

True, except... "They stayed up really late last night, Elliott. Maybe this morning was extra hard on her."

"She does this almost every morning, Abel. Today was just worse than normal because of the late night. She refused to put clothes on, so I let her go to school in her jammies..."

"Good call," I agree.

"Then on the way to school she demanded I buy her a donut."

"Wait, she didn't get breakfast before school?"

"No." Elliott looks really miffed now. Which I understand, except...

"Elliott, you can't keep food from a kid as a punishment."

She reels back. "Really? That's what you think happened? Abel, she was given multiple warnings about missing breakfast if she didn't get up, and she refused to comply. She knew the consequences. She was testing me."

I don't doubt Elliott is telling the truth. Mabel can be a little shit. She's my kid. I know that more than anyone. But I'm having a hard time believing she really is this bad. I mean, I know the school says she has some behavior issues, but I've never seen it for myself, so it's hard to gauge exactly what everyone is talking about.

"Listen, Abel." Elliott's tone changes from one of anger to one of understanding. "I know she's still grieving over May leaving. And I'm trying really hard to be sensitive to it, ya know? Not pushing her too far or crossing over some invisible parenting boundary. But I can't allow my kid to be late to school either because yours is dead set on punishing me for something I didn't do. That's not fair to Ainsley."

I put my hand on Elliott's shoulder and begin rubbing her neck. "I know. And you're right. You're in charge in the mornings as much as I'm in charge in the afternoons, and she needs to not make things hard on you."

Elliott smiles shyly. "I'm not even asking for her to be nice to me. I'm asking for her to respect our morning routine before school."

"I get it. I'll talk to her."

"Yeah?"

"Oh course." I lean in closer. "And next time, tell me before it gets to this point, will you?"

She replies just as quietly. "You've seen it firsthand, remember?"

I grimace because she's right. I have seen the disrespect and the mouthiness and haven't pressed the issue very hard. "I'll call her out on it more. It's a fine line letting your kid process their own grief while still being a nice person."

"Necessary skill, my friend." Elliott turns back to her food and the heaviness of the conversation dissipates almost immediately. If this was our first conflict, it wasn't too bad.

I dig into my food and get ready to comment on her choice of meal when Rian comes stomping our direction.

"Tabitha!" I yell to give her a heads up. "Customer!"

"On my way!" she shouts back and immediately steps up to her station to make another smoothie. How did she get out here so fast? Sometimes I wonder if she's a ninja, always knowing when someone is approaching and always knowing what they want before they even order.

My usually-favorite client, on the other hand, is taking her sweet ass time probably because she's wearing work clothes, which includes shoes that don't look very comfortable. I say "usually-favorite" because I have a strange feeling she's about to lose the coveted title if the fire in her eyes is any indication of what's about to go down.

"You!" Rian points a finger in my face. "You got me knocked up."

Except for the sounds of the blender, the room goes completely silent. Keely, who happened to be walking by, stops and backs up by two steps to see what's going on. Even Elliott's eyebrows rise.

Those words coming out of any woman's mouth sparks fear in men young and old. However, I am cool, calm, and collected. I may have been around the block a few times, but I was married when I met Rian, and she began dating Carlos not long after my divorce.

She's cute and all, and maybe in a different lifetime we'd hook up, but we're more like brother and sister than love interests.

Swallowing, I slowly wipe my mouth with a napkin, drawing out the moment. I feel like this is something I need to be prepared for before speaking.

"I know we've never done the nasty, so I'm gonna need you to clarify."

Rian's face contorts in a myriad of emotions—anger, overwhelm, fear. The one I don't see is joy. Although if sarcasm is an indicator, she hasn't lost that completely yet. It's just hidden by everything else.

"'Clean eat,' you said. 'You'll feel better,' you said. What did you didn't say is, 'It'll make you fertile, Rian.'"

"First, I don't sound like a cartoon character." I dodge her punch as she half-heartedly goes for my shoulder. "I also never said not to use birth control, Rian. That's kind of up to you."

"I thought this one was shooting blanks." She gestures behind her with her thumb.

And here comes the man at fault now. Carlos practically bounces up and the joy that's missing on Rian's face is all over his. "She was wrong. So wrong. I'm not shooting blanks. I'm shooting babies. My babies!"

I shake his hand, smiling wide. I remember that feeling of pride, knowing your child was coming into the world. There's nothing like it. "Congratulations, man. You look really excited about this."

"I am." Really, there is no doubt. I've known Carlos for a while and he's never smiled like this before. Come to think of it, I've never seen his hair look disheveled before either. He must be really focused on this baby for a hair to be out of place. "I didn't even want kids, but suddenly the prospect of having one is overwhelming. I can't even describe it. I can't wait. Tabitha!" Carlos turns to our smoothie bartender who's been standing by the blender and has missed this entire conversation.

"What's up, Carlos?"

"Drinks on the house. I'm having a baby!"

Tabitha's eyes widen and her jaw drops. "What?!?"

"No, no, no." Rian wiggles her finger at him. "You aren't actually having the baby. You're not doing anything except ordering baby shit we can't afford from Gucci or wherever."

"Our baby deserves only the best. In fact, I need to see how long the wait list is for that Italian crib maker. It's pricey, but worth it."

"Oh my god. I'm having a baby," Rian whines. "I'm having a baby, and my boyfriend has gone off his rocker already."

"Oh, a rocker!" Carlos exclaims, whipping his phone out, presumably to add to his list of furniture that needs to be purchased.

"No! No rocker! Oh geez. We're gonna have to implement Code Pink again. Only this time, I won't be the buffer. I'll be the one calling it. I can't believe this is happening."

Carlos leans over and talks to Tabitha, who is trying to hug him over the counter and only succeeding in squishing them both. Since they're distracted, I take a moment to grab Rian by the arm and walk her away from the crowd.

"Are you okay with this? You know you don't have to have this baby, right?"

Rian sighs deeply, and I swear tears are shimmering in her eyes. "It's not that I don't want to do this... it's just really, really new. I can't quite wrap my brain around it. I'm old, Abel."

"You're in your thirties. Exaggerate much?"

"I'm in my late thirties and my boyfriend is forty-three. We're going to be the old parents at the school. The mom people think is the grandma."

I snort a laugh. "That's not likely to happen. And if it does, make sure to tell me so I can have a good laugh." She crosses her arms and glares at me. "But it won't. See that woman over at the counter?" I point to Elliott, who has joined the conversation with Carlos and Tabitha. I have no doubt she's giving her opinion on whatever baby gear Carlos is showing her on his phone. "She's in her forties and her daughter is in my daughter's class. No one can tell a difference in our ages."

"I can tell. Aren't you like, twenty-one?" Rian sasses.

"Har. Har. You're funny. Seriously. Would you ask her if she was Ainsley's grandma?"

"I assume Ainsley is her daughter, which brings more questions to mind, but to answer your original question, no. I wouldn't ask her."

"You will be her age when your kid is in school." I rub up and down Rian's arms, hoping to calm her fears a bit. "It's gonna be good, Rian. We'll keep you working out and eating right so you're as healthy as you can be. It's always scary, but I know you can do this. Hell, Carlos already has everything you need being delivered as we speak."

Rian's turn to snort a laugh. "No doubt." She takes a deep cleansing breath, and I know she's trying to build up her own self-confidence. "Okay. I can do this."

"You can do this," I reiterate, hoping my words sink in. Eventually. Probably three years after giving birth, but she'll get there.

"Thanks. We need to get back to the office. I just wanted to swing by and—"

"Berate me?"

Her eyebrow quirks up. "Tell you the news."

"Yeah, well next time you want to say the words, 'you got me knocked up,' maybe don't say it as loudly in front of my boss."

"No guarantees."

As if I would expect anything less from her.

"Oh, and hey Rian," I call after her as she walks away, "can you write me a testimonial now? I bet I can get some good referrals off your news and how working out helps with breeding."

She flips me the middle finger without looking back, something she's never done in the year or so I've known her. It makes me laugh.

This is going to be a fun nine months.

CHAPTER TWENTY-TWO

ELLIOTT

"Ainsley! Come on!" I yell up the stairs. "Your dad is here!"

It takes all my self-control to not add on a quiet disclaimer that I don't really care if she's taking her time. I just don't want to spend any more time with Derrick than necessary. Especially since he seems to have forgotten what boundaries are. He's already made his way into the living room and is inspecting all the pictures.

"Where's your roommate?" The distain practically drips from his voice. Two years ago, it would have really bothered me. Now, it's an irritation. Like when you accidentally walk through a swarm of gnats and you have to stop and get them out of your hair, and if you're really unlucky, one of them gets squashed between your eyelids.

Some days, I'd really like to squash Derrick. I will never understand what I saw in him all those years ago. Was I drunk? Maybe that's it. I was a regular at Happy Hour way back then. No telling what was actually in those Bloody Marys.

"He's not here." I answer with a bored quality to my voice. I learned about six months into our divorce that the less emotion I show—excitement, sadness, happiness, fear—the less interest Derrick has in me. Call it narcissistic tendencies or just plain self-absorption, but monotone feelings bore him, which in turn keeps him from putting me on his radar as a person of interest in any way. I'll take it.

Derrick turns and subtly pouts his lips at me. "You'll be all alone tonight. That's so sad." I can practically hear the victory in his voice.

"Don't worry about me," I shoot back quickly. "He'll be back with takeout later."

Okay, okay. Not the smartest thing to say considering my overall goal is to not have Derrick think about me ever, unless it's "Elliott will have my balls if Ainsley gets hurt in my care." But his morphing expression from one of mock sadness as a front for triumph into shock that I do in fact have a life beyond him, makes it worth it. This time. I'm still smart enough to know I need to tread lightly, if only for Ainsley's sake.

Speaking of, the little diva finally makes her appearance wearing a plastic, sparkly tiara, matching dangly earrings, and bright red lipstick.

"What in the world are you dressed up for? And who told you to use my lipstick?" I'm really not angry. It's actually pretty funny that she's going to make her dad take her out like this.

"I wanted to dress up for Daddy." Grabbing her coat, Ainsley looks pleased with herself for putting in the extra effort for her father.

"Well, you look lovely," Derrick says while he helps her bundle up. Odd, but I've got to give it to him—he sure can play the role of her Prince Charming when he wants to.

Ainsley has clothes and toiletries already at her dad's house since she's there every other weekend, so there's no reason for her to pack, but her beloved tablet and favorite stuffed animal usually go back and forth. As we go through the normal verification process that yes, those items are in fact in her bag and there will be no hysterical moments at midnight requiring me to trek across town to appease her, they're ready to head out for the weekend. Two days also known as my mom-cation weekend.

That thought process might make me seem like an uncaring mom to some, but finding the silver lining to a joint custody agreement has done wonders for my emotional well-being. In addition, it helps me rest better when I'm focusing on self-care instead of worry. As a single mom, rest is priceless these days, so I'll suffer through having mom-guilt because I don't have mom-guilt.

Pretty sure only another mom can understand the logic of that one.

Just as they reach the door, it flies open and Abel steps through. With his bulk and the fact that spring is right around the corner, he's dressed in boots, jeans, and a bulky sweater. No coat. After so many months of cold, it makes me irrationally happy to know warmer temps are coming. Plus, he's holding a bag of food, which also delights me.

"Hi Abel," Ainsley says like the two men in her life staring each other down isn't awkward at all. Well, Derrick is staring Abel down. Abel doesn't even acknowledge Derrick is here.

"What's up, Tiny Dancer? You heading to your dad's?"

"Yep." She flings her backpack across her shoulders. "I've got my tablet and my lion, and I'm gonna sleep there and maybe see my grammy."

Abel smiles at her like she's the most precious child in the world and my heart melts. Every child should have a male role model look at them that way, and the fact that she's not his daughter and he still doesn't hold back, proves what kind of man he is. The more stuff like this happens, the more I like him. He makes it easy to fall for him.

Not that I'm falling for him. He's my friend and my roommate. Well, and the guy I'm seeing. So, I definitely like him, but falling for him? Yeah no. Not yet.

I don't think…

"Well, I hope you have a fun weekend. You look absolutely beautiful for your night out with your dad," he adds with another drop-dead gorgeous smile. The smile turns into a menacing smirk as he looks up at Derrick.

For a split second, I worry there's going to be a beatdown, which is not what I have planned for the night. I'm hungry and broken noses tend to kill my appetite. Not to mention it really sucks trying to get blood out of carpet. I'm pretty sure Derrick has the same thought. But no. Abel isn't that kind of a man. He just gives Derrick a curt nod and walks past them toward me.

"Hey." That smile is back and this time, it's all for me. "I didn't think you'd want chicken again, so I got you some sushi."

My eyes light up as I peek into the bag he hands me.

"Sushi!" Ainsley yells excitedly.

"We'll get some on the way home," Derrick immediately responds and quickly ushers her out the door.

I save my own verbal reaction until after I hear the door close behind Derrick. No sense in giving him ammunition. Or encouraging my daughter. She loves sushi as much as I do. I have no doubt that kid would have tried to steal it all if she'd stayed any longer.

"Ooh! You got my favorite kind with the special sauce." I clutch the bag to my chest, a dreamy smile on my face as I look at my knight in shining... well, boots. "Thank you."

"You know that's not actual sushi, right?"

I look over my shoulder at him like he's nuts, beelining for the plates and silverware. I'm about four seconds away from this hunger turning into hanger. Ain't nobody want to see that. "What? Of course, it's sushi."

Abel follows behind me with his own bag. Probably that nasty chicken he mentioned. "The fish is cooked and there is creamy sauce on it. Not to mention the avocado inside which isn't native to Japan at all. They don't even use it in their rolls in Asia unless they're purposely trying to Westernize the food."

Grabbing everything I need to finish fixing my dinner, I'm singularly focused on getting this food in my belly, even as Abel tries to ruin it. "That's not true. How do you know that?"

"I asked the guy at the sushi counter." Abel takes one of the clean plates off the small stack and we work in tandem, making our personalized meals. Being able to cater to my personal taste buds instead of eating whatever the kids are having might be my favorite part of these weekends.

"Whatever. It's got seaweed wrapped around it and sticky rice holding it all together. Cut in pieces. Soy sauce and wasabi on the side—yep. Sushi." Mixing the two extra flavors together, I dip a piece in the spicy/salty combo and pop it in my mouth. I can't help my moan because this is so. Damn. Good. "Oh yeah. That's good sushi too."

Tearing my eyes way from my food, I look at Abel who is frozen in place, a weird expression on his face. "What?" I ask around my bite.

He licks his lips and swallows, Adam's apple bobbing. Something in the air has changed. The energy is suddenly different. Charged. Sensual, somehow. Or maybe that's just my love of sushi, but I don't think so. I think it's Abel.

"Do you moan like that during sex too?"

I freeze, another bite halfway to my mouth, and it takes everything in me not to drop it on the floor. Especially with my lady bits suddenly tingling like they are. Now I understand the energy change in the room. It has nothing to do with my dinner at all.

Slowly and carefully, I put my chopsticks down, making sure not to drop anything. Dinner may be over for now, but I don't plan to waste any of this later. I always get hungry post-sex, and I have a feeling I'm going to be starving later.

Once everything is situated, I turn back to Abel and lean against the counter. "Depends on if I have something to moan about."

In half a second he is on me, his arms around my waist, holding me close as he dips his tongue in my mouth, sucks on my tongue, bites my lip. I fully reciprocate, enjoying the raw passion we both feel and can finally focus on.

"When does Mabel get back from your mom's?" I ask against his lips and dive right back into the moment before he can answer.

Pushing back to give him enough room he answers, "Not until tomorrow. They decided last minute to have a sleepover, so they won't be here until about eight," and thrusts his hands in my hair, tilting my head to the side to give him easier access.

I try to shut off my thoughts, but my mom-brain has to do a teeny tiny bit of organizing before I can be completely in this moment. It's a hazard of the toughest job in the world, I suppose.

"Hang on. Let me think." Abel rests his forehead on mine, breathing heavily while I quickly sort through my thoughts.

"Ainsley is with her dad until Sunday. Mabel is with her grandma until tomorrow. I'm pretty sure you have condoms in your drawer—"

"Roger that."

"Okay. We have approximately fourteen hours to make good on this."

Not wanting to waste any precious time, I grab the hem of his shirt and help him rip it over his head. The sight before me stops me dead.

He. Is. Beautiful.

I've seen Abel without his shirt before. It's part of living with someone who uses the hall bathroom. I always knew he had a phenomenal physique, but somehow, knowing this body is about to be on top of mine makes him even more attractive. Call it hormones or pheromones or being horny, this sight is definitely in the top ten most beautiful things I've ever seen. Maybe even top five.

Running my fingers over the smooth, hairless six—no, eight pack —I can't help remembering that I don't come close to looking like this at all. Not that it's going to stop me. I'm not a crazy woman. It's just mind-blowing that he sees the same kind of beauty in me that I see in him.

"How can I compete with these abs?" I breathe, still exploring with my touch.

"You're not supposed to compete with them," Abel says quietly, holding still as I touch him. "You're supposed to complement them."

Um, what? "Compliment them? You want me to tell them they're pretty?"

Abel rolls his eyes, like I'm the one being confusing here. "Complement," he tries to explain. "Like match." There is a possibility the blood has already stopped circulating to his brain already, because he's not making much sense.

No, with that bulge, there is a good probability his brain isn't functioning at normal capacity. Because he's wrong.

"My abs will never match these."

"No, not like that." Now he's getting frustrated. "Like apples and oranges. Combined they make a fruit salad."

I crinkle my nose in disgust. What kind of fruit salad has he been eating? "No, they don't."

He huffs, which makes me want to laugh. "Fine. Like the drama mask." He waves his hand around like he can conjure up the image he wants me to visualize.

I know I'm ruining the mood here, but I can't help myself. I think I know what he's trying to say, but all the words are not making sentences that mean anything. It's too funny to ignore. But this is what we do. It's who we are. We laugh and joke and keep each other on our toes. Sure, it delays sex a little bit, but one of the things I learned in my marriage is that sex isn't everything. It will get stale and stagnant at some point, even with the best effort. Hell, once you get to a certain age, it may not be a priority at all anymore.

But you know what will keep a relationship sexy? Humor. Humor and laughter and fun. So, to hell with worrying about getting to the bed any faster. This moment is plenty sexy enough for me.

Feigning innocence, I say, "Your abs make me happy and my abs make you sad? That's not very nice."

Abel nostrils flare with annoyance. "You are driving me crazy, woman." He immediately attacks my neck with his lips, kissing down the column of my throat and making me moan again. The sound throws him into a frenzy and his kisses become harder and more intense. I lose my thoughts, too busy enjoying the touch of his lips on my skin, his fingers on my waist, the air on my body when my shirt disappears.

Holy shit. My shirt disappeared!

"How did you do that?" I ask, looking down at the lacy bra barely containing my breasts. Abel chuckles, but never looks away from where his hands are roaming my now naked flesh. "Seriously. I didn't even feel you pull it over my head."

"I told you I have skills. Imagine what kinds of things I can do when the rest of your clothes fall off."

"Maybe it's time to stop bragging and start doing."

He wastes no more time, picking me up and carrying me to my bedroom.

I had no idea he could lift me and my mom-bod, let alone haul it upstairs without heavy breathing. Yet here I am, my forty-two-year-old self about to make love to a guy whose insides are as beautiful as his outsides.

Make love?

Yeah. That's about right. Because no matter where this relationship goes, no matter if or how it ends, this is love right here. It's not the kind that bowls you over so nothing else matters. It's not the kind that fizzles when the lust is gone. It's the kind that starts with two people being best friends and grows until they become "your person."

That's the best kind of love there is.

CHAPTER TWENTY-THREE

ABEL

B leary eyed, I stumble down the stairs, trying not to fall. Technically I slept in so I should be wide awake, but considering I spent most of the night buried between Elliott's legs, "sleeping in" felt more like a nap.

Totally worth it.

I've never been with anyone like Elliott before. Granted, I haven't been with anyone besides May for a very long time. I never cheated on her, so the only real experience I have is with my ex-wife and anyone before her. That was a long time ago, though. I'm a lot older and wiser. This is the body of a full-grown man now, and last night I was making love to a real woman.

Yes, I said making love. Because there is something very different about sex when it's with someone you consider one of your very best friends and not someone you've only known in a dating capacity.

I shouldn't compare. But I'd gotten so used to being with May, whose goal has always been to be a supermodel, I'd forgotten what it was like to be with someone who has some meat on her bones. It didn't disappoint. At all.

I enjoy feeling Elliott's softness against me as I thrust inside her.

I like digging my fingers into soft flesh while she rides me. I love seeing the roundness of her ass when I take her from behind.

Annnd now certain body parts are awake while the rest of me is still half asleep. Quickly, I shift my thoughts to the coffee I hope is brewing. I can smell it, but I don't know if my mind is playing tricks on me in my morning fog, or if it's real.

The hand that shoots out as soon as I step into the kitchen clears things up. It's holding a mug of coffee just for me.

"How did you know I needed this?" I ask groggily, and moan in appreciation at the rich, bitter taste sure to wake my sleepy-ass up.

Elliott is leaning against the counter opposite of me, giving me a playful smirk. "First of all, you need it every morning." She's not wrong. "Plus, you did most of the work last night. Or maybe it was this morning. Either way, I figured you'd need a little caffeine boost. And since the new machine doesn't need any corporal punishment to work, I figured it was the least I could do."

I raise my eyebrows flirtatiously. "You enjoyed last night, huh?"

"I enjoyed it..."she pauses and counts on her fingers quietly. "Four times."

So much for curbing my wayward thoughts. Placing my mug on the counter next to me, I stalk over to her, intent on completing that kitchen fantasy I keep having. "Only four?"

Recognizing the lust in my eyes, she puts her own mug down but keeps up the banter. "Well there was that almost-fifth time."

"*Almost* fifth?"

"It doesn't count if you pull out in the middle of an orgasm."

"It does in my mind." Putting my hands on her waist, I rub my nose up and down the side of her neck, smiling when she shivers. "Especially when I went right back to work and made you come even harder after that."

"Mmm. Nope. Maybe you should try again."

Hooking my thumbs into the waistband of her pajama pants, I begin slowly pushing them to the floor, enjoying the feel of her skin on my fingers as I do. "I think I'm up for the challenge. But why are you wearing pants?"

"I got cold this morning." She breathes before all talking is done.

Unable to keep my lips off hers, I kiss her deeply, my tongue diving in for another taste of this woman I can't get enough of. And then, despite my best efforts, I start laughing because of what I discover.

"Sushi? Already?"

Elliott giggles in response. "I didn't eat last night."

"Really?"

She rolls her eyes and then smiles at me. "Let me rephrase, I didn't eat anything of substance." I open my mouth to respond, but she cuts me off, finger to my lips. "Yes, your sausage is substantial, but I still woke up hungry, okay?"

"Good enough." I lean in again, ready to make good on my promise of a fifth orgasm. I can feel her breath on my lips, feel her warmth in my hands, feel her body quiver in anticipation—

Ding-dong.

Aaaaand the moment is gone.

Sagging into each other, we both take a second to calm down. And pray that whoever is at the door leaves.

No such luck. The doorbell rings again.

Glancing at the clock, I realize why there is such persistence behind noise. It's a few minutes after eight.

"Shit. It's Mabel. Wait... I don't mean it like that."

"I know what you meant." Elliott nudges me gently. "Go. Don't leave her in the cold. This can wait."

I give her a quick peck, knowing it's the last one I'll get for at least the rest of the day, and pad my way to the door. Quickly glancing down to make sure there's no unwelcome bulge greeting my daughter at eye level, I fling it open.

As expected, my mother is sitting in the car on the street, engine running. There's so little parking in this neighborhood, I'm not surprised she opted to drop and run instead of risking a ticket for double parking. She waves at me before driving off, satisfied that she is officially off duty.

Mabel, on the other hand, is glaring at me as she eyes me up and down. Weird.

"Why aren't you wearing a shirt, Daddy?"

"Because I was asleep, baby girl." I wave her in so I can close the door. March still has a chill to it, even if it's not snowing anymore.

"But, Dad," Mabel scolds. "Elliott's here."

"I don't think Elliott minds, honey. Now let's eat. I got you powdered donuts, and I know you can't resist those." Apparently, sometime between last night and this morning, she has learned a ridiculous amount of self-control, as proven by the fact that Mabel glares at me but doesn't move from her spot. "What?"

"She is not my mom."

Did I hear her right? I think so, but surely my daughter isn't putting together that Elliott and I are together based on the fact that I'm not wearing a shirt. Is she? I work really hard to make sure my eyes don't widen with admission.

Deflect, deflect, deflect...

"No one thinks that, baby. Come on, Mabel. We have breakfast waiting for you." Sure enough, Elliott already has the donuts on a plate and is setting them on the table. But Mabel is having none of it.

Instead, her mouth opens wide and she clenches her fists at her side. Apparently, the word "we" is just the thing she needs to come up with the exact conclusion I've been avoiding her coming to.

"I won't eat it!" she finally screams, stomping her feet. "You can't make me! I don't care if she's your girlfriend. She is not my mother!" Mabel races up the stairs, and within seconds, her door slams so hard, it reverberates down here.

I run my hand down my face, trying to wipe away the last few seconds from my brain, but it doesn't do any good. Instead, I'm pretty sure I got powdered sugar in my eye. Although, where it came from, I have no idea.

As I try to wipe it back out, Elliott sits on the couch adjacent to me, a cup of hot coffee in her hands.

"I guess we weren't as stealth as we thought," she remarks calmly.

"Apparently not."

"What do you suggest we do now?"

I look at Elliott, with her bedhead and cute fluffy pajamas. She makes me smile. She makes me laugh. She makes me feel like I'm special. Like there's more to me than being a meathead. Last night was more than sex for me. It was about my feelings for her. For us. For what we could be. And call me selfish, but I don't want to let it go just because my daughter misses her mother. A mother who isn't coming back. But how the hell do I make an eight-year-old accept the fact her dad isn't going to be single forever? First things first, though, we need to make sure there's no more surprises about this situation.

"I think maybe you need to get Ainsley up to speed before Mabel spills the beans."

Elliott nods her head. The movement is subtle, but it's there, and I know what she's thinking: things are about to get a whole lot more complicated.

CHAPTER TWENTY-FOUR

ELLIOTT

The rest of the weekend is spent with a lot of tense moments and rolled eyes. Mabel's, not mine. However, I did think about reacting with equal immaturity but never followed through. It's a little less acceptable for the adult to behave that way than the child; not by much though. Or maybe that's just me and my aversion to this kind of behavior.

Or maybe my feelings are a little hurt.

It irks me that Abel never tells Mabel she's being rude or makes her stop acting like I'm the enemy. I'm trying to give him the benefit of the doubt. He's struggling with his own guilt as a dad, which I understand completely. Don't we all have some sort of internal conflict when one parent leaves our child, no matter what the circumstances? It's a process. I know that. I just wish his process would hurry up so I could be comfortable in my own home again.

Er, Abel's home.

Whatever. I pay rent. I deserve to sit in the living room and watch TV if I want to and not feel pressured to hide in my room from an elementary-school-aged bully.

Although, he may have talked to her and I don't know about it. Lord knows, her behavior hasn't changed, but we're not together every second of every day, and that's not a conversation I necessarily need to be privy to anyway. It would be nice to know it, but I don't think it's information I can demand from him at this point in our relationship.

Thankfully, Ainsley made it home on time, and her return seemed to brighten Mabel's mood considerably. See what a good mom I am? I'm using my child as a buffer from a pint-sized devil. *Awesome work, Elliott.*

But at least the tension eased in the house and Mabel finally brightened up a bit and got some pent-up aggression out on the Wii. After an hour or so of doing summer Olympic sports in the basement, Mabel was much calmer. Dinner ended up being not-horrible, not that I wish we were still sitting around the table. It wasn't fun either. Just more... neutral. It cemented the understanding that there's still a lot to work on if Abel and I are going to go the distance. I'm sure this is one of many hurdles we'll encounter together.

My next individual hurdle, however, is to have the dreaded conversation with my own child. Now that dinner and baths are over and things are settling down for the night, I have no excuses. Ainsley is ready for bed, I'm about to tuck her in, and it's about to go down.

The cat is about to be out of the bag.

The secret is about to be revealed.

Okay, now I'm slipping into melodramatic territory myself. I'm not sure what I'm worried about. Ainsley really likes Abel. He does a great job caring for her in the afternoons. They have their own small inside jokes (that he always tells me about later, so I know what the heck is going on) and I trust him with her completely. So, what's the problem?

Actually, I know exactly what the problem is. It's multifaceted. One, I don't want her to react like Mabel did. I can only handle so many little devils in one house. And two, I don't want her to give her the impression this makes us a family. None of us are ready for that, despite how odd our circumstances may be.

Still, I can't avoid this conversation forever. I can't even avoid it for another ten minutes. It's go time.

Time to put the pedal to the metal.

Time to put on our running shoes.

Okay, enough Elliott. This isn't about you. It's about Ainsley.

With that thought in mind, I try to ease my way into this awkward conversation. "Did you have fun with your dad this weekend?" I ask, as she climbs under the covers and slides into her bed.

Ainsley nods her head, freshly washed hair falling in damp clumps of blond around her face. "Yeah. We ate sushi, and I went to Grammy's house."

"Sounds fun," I say absent-mindedly as I settle myself in next to her for our nightly talk. "What did you do with Grammy?"

"We made cookies and watched a movie and took Roscoe for a walk. And then we went to the grocery store and made spaghetti."

I furrow my brow. "Wow. You did a lot of stuff."

Ainsley snuggles in deeper and pushes her little body against mine. "I spent the night there."

My eyebrows rise, but I say nothing. It's irritating that Derrick passed off his weekend to his mother, especially since I've made it clear from the beginning that any time his mother wants to see Ainsley is fine with me. It's not hard to incorporate my daughter's extended family into her everyday life.

But it's also not my job to force any of them to be adults, so if Derrick wants to share his custody time with his mother instead of doing it the smart way, not my problem.

"I'm glad you had a good time." Kissing her on the head and stroking her hair, I add, "I missed you, ya know. Mabel spent the night with her Grammy, too, so it was just me and Abel."

A giant yawn comes out of her mouth, and I know I'm running out of time before she falls asleep. "Did you watch a movie with him?"

No. No movies for us. We were too busy doing other things. I can't say that though, so I stick with, "No. But I ate a lot of sushi."

Ainsley nods and rubs her fingers over her fuzzy blanket like she does every night to fall asleep.

Okay, Elliott. Now or never. Tell her the truth before Mabel does.

I take a deep breath to steady my nerves. "Um, you know how Abel and I work together and help each other around the house?"

"Yeah."

"Abel and I... kind of ... we sort of..." *Why is it so hard to say it out loud to my daughter?* "We like each other."

"I know, Mom."

"I mean, we *like* like each other."

"I *know,* Mom."

"What do you mean, you know?"

Ainsley rolls her eyes, no doubt a habit learned from Mabel. "I mean, I know you are Abel are dating."

"Wha—?" My eyes widen and my mouth drops open. Of all the ways she could have responded, her already knowing never crossed my mind. "How? Did someone tell you?"

"I heard you."

Her eyes close and she snuggles in tighter still, oblivious to the fact that my blood is running cold as I wonder what exactly she heard. Did she hear us having sex? Wait, she wasn't here last night and that was the first time we were together. I should be safe. I think.

Did she hear us kissing? Do kids even know the difference between the sounds? What does she know?

Okay, Elliott, calm yourself. There's only one way to find out...

Pushing myself up on my elbow I decide to get to the bottom of this. "What exactly did you hear?"

"You and Abel talking."

Okay, phew. That's much better than it could have been. But now I'm really curious.

"Have you been eavesdropping?"

Ainsley giggles like she has her own secret. "When you're in the kitchen, we can hear you in the basement."

I wrack my brain, trying to figure out how they can hear us from so far away. Surely, the sound doesn't carry down the stairs loud enough to be heard over the Wii. But how else would they be able to hear us?

Ainsley answers my silent question, dispelling all the myths. "There's a vent thingy above the TV. We can hear you through there."

Sure enough, I know which vent she's talking about. I knew these older homes had some weird ventilations systems. I just didn't know the basement vent was connected so closely to the one in the kitchen. Which brings up a more important question.

"Are you kidding me, you little sneak? How long have you been listening to our conversations?"

"Since we moved in." Ainsley's little girl giggle makes me laugh too. The idea that she got away with this for so long seems to make her thinks she's a sharp cookie. I suppose she's not wrong. Except...

"Wait... is that how you knew what you were getting for Christmas?"

This time she belly-laughs as she nods.

"I knew you weren't as excited as you should have been for that Hatchimal!" I dig my fingers into her sides, tickling her and making her howl with laughter.

"I was still excited, Mommy. I didn't know which one you got me."

Dropping onto the bed, I raise my arm over my head to relax. "I can't believe you've been listening to me all along and pretended this whole time."

She rolls over, wide awake from the fresh exertion. "I was gonna tell you, but Mabel doesn't want her daddy to know. She doesn't want to get in trouble."

Somehow, this doesn't surprise me. It also makes more sense why Mabel seems to be getting more and more angry. She's listening in on conversations that not only should no child hear, but that her little brain isn't old enough to process anyway.

"Well, now that I know, I have to tell him. You guys are still children and some adult talk will be too hard for you guys to understand.

I want to make sure we talk to you about any important things the right way, okay?"

"Okay." Once again, her eyes get heavy, her fingers rub her blanket as she yawns. She's about to drop into sleep when she suddenly says, "Abel's nice, Mommy. I'm glad you're dating him."

Caressing her hair, I smile at her, even though she's already drifted off. I have no idea how I was blessed with such an amazing kid.

"Me too, baby. Me too."

CHAPTER TWENTY-FIVE

ABEL

"Come on, Beast! Get it!"

Joey's yells reverberate in my ears, but I barely hear them. I don't feel the sweat sliding down my face or the hear the music pumping through the speakers.

The only thing I see is the spot on the wall I'm staring at as I concentrate.

The only thing I hear is the sound of my heart beating as I strain.

The only thing I feel is the tension in my quads as I slowly squat, lowering myself and an additional four hundred eighty-six pounds to the floor. Just a little lower...

...a little more....

... a few more inches...

"Go Beast! Push!"

That's all I need to hear to know my form is bang on and I've hit my mark. All I have left to do is stand back up.

My legs are practically quivering. My core is tighter than it's ever been. It's grueling, but if I can do it, I'll have beaten my own personal best.

"Aaaaaaaarrrrrrrrrrrrrrggggggggggggggghhhhhhhhhh!" A roar emanates from deep within me, my face probably a dark shade of red as I use all my might to stand. And when my legs are straight again, a smile crosses my face as the crowd around us explodes.

Joey and Tommy, another trainer we know, each immediately grab a side of the bar and help me rerack the weight. Even with two of them, they're grunting from the strain, which only makes me feel better about raising the bar on my personal best. It happens to be the gym best as well, but I'm less concerned about that. For me, it's about smashing my own goals.

Someone tosses me a towel and a water bottle, while others pat me on the back and congratulate me on my accomplishment. It's all I can do to get some water in my system while trying to catch my breath.

"Holy shit, man," Joey exclaims when the crowd begins to disperse. "That was insane! I can't believe your legs held out."

I shake my head with my own disbelief. "For a second there, I didn't think they would." They actually still might not if they keep quivering like this.

"Nah." He claps me on the back. "I never doubted you. I can't wait to see the new plaque on the wall with your picture on it. Maybe they'll spring for a trophy this time instead." His eyes widen as he jokes. "Oh! It would look great on the shelf behind the trainer desk."

I groan before taking another drink. "The destruction of that stupid plaque was the only good part of that fire."

Joey chuckles because he knows I'm right. The last time I beat my personal record, management thought it would be fun to promote it. Something about making sure customers know "one of their own" was a client too, working hard to reach their goals like everyone else.

Not only did it seem a bit over the top to have the weight I squatted on a shiny plaque, they took the picture right before I sneezed. It looked like I was smelling a fart. And since he who smelt it, dealt it...

Yeah. I got a lot of shit from Joey about that picture.

"Make sure you don't sneeze when they pull the camera out this time."

See?

I shove him with a "Shut up, man."

"They'll give you some notice so you can prepare, right? You can check the pollen count at least. Should I bring you some Claritin?"

He'd be funny if he wasn't so obnoxious sometimes.

"You're a dick, you know that?" Looking at the clock, I realize I have a few short minutes until school pickup. I could shower here, but I'm still so hot, it'd be pointless. I'd be sweaty again before getting fresh clothes on. My best bet is to get the girls first and shower at home. I need to let Elliott know I'm heading out.

"Speaking of dick," Joey continues like I'm not ignoring him and walking away, "has yours gotten any yet?"

I flash him a disgusted glare over my shoulder as we head to the locker room, me to grab my stuff, him to harass me some more. "You really are a pig, you know that? I get why none of the women here will touch you with a ten-foot pole."

"Eh. Their loss." He shrugs like he really doesn't care what other people think. I've known him long enough to know it's not an act. If there's one thing Joey is good at, it's being confident in his own man-bun. To a fault sometimes. This is one of those times. "I'm not asking for details about your sex life, man. I just wanna know if you've finally gotten a piece of ass."

Pulling my locker open, I rummage around for my deodorant. The least I can do is cancel out some of the odor before making the girls walk home with me. "I don't know why you think that's any business of yours."

"It's not." He plops down on the bench and leans back to relax. "I just know it's been a really long time for you, and I wanna make sure you aren't gonna back up or something."

Something about that sentence makes me pause. Did I hear him correctly? "Back up. What are you talking about?"

"You know..." He gestures towards my crotch, which is a little worrisome. Since when is Joey concerned about my junk? "Like... a clog. Of spooge."

"What the hell are you even talking about?"

He sighs, as if this conversation is paining him. But did I bring my testicles into this little chat? No. No I did not. And now I want to know why he did.

"Seriously, Joey. Spill. Why are you suddenly worried about my schlong?"

Unable to look at me, he pulls out his phone and starts scrolling. "Elliott sent me this article the other day and it has all these statistics on testicular cancer and different kinds of bacteria that can build up inside and kill you."

Weird. Why is she sending him medical articles about penises? Is there something going on with him I don't know about? None of this sounds right to me.

"One of the things the article says is that in order to protect ourselves, we men need to be ejaculating a minimum of twice a day. Three times is actually ideal."

"Wait, what?" I feel like I'm missing a key of very important information, so I let him ramble.

"Yeah. See?" He holds out his phone for me to read the article he has pulled up. "It got me thinking that this relationship with you two is new, and maybe you were holding back until you got to know each other better since you've got all this integrity and whatnot," he says with a wave of his hand. "But we're not getting any younger. You need to take care of your testicular health."

The more I read, the more I have a suspicion of what's happening here, and the more I try to hold back my laugh. Finally, though, I cave.

"Are you saying...?" A belly-laugh bursts out of me, and I can't stop long enough to finish my sentence. "Does this mean...? Oh, holy hell, I can't stop laughing..." He looks at me like I've lost my mind when he's the one who fell for this whole thing. He just doesn't know it yet. This is going to be fun. "You've been jacking off three times a day for how long?"

"I don't know. It's been about a week since she sent it to me." That sends me into yet another round of laughter, this time complete with tears running down my face. "It's not funny, man. Penile health is nothing to laugh at."

That does it. I crumple to the floor, unable to stand up straight anymore after my workout followed by this mess.

Things only get worse, or better, depending on who you ask, when Frank exits the dressing room area, his gym bag in hand.

Frank is like the resident cool grandpa everyone wants to grow up to be like. With white hair and always dressed to the nines, he looks like the last remaining member of the Rat Pack. He's classy like that too. And he's a staple here at the gym, spending much of his time at Tabitha's smoothie bar chatting up other patrons. He knows almost everyone's name and is always kind, even when he's poking fun.

As Frank passes by, a conspiratorial smirk on his face, he pats Joey on the back. "Listen here, fellas. I like masturbation as much as the next guy…" That statement alone throws me back into my hysteria. "But that's not testicular health. That's fake news, and you got duped by it. Let me know if you need a recommendation for something to clear up that chaffing."

Joey looks back down at his phone, discreetly adjusting himself —or maybe trying to relieve some of the tenderness from overuse— with shock written on his face while Frank saunters off.

"Seriously?" Joey looks even more stumped now. "But it looks real. It even cited the *Journal of United States Medicine*."

Another laugh barks out of me. "That's not even a thing. It's the *Journal of* American *Medicine*. That's an Onion article, Joey!"

"Son of a bitch, I didn't even notice." Now that he's up to speed, my laughter begins to subside until he yells, "Frank! Don't tell Tabitha. Please? Frank!"

There's no response because Frank is already gone. Which means, this news is about to spread like wildfire. Only better. The only damage will be to Joey's reputation. Actually, no. His current reputation will only confirm this whole incident is plausible, and that makes it even more fun for me.

Zipping up my jacket, I toss my bag over my shoulder and head to the childcare center to let Elliott know I'm heading out. This is our normal routine, so I know she isn't worried. But I find it to be common courtesy to let her know. Besides, she needs to know her little article worked. She's going to get a kick out of this.

"I don't get it," Joey says as he catches up to me. "Why would Elliott send me that article then? Did she send it to you?"

"Nope."

"But if she was so worried about this, why am I the only one she sent it to?"

"Really? You can't figure out why she would want to trick you into whacking off three times a day and overusing your... hand?"

For a split second, I see a flicker of understanding. And then it's gone. "You think she did it on purpose?"

I shake my head and pull the glass door open. "Maybe you should ask her yourself."

Speak of the she-devil, Elliott's already in the process of pulling out tables for workstations, like she does every day at this time in preparation for the older kids.

"Hey," I call out to her. She looks up and smiles at me. I love that smile. It's not saccharine sweet or fake. But it is different than it used to be. It's more... mine. Like everyone else she's friends with gets a certain look, but this one is that of a friend, roommate, and lover. More intimate somehow.

Oh Lord. I must have sweated out every bit of testosterone in my body during that last squat to be thinking like this. *Now where did I put my man card?*

Elliott stops what she's doing to come talk to us. "Did you beat your record?"

The fact that those are the first words out of her mouth make me want to puff out my chest and maybe beat it a little.

Found the man card.

"You should have seen it, Elliott," Joey exclaims wildly, forgetting the whole reason he followed me in here. "This guy barely flinched. Like he was just picking up Mabel or something, not almost three hundred pounds. It was awesome."

Elliott's eyes sparkle as she listens intently to Joey ramble on about the crowd and how red my face was, like this is the most interesting thing she's ever heard. Damn, I love this woman.

Yeah, I said it. I love her. Not as my friend anymore, but just as her, and it doesn't wig me out at all.

"We could hear the cheers from here, so we figured you'd done it."

I chuckle, a little embarrassed that the crowd was so loud. "Yeah, it would've been a totally different reaction if I'd fallen over."

Joey claps me on the back. "No way that was gonna happen. He did great, Elliott. You should be proud."

"I am," she says quietly and smiles shyly at me. Not that she has anything to be shy about, but I'm pretty sure she's having the same thoughts as I am—our feelings are getting deeper every day, just from the little things that happen. The small victories we share. The secrets we keep. The sex.

Let's not forget about the sex.

"But hey, Elliott, I have a question," Joey says.

Or maybe we need to forget the sex for now.

She tears her gaze away from mine. "Sure, Joey. What's up?"

He turns his phone to show her what he's looking at. "Did you know this article was fake? There isn't really any risk of a semen back up."

Dinah happens to be walking by with a baby in her arms and stops. "Um, guys. I don't know what you're talking about, but can we be careful with our words about certain bodily functions while in the vicinity of small ears?"

Elliott takes the phone out of Joey's hands and gives it to her boss. "He's asking about the validity of the article I sent him the other day." If I didn't know better, I'd say my girlfriend was sporting a victorious smile with a little bit of maliciousness mixed in.

"Wait. You knew this wasn't real?" Joey's still baffled as to how Elliott didn't know this was all misinformation. As if the idea of her sending it on purpose is perplexing to him.

The more she reads, the more Dinah starts to laugh softly.

"Of course, I knew," Elliott confesses.

Poor Joey looks stumped now as to why his most prized possession would become the butt of a joke. Actually, that sounds like a joke within itself, but I refrain from saying as much. I don't think his poor, wounded ego could take much more.

"Why, Elliott? Why would you send that to me, knowing it would end in chaffing so bad, no medicated lotion could fix it?"

Dinah and Elliott both get wide-eyed. "You've actually been... you mean... Joey, three times a day?" Dinah barely gets the words out, clearly not sure if she should laugh or offer him some sort of help.

"Of course." He holds up his hands like it's a no-brainer to spend half your day spanking the monkey. "Who jokes about this kind of thing? I'll tell you who—a sad, sadistic woman, that's who."

Dinah loses her battle and starts laughing. Elliott, on the other hand, crosses her arms over her chest. She may have won this battle, but she's waiting to see if she's started a war. "More like a woman who was getting you back for telling everyone at work about my love life."

"That's what this was about? You're mad a few people know about you're bumping uglies with this meathead?" I shake my head when he gestures to me. Joey will never learn. I often wonder how many times he was dropped on the head as a baby.

"Wait a minute," Dinah butts in, bouncing the baby in her arms and rocking back and forth. "You guys are together now? Like *together* together?"

Elliott eyes widen briefly as she realizes she just let her own cat out of a diaper bag. When all else fails, her go-to defense mechanism is to deflect, deflect, deflect. "Isn't there a baby who needs to be changed or a fistfight between three-year-olds happening that you need to break up?"

"No, things are pretty quiet right now," Dinah quips back. "And this is really entertaining to be honest. I'd rather stand here."

Cue Elliott's dramatic eyeroll. She should know better than to think she was going to get off that easily. Frankly, I'm shocked Dinah didn't know about our new dating status until now. Tabitha is usually more on her game with the rumor spreading. Either Carlos is keeping her super busy with his baby gushing, or she's dying of something terrible. Someone should probably check on her because, either way, I'm sure it's super painful for her.

"Fine." Elliot finally sighs, again with the dramatics. "We were trying to keep it under wraps because there are kids involved but Perez Hilton here," she says, gesturing to Joey, who mouths, "Who me?" as she rolls her eyes, "can't keep his trap shut."

"Well, that's kind of your fault for thinking he could keep a secret in the first place," Dinah cuts in, quickly glancing around the room to make sure all hell hasn't broken loose while she gets her daily entertainment news.

"It's not like he found out on purpose. So, to answer your question," Elliott continues, "yes, Abel and I are... um...taking things slow."

"Together," I interject. "She means we're together." Elliott's jaw drops, and I respond with, "No use in pussyfooting around it, babe. You know Dinah is going to come to her own conclusions otherwise. Joey did."

"Well, I know but... I don't know."

"I know. It's still new. You're still wrapping your brain around it. The girls are having a tough time of it. I know."

Elliott looks back and forth between Joey and Dinah, pleading in her eyes. "This is why I wanted to keep it private for a while. It's a complicated situation."

Dinah gives her an incredulous look and shifts the now squirming baby in her arms. "What's complicated about it? Man and woman meet. Man and woman boink. The end. The most complicated thing about it is how I'm a much better matchmaker than I knew."

"How come you can say *boink* in here, but I can't say semen?" Like I said, Joey never learns.

He takes a full step backward when Dinah hisses at him. Serves him right.

Elliott throws her hands up and grumbles something about giving up on caring anymore and goes back to setting up her tables, waving her hand in my direction when I yell that I'm leaving to get the girls.

At least she noticed. Dinah and Joey are too entrenched in their standoff about kid-friendly words to even notice me walk out the door.

CHAPTER TWENTY-SIX

ELLIOTT

Today has been a long, painfully hard day. And I mean that in the most literal sense of the word.

Not only did one of our "energetic" four-year-olds kick me in the shin when he got angry about having to share the train table, but one of the homework tables collapsed and landed on my toe while I was putting it away.

This is probably the only time in the last six months I've been glad cold weather lasts so long around here, because I have no desire to shave my legs or wear flip-flops with all the black and blue I'm sporting right now. All I really want is to sit down on the couch, take my shoes off, put my feet up, and not move.

Maybe if I'm lucky, Abel will bring me dinner on a TV tray, and I won't have to get up once I sit.

Thoughts of Abel catering to me as I rest quickly morph into me lying on a lounge chair by a fabulous pool with sparkling blue water, wearing a fabulously expensive deep yellow bathing suit and fabulous super dark sunglasses. Glam is the only way to describe it. Especially when I shake out my Pantene-esque hair. And Abel walks up wearing a tiny little Speedo to feed me grapes.

A smile graces my lips as the world around me fades, only my fantasy to keep me company as I limp down the street to the house. My mood elevates with each grape my fantasy-self eats, and I find myself practically floating instead of walking. Nothing can change how I'm feeling right now, as if nothing can go wrong and everything is right in the world—

Splash!

Odd. That water isn't warm like the pool I was just sort of not really sitting next to. It's cold. And slushy. And only up to my ankle. *What the...?*

Looking down, I find the culprit of my lost happy attitude.

"A freaking puddle? What else could go wrong?" I grumble to myself, as I shake my now freezing foot off and continue with my trek home. "And when the heck did it rain?"

Fantasy bubble now burst, I concentrate on finding the right townhouse. With the way things have gone today, I wouldn't put it past me to walk into the wrong building.

Fortunately, my key fits when I finally make it to the front door. That means I'm in the right place.

"I'm home," I yell as I step into the tiny foyer area, stripping myself of my shoes and socks before ridding myself of my coat. Thank goodness there is a pile of clean towels on the banister waiting to be carried upstairs. At least I can dry off my poor foot before limping to the couch.

Abel's head pops out from around the corner, and I assume from the smell he's cooking dinner. "Hey!" His face looks bright and happy, the exact opposite of my mood. It's charming and irritating at the exact same time. I would question that thought more except Daniel Tiger taught me a few years ago it's okay to have more than one emotion at the same time.

Damn Daniel Tiger and all his preschool-aged wisdom.

Still, my mother raised me to not be rude. "Hey." A grumble is better than nothing, right?

Apparently not, because Abel's face changes to one of concern as he comes closer. "What's wrong? Did something happen?"

"Yeah, something happened. Lots of somethings happened. I had a terrible day complete with several injuries, a giant cold puddle, and now you're not wearing a Speedo."

He looks down at the clothes he's wearing and back up at me as I finally plop down on the couch. "Uh... I didn't realize there was a particular uniform for cooking dinner."

"If we're not having grapes, it doesn't matter anyway." Looking at my now bare toe for the first time, I realize it's red and swollen, and a bruise is clearly forming. No wonder it hurts to walk on it. Pressing gently on different areas, I wince. "We don't have an ice pack or something, do we?"

"Let me look at that." I lean back on the couch as he sits on the edge of the coffee table and gently takes my foot in his hand. "Holy shit, Elliott. What did you do?"

"Dropped a table on my toe."

"That'll do it." He continues to examine the injury and various parts of my foot. "It looks like it might be broken. Do we need to take you for an X-ray?"

I shake my head, enjoying the feel of his gentle hands on me. I never got to this part of my fantasy, so I make sure to lock it into my memories for the next time I need a moment away.

Also, he better remember to wash his hands when he goes back to cooking.

"It's a broken toe. What are they doing to do? Tell me to tape it and send me on my way. I'd rather save the money. And I'd rather stay right here on this couch. Where are the girls anyway?"

He raises an eyebrow in response.

"Ah," I say, understanding perfectly. "On the Wii."

"Where else?"

"They're not playing kickboxing right? They're getting a little too aggressive with that one."

"Nope. They begged, but I reminded them of the close miss the other day. Joey can be a real baby if he gets kicked in the face." Abel pats me on the leg and stands up. "I was actually about to call them up for dinner. I assume you want me to bring yours on a TV tray?"

Oh! That's how my cabana boy fantasy started! If things continue this direction, my night is about to get a lot better.

"That sounds perfect."

Abel leans over to gently kiss me on the lips. "Don't get any crazy ideas about it. I'm still not putting on a Speedo."

Drat. So much for my good night. At least he's letting me rest for a few minutes before taking over my mom duties again. For that, I'm grateful.

Closing my eyes, I do that mom thing where I zone out but am still listening to everything around me. Especially when Abel calls the girls for dinner. As always, they come barreling up the stairs, giggling the whole way.

"What are we having for dinner, Daddy?" Mabel asks excitedly.

"Yeah! What are we having?" Ainsley immediately parrots. "And when is my mom getting home?"

"She's already here, but she had a hard day. She's on the couch if you want to go say hi."

"Mom!" Ainsley yells, and I hear her run into the living room. "You're home!" She launches herself onto my lap before my eyes open, hugging me.

"I got here a couple minutes ago." Smoothing down her long blond hair, which is falling out of her ponytail from all her afternoon activity, I kiss the top of her head. "How was your day? Did you take your spelling test?"

She nods and tightens her arms around my waist. "I got a ninety on it. I forgot the E on the end of jive."

"Hmm. Those E's sneak up on ya sometimes, don't they?"

"It's okay. I think we're done with silent E's for a while. Now we're doing long O's."

Mabel comes walking in the room, not nearly as happy as Ainsley is to see me. Still, I'm the adult here, so I greet her with a smile on my face like I would anyone else.

"Hi, Mabel. Did you have a good day at school?"

Glancing down at my foot briefly, she ignores my question,

opting to glare at me instead. "Why do you have your feet on the table?"

Leaning forward, I take a closer look at my injury. "I think I have a broken toe." Ainsley gasps and also leans in to inspect the bruise. Mabel has virtually no reaction. Except for spite and malice, of course.

"You're not supposed to have your feet on the table. Dad says so."

I have had a horrible day and am way too irritated for a pissing match with an eight-year-old. So, I have a very methodical choice to make. I can tell Mabel to shove it. Or I can show Ainsley what it means to turn the other cheek and have some integrity. I'm honestly torn between the two responses.

Okay, fine. I know I'll pick the latter because that's who I am. But I may or may not have just had another brief fantasy that included it not being illegal or immoral to stuff a wet sock in a child's mouth.

"Your dad already knows and is bringing me an ice pack to put on it."

"Why ice, Mommy? Won't that hurt it?"

She's not wrong. I hate that part. But it still beats an ER co-pay.

"Just for a few minutes. But then, it'll make the swelling go down, which will make it feel better."

Ainsley jumps up and races out of the room yelling, "I'll get it for you, Mommy."

The conversation about ice between her and Abel is nothing more than murmurs and the sound of Abel ratting around in the freezer. It's nice to see that my daughter and my boyfriend can get along. *His* daughter and girlfriend apparently cannot. The current stare-off I'm finding myself in is proof of that.

I don't know how we end up locking eyes, but I'll be damned if I'm going to back down. It's not about winning. It's about not letting her run over me. She tries to get my goat every single day, and since Abel won't intervene enough for it to stop, I don't feel like I have much of a choice left.

Finally, having enough of this situation, I draw out all the mom-jo I can find and put myself into position—leaned back, arms crossed, lips pursed in irritation, one eyebrow cocked, and my head slightly tilted. It's the universal body language that means "bring it" used by millions of teachers, moms, and step-moms around the world.

For a split second, Mabel's eyes widen. She knows exactly what I'm saying without using words. The look is gone almost as soon as it happens, and Mabel turns on her heel and stomps out of the room, passing Ainsley who is running back in.

"Abel doesn't have an ice pack, Mommy, but he gave me a bag of peas."

She hands me the bag and a rag, so I don't accidentally get frost-bite, then proceeds to chatter about how there is no way we'll get her to eat these peas now that they've been on my foot. I kind of don't disagree with her.

As she helps me get situated—and "helps" is a relative term— Abel carefully walks in holding a plate and some silverware. He slowly pulls out an actual TV tray I didn't realize was here and sets it up next to the couch for me. He's not a moment too soon because, on top of everything else, I'm starving.

"Oh, thank you," I gush, because truly, I don't think I could sit at the table easily with my foot up and balance frozen peas on it.

He flashes me the smile that I'm learning is much different than the one he gives anyone else. The one that says our feelings are continuing to grow deeper than they were a month ago. A smile that proves he was right when he said the best relationships start out as friends.

"You don't have to thank me." He moves the tray a little closer so I can reach the food without much effort. "It's just shredded chicken, cauliflower potatoes, and green beans."

"Cauliflower potatoes? Where did you get that idea from?" I crinkle my nose, not sure what to think of a cauliflower posing as a potato.

"Oddly enough, I got the idea from Rian. My client who is pregnant."

I smirk at him. "The one you helped get pregnant?"

"Not in front of my boss, *or* my kid, okay?"

We both laugh as he runs back to the kitchen to bring me a drink and a few napkins.

"Seriously, Abel," I gush, "I really appreciate you thinking about how to make my night easier. I know it's hard to be up early and keep the kids all afternoon."

He shrugs sheepishly. "This is what you do in a relationship, Elliott. Or at least, it's what I do."

I open my mouth to respond with "It's what we all should do," but the moment is stolen from me by a snot-nosed, soon-to-be pre-teen who suddenly screeches, "How come *she* gets to eat in the living room and I have to sit at the table?"

If it weren't for the pain I'm in, the bad day I had, and the fact that Mabel just said

"she" like I'm the most vile, disgusting thing she's ever seen, I'd let it go. But I am in pain and I did have a bad day. And I'm already anticipating how much worse it's going to be tomorrow morning when I need them to help me help them get ready for school.

It doesn't help when Abel's only response is to say, "Because she has a broken toe, Mabel. When you have a broken toe, you can eat out here too."

Suddenly, my dinner doesn't look as appetizing as it did a few minutes ago.

When I push it away, Abel looks at me quizzically. "What's wrong? Are you starting to get nauseous?"

"You have no idea," I say under my breath.

Sitting down next to me, he puts his large palm on my forehead. "You don't feel feverish. That's good. Maybe you need an antacid? Sometimes injuries like this can make you feel sick once the adrenaline wears off."

Rubbing the bridge of my nose, I take a few deep breaths. "It's not the food, Abel."

"Then what is it?"

I don't want to have this conversation. I really don't. We've had it before, and nothing changed. But this time I'm in legitimate pain, which makes the filter between my brain and my mouth not as strong.

"I can't keep doing this, Abel."

"Doing what?"

He looks genuinely confused by what I'm saying, and I can't help but recognize the sweetness that goes with a father who thinks his baby girl is wonderful. Every father should feel that way . But this baby girl is going to be a menace if he doesn't take a step back and look at things objectively.

Thinking about how to best approach this topic, I settle on yet another work around. "This is your house, but it's my house too, ya know?"

He nods in agreement. "Of course. You pay to live here, and as far as I'm concerned, that means we share the house equally."

Good. I'm glad to see we're on the same page so far.

"I've always been of the mindset that your home is where you should rest. It's your sanctuary."

"Absolutely."

"And if I'm being honest here, this doesn't feel like a sanctuary to me."

There. I said it. No take backs.

Abel pauses for a few seconds before getting to the crux of the issue. "Because of Mabel?"

I nod once, not wanting to be overly dramatic. "It's not that I don't care for Mabel. She's energetic and funny. Some of her sassy comments make me laugh really hard. But her attitude toward me is terrible."

"I know she's not always kind with her words. But I told you we're working on it. I talked to her about it the other day. About how you're not her mom, and she needs to not take her anger out on you."

I knew Abel would say that. And while I appreciate it, clearly it didn't work.

"And yet it keeps happening."

"It's going to take time."

"I know that. But, Abel, look at it from my perspective. I'm in pain and needed to come home to rest. But instead of resting, I'm sitting on pins and needles because I've already had one showdown with her over my foot being on the table."

Abel huffs a laugh. "Yeah, that girl likes her rules."

"First, it's not funny. Second, it's not true. If she was so into rules, she wouldn't have worn her jammies to school the other day simply to prove I couldn't make her get dressed."

Abel throws his hands in the air. "Well, I don't know what to do about it. I'm trying here, Elliott. I really am. What am I supposed to say, 'I'm sorry your mother left, and you have all this anger inside you, but if you do it again, I'll take away the Wii.'?"

"Yes! That's exactly what you say!" Our voices are raised now, and I'm sure the girls can hear us, but I don't care. This has to be hashed out. The future of our relationship and living arrangements depend on this. "Look, I know she's hurting. I know. And I give her leeway because of it all the time." He opens his mouth to interrupt me, but I hold up my hand to stop him. "To a certain point. But she is crossing lines left, right, and center, and pain isn't the reason."

"Then what's the reason?" He doesn't ask because he wants a real answer. This is a challenge question. And this might all blow up in my face if he doesn't like the real answer.

"Because no one makes her stop. And by no one, I mean you."

Abel looks away, mashing his lips together. I know he's angry with me, but I also know it's about not wanting to make a mistake as a dad and not knowing how to fix this.

"Look, Abel. Mabel has every right to feel angry. But what she does with that anger is important. If she doesn't learn how to channel it appropriately now, where will she end up? Probably in New York City with her new agent boyfriend."

Abel's jaw drops, and I know he feels like I slapped him. "You crossed a line."

"I know." Because I do. Unfortunately, teetering on the edge of that line wasn't making a difference. "But if you think about it when you're not mad at me, you might realize I'm also right. When you grow up getting everything you want, you become an adult who still takes whatever you want."

Gingerly, I push myself up to standing and drop the peas on the table.

"Thank you for making dinner. When Ainsley is done, will you please send her upstairs?"

He doesn't answer, gaze glued to the floor as I hobble up the stairs into the safety of my bedroom and shut the door.

CHAPTER TWENTY-SEVEN

ABEL

Elliott's words stung. It's still stinging a couple hours later.

It's not that I don't understand where she's coming from. I do. No one should feel uncomfortable in their own home. Even if that home is shared with another family. But no one should be backed into a corner and have to choose between their girlfriend and their child either.

I know that's not what Elliott said. But it definitely felt that way. Like if I don't discipline Mabel the way she sees fit, it's a deal-breaker for Elliott. But what if I don't think Mabel is doing anything all that wrong? Sure, she's being mouthy, which we definitely need to talk about. But she's a kid. They process their anger and grief in different ways.

Right?

These thoughts were running through my mind the entire time the girls and I were eating dinner and all the way through my cleaning up afterward. The only conclusion I have come up with is… I don't know what the right thing to do is. I don't know if I'm being too harsh or too lenient. Maybe both. Maybe neither. I'm stumped.

The kicker of it all is I thought I had this parenting thing nailed, but after tonight, I'm second guessing everything I thought I knew.

I've based my entire strategy as a parent by being stricter than my parents were. They basically let us run wild and do whatever we wanted. By the time we were teenagers, that meant no curfews and very few rules. As long as it was legal, it was fine.

Unfortunately, not all of us stayed between the very lax boundaries, which is probably how my older brother ended up doing a short stint in the state prison. And why my sister ended up dropping out of high school, only to finally go back and graduate after realizing fast food wasn't going to pay for diapers, and without an education, she wasn't going anywhere.

Don't misunderstand—my parents are great. They're fun and loving and want their kids to make good choices. They just fell more into the "friend" role than "parent" role. With our strong-willed personalities, that may not have been the best way to go.

Which is probably why my younger brother is still single, and why I'm adamant about having a regular bedtime and making Mabel eat her vegetables. She's as stubborn as I was, so I want to make sure she had more guidance than I ever got. Now, though, I have this uncomfortable pit in my stomach that has me questioning it all.

The one thing I know for sure is I need to talk to Mabel. I need to find out why she has such animosity for Elliott and what she needs from me to help curb it. And I need to figure it all out soon.

"Hey, Mabel."

Freshly bathed, my little girl is climbing into her twin bed, settling between her bean-bag-style basketball and the My Little Pony stuffed animal May sent her for Christmas. That damn pony is a harsh reminder of why I'm trying so hard not to cause my child to feel any more rejection.

Mabel sleeps with it every night. She doesn't like cartoons and has never seen the show, but she won't part with it, and it has a pride place on her pillow during the day. I guess when your mother leaves you and doesn't make much effort to visit, you cling to any present they send you, no matter how ridiculous it is. Seeing it now makes it so much harder to have this conversation.

Biting the bullet, I go for it. "Why don't you like Elliott?"

She looks at me and if she was a few years older, I'd swear she was thinking, "Really? We're doing this now?" But she's not old enough to have those kinds of thoughts yet. I hope.

Instead she grabs her pony and hugs it tight to her chest. "Because she's not my mom."

Sitting on the edge of her bed, I make myself comfortable. "Neither is your teacher, but you don't say ugly things to her."

"My teacher doesn't live here and try to be my mom."

Finally, we're getting somewhere. She's wrong, but at least she's being honest. "Mabel, Elliott isn't trying to be your mom."

"Yes, she is, Dad. She makes me get up in the morning. She makes me breakfast, but she makes the wrong kind and won't make me what I want to eat."

"Honey, she does all that in the morning because I asked her to. That way you can sleep in and don't have to go to the gym with me in the mornings. Just like I pick up you and Ainsley in the afternoon while she works."

Mabel lays her head on her pillow and closes her eyes. I know I'm going to lose this battle of wills soon. When she doesn't want to talk about something, she literally shuts down. Usually in the form of falling asleep. But this time, it's not before she gets in one more dig.

"She doesn't even wear eyelashes," she scoffs.

Furrowing my brow, I'm not sure I heard her correctly. "What?"

"I said, she doesn't wear eyelashes. And doesn't she notice the wrinkles on her face? Someone needs to get her a good face cream to help with that. I'd probably like her better if she didn't look old."

I'm stunned into silence. Not because that was probably the snottiest thing I've ever heard my child say, but because it confirms everything Elliott was trying to tell me.

My child is turning into a mean girl.

My mind is racing with scenes from when May and I were married and the things she would say about other people when I was only halfway paying attention.

"She would be so much prettier if she got better clothes."

"That's her style? Are you sure she isn't trying to imitate Cindy Lauper's early years?"

"No woman should leave the house without lipstick. It's a cardinal rule or something. It makes you look poor."

I never really paid any attention when May was going on about other people. I had learned to tune it out when we were in that brand-new honeymoon stage, so I wasn't really listening to what she was saying for the remainder of those years. But our daughter was. And despite May not being here, her influence is still very much in this house.

"Mabel." She ignores me, pretending to be falling asleep, but I know her better than that. "Mabel, look at me."

She sighs dramatically. "Daddy, I'm tired. I need to go to sleep."

"And you will after you listen to me."

Finally, she opens her eyes and turns toward me.

"Mabel, Elliott is a nice woman. She takes care of you when I'm not here. She makes sure you aren't forgetting anything when you go to school. She leaves notes in your lunchbox sometimes, right?"

Mabel nods and I can see her expression softening a bit. She didn't know I knew about the notes. She also doesn't know I found the box she keeps them in. I won't admit to that little tidbit, though.

"Elliott is my friend. I know you wish your mom was here instead of her, but she's not. She's not going to be. That's a choice she made. I know it's hurtful to you, but Elliott didn't do that. Elliott just wants to have a nice, safe place for her and Ainsley to live. And she deserves for you to at least be civil to her."

"I don't know what that means."

"That means you listen when she tells you to do something like get dressed for school."

Mabel scowls, although I'm not sure if it's because I'm calling her out, or because apparently wearing Disney characters on your clothes isn't the way to make yourself popular in second grade. Elliott was right on that one—the natural consequences seem to have worked.

"It also means you stop trying to make her follow your rules and you remember she's the adult here. You need to be respectful and mind your manners."

Mabel doesn't say a word, only stares at me. I can tell she's battling her own pride right now, and I don't want to push her. Just admitting why she doesn't like Elliott is a good step in the right direction.

"Look, I like Elliott. And I know it's weird she's my girlfriend—"

"I don't want you to marry her," Mabel blurts out.

Now how do I answer this one? "Marriage isn't an option right now, baby, so you don't need to worry about it. But if someday we decide to get married, that's something we would have to discuss."

"No."

"No what?"

"No, it's not something I want to discuss."

I sigh. We're getting off track. "There's no reason to discuss it now anyway. All I'm asking is for you to obey Elliott and be respectful instead of acting like you hate her. Whether you like her or not, having her around makes things easier for all of us. I don't want us to lose that."

Mabel rolls her eyes to the ceiling and stares at nothing, huffing her annoyance. It's a look I've seen her mother make before, and that bothers me. I don't want Elliott to be right, but when Mabel does stuff like this, I can understand the comparison.

Finally, she looks back at me. "Fine. I'll listen to her in the mornings."

"And not be ugly to her."

"I said fine."

Nodding my approval, I lean down and kiss my daughter on the top of the head then tuck the sheets around her. "That's all I'm asking, baby girl."

I'm actually asking for more than that, I think as I shut off the light and walk out of the room. I'm asking for them to get along and maybe, eventually, even like each other. But this is a good start. For now.

CHAPTER TWENTY-EIGHT

ELLIOTT

I don't know what Abel said to his daughter, but things were not as rough the next morning. They weren't amazing either. But at least Mabel got out of bed and got dressed, and actually tried eating her scrambled eggs for breakfast without complaining.

Of course, she gagged and pushed the plate away, but I still consider it a small blessing she didn't yell at me for making her eat the souls of unborn chickens again. It took almost a week for Ainsley to finally eat her favorite deviled eggs after that one.

That's not to say there aren't still nasty glares and lots of eye rolls. It's irritating, but so much easier to ignore. She's going to be delightful when she hits puberty. At least she's learning to bite her tongue at a young age. I'll have to focus on that.

A little sleeping in did us all some good this morning too. At least it did for me. I enjoy sitting in my jammies, sipping on a cup of coffee, no pressure to walk out the door on time. That's part of why I got a late start on making lunch for the girls. I know it's the weekend and I could let them graze as they want to, but then I have to try to get them back into the routine on Monday again. It's not worth it. I'll wait until summer break to let our hair down completely.

Ugh. Summer break. The thought of it already gives me hives.

"Girls! It's time for lunch!" I finish putting half an apple on each of their plates. Three months ago, I would have gone for chips, but between Abel's healthy eating and my lack of funds, we don't have any. I never thought I'd see the day, but I also can't say I hate it. Not only is it better for us, but I may have dropped a few pounds off my mid-section. Nothing wrong with that.

Realizing they never responded, I call out again. "Girls! I said its lunchtime! Let's go!"

I hustle to put the plates on the table, knowing I'll likely get run over if I don't hurry, then head back into the kitchen for drinks. It's not until both cups have juice in them that I realize the girls have ignored me twice. I know they can hear me. I'm loud enough, but I'm also standing by the vent. And where the heck is Abel? How many lightbulbs needed changing in this house?

Tamping down my frustration, I walk to the doorway and peer down the stairs. I can hear them roughhousing, which will probably not end well. Hopefully it will end quickly though when they hear how agitated I'm starting to become.

"Girls! This is the third time I've called you. Get your butts up here for lunch!"

The words are barely out of my mouth when I hear a weird *thwack* sound followed immediately by the sound that makes every mother's blood run cold. It's a primal shriek followed by a wail of pain and instinctively, I know my child is hurt.

Running down the stairs, my heart beating rapidly, I find Ainsley with her hand over her face, blood running down her arms and dripping to the floor.

Racing to her, I focus on staying calm and getting her to do the same. "Ainsley. It's okay. Breath. What happened?"

"It wasn't my fault!" Mabel yells, but I don't have time to find out what happened. I need to focus on what needs to be done to fix it.

"Let me see, baby." I gently pull her hands away from her face. Ainsley's eyes are wide, and she resists the movement, but I see why as soon as her hands are far enough away. Her front tooth, her very first adult tooth, is completely knocked out.

Letting her hands go, I shush her before she starts crying again, trying to get as much information as I can. "Did you swallow your tooth?" She shakes her head in response just as I hear Abel come racing down the stairs.

"What happened? Is everyone okay?" His eyes look as wide as Ainsley's are. Good to see I'm the only one who stays in control during a crisis.

"It wasn't my fault! She stepped in front of my foot!" Mabel yells again, but we all ignore her.

"Ainsley's tooth got knocked out. See if you can find it," I instruct and go back to keeping Ainsley calm.

Within seconds, Abel calls out, "I found it! Be right back!" and runs up the stairs.

"Mabel, honey," I say calmly, keeping my eyes focused on my daughter, who looks like she's about to pass out. "Can you please get me a couple of rags?"

"I didn't do it, Elliott. She stepped in front of my foot."

I don't have the time or the desire to have this discussion with Mabel. What I need is her help so I can get Ainsley to the dentist quickly. I've never dealt with something like this before, but I know enough to know we have a certain time limit before Ainsley will lose that tooth forever.

"I'm not talking about any of that right now, Mabel. I need help cleaning some of this blood up. Go grab me a rag, will you?"

As if she is finally realizing what is going on, Mabel steps forward, takes one look at the blood dripping down Ainsley's arms, grimaces and says, "Eeeeeewwwwwwwwww."

"Mabel!" I snap. "This is an emergency. Please go get me some rags. And for heaven's sake, where is your father?"

"Right here." Abel comes ambling back down the stairs, supplies in hand. "Her tooth is in milk upstairs, so hopefully that'll help. Here's a couple of rags. What is her dentist listed under in your phone?"

Handing me the towels, he swipes open my phone.

"Dr. White."

While Abel calls the dentist, hoping to get an emergency appointment on a Saturday afternoon, I wipe as much blood off Ainsley as I can. She's still whimpering, with a few tears falling every now and then. But the initial adrenaline has definitely worn off. I take this time to figure out what happened.

"Girls, I need to be able to tell the dentist how Ainsley's tooth got knocked out so he can figure out how to fix it, okay?" Ainsley nods. Mabel might also, but she's still behind me so I can't see. "Tell me exactly what was going on."

"I told you," Mabel says briskly, "Ainsley stepped in front of my foot."

"I know that part. But I'm trying to figure out why her face was on the floor in the first place." I know my answer is snarky and kind of rude, but I can't seem to get any answers from her. Ainsley can't talk without blowing air across exposed nerves, so I've only got one option and she's not being very helpful.

"We, um… we were playing kickboxing."

"You were what?" Abel bellows. I guess he's off the phone.

I turn to see Mabel's eyes fill with tears. "We were playing, Daddy. And Elliott called us for lunch and Ainsley ran right in front of my foot."

"You guys were told not to play that game, remember?"

"I know, but Ainsley really wanted to play."

I look back over at Ainsley whose eyes have gotten wider, if that's even possible, and is shaking her head back and forth vigorously.

"Regardless, you should have told her no," Abel says, and Mabel bursts into tears.

I can feel my anger level start to rise, but more than that, I can feel my panic start to set in. I know we need to get to the dentist as soon as possible.

"Can we discuss this part later?" I demand, and they both stop and look at me. "We need an Uber or taxi or something here now."

"Already ordered. They should be here in less than five minutes."

"Okay then. Ainsley, let's head upstairs, okay?"

Carefully, I guide her up the stairs into the living room by the door. It's still chilly outside, but I don't dare make her move her hands. Now that she's biting down on a rag, the blood part is relatively contained, but draping her jacket over her shoulders still seems like the best idea.

Not all of us are full of good ideas right now, though. For whatever reason, Abel seems to think badgering Mabel is going to get us somewhere. The only thing it's doing, though, is frustrating me even more.

"Mabel, do you have anything to say to Ainsley before they leave?"

"Um… I hope you feel better?"

I won't give her an A for effort on that one, but I wouldn't call it an F either.

"No, Mabel," he chides. "Maybe you need to apologize."

"For what?" she demands angrily.

"For knocking her tooth out, that's what."

"But she stepped in front of my foot! I didn't do anything!"

Fortunately, a car drives up before I'm forced to hear any more of their fighting. I'm praying it's the Uber and not a random delivery person. Or someone going to the neighbor's house. Or a serial killer. Because at this point, I'll take my chances.

"Come on, baby." I put my arm around Ainsley's shoulder and guide her to the car.

"Call me when you know anything," Abel calls after us. I appreciate his concern and all, but right now, I'm all too happy to be out of that house to even care.

CHAPTER TWENTY-NINE

ABEL

Five hours. It's been five hours since Elliott climbed into that car with Ainsley without so much as a goodbye. Five hours of wondering what's going on and how Ainsley is doing.

Five hours of thinking long and hard about how Mabel responded to my suggestion of her apologizing. I didn't like it.

I've left a couple of voicemails for Elliott and have gotten no response. I switched to texting, thinking maybe it was too hard to answer the phone at an emergency dental visit. There are "no cell phone use" signs all over my dentist office, so maybe it's the same at theirs? That was my hope, but texts have gone unanswered too. Either Elliott is really busy right now or she's ignoring me.

Five hours is enough time to know that most likely she's ignoring me.

Once I cleaned up the blood downstairs and tried in vain, again, to talk to Mabel about her behavior, I started pacing. I've been at it for so long now, the carpet might have a worn path. I can't get rid of this antsy feeling running through my whole body. I want them to come home. I want them to be here so I can make sure Ainsley is okay and see what I need to do to make Elliott okay as well. It's too quiet in this house without them. It's too empty.

When they moved in, I didn't anticipate they would become this part of my life that just fit, but that's exactly what happened. They slid into this empty spot I didn't know was there. But now I know what I was missing, and that part feels empty again. And I'm terrified it's going to stay empty permanently.

Somewhere along the way, despite our best intentions at keeping solid boundaries, they became my family. The thought of losing them is terrifying. Even more so than when May left. That was nothing compared to losing them. To losing Elliott. The woman who is no doubt the best friend I've ever had.

I can't think like that. I have to focus on reality—Elliott and Ainsley live here. They pay rent. All their stuff is here. Even if they decided to move out, they have to come back. And legally, the only person who can actually break a lease agreement is Elliott, so she can't send her mother over to do her dirty work. Not that if it's what she really wanted, I wouldn't give it to her. I'd give her anything.

Knowing my thoughts are starting to spiral into dangerous territory, likely because this feels similar to when my marriage suddenly dropped dead, I force myself to stop assuming the worst. Instead, I take a chance and call Elliott again.

It rings three times and I can feel myself starting to give up, the moment of anticipation turning into deflation. I'm about to hang up instead of being sent to voicemail again when she finally answers.

"Hey."

Relieved to hear her voice, I lose my footing and quickly sit down on the couch behind me.

"Hey, how's Ainsley?"

"Good. Better. Dr. White was able to save her tooth, so that's good news, anyway."

I let out a deep breath and allow my body to finally relax a bit. "I'm so relieved to hear that. And it's not going to change color or anything?"

"It shouldn't. He said we got here fast enough and did everything right, so the tooth never died. The only thing we could have done better is to actually push her tooth back into the socket."

I shudder at the thought. "I'm kind of glad I didn't know that was an option."

"I said the same thing to Dr. White." Elliott laughs softly. Hearing the sound makes me feel better. Like she's exhausted, but the worst is over.

"Is Ainsley in a lot of pain?" In my mind, I'm taking inventory of how much children's pain reliever we have, and if I can open that bag of peas to make smaller bags for Ainsley to put on her mouth.

"It's hard to tell. I think her tooth feels better, but she still bursts into tears every once in a while." Hearing that my tiny dancer keeps crying breaks my heart. "But I'm not sure if it's from physical pain or because she's grounded from the Wii for the next month."

Wait, what?

"Um, she's grounded from the Wii?"

A combination of guilt and confusion flood my mind. Guilt because I'm listening to the sounds of *WipeOut* wafting up my basement stairs as Ainsley cries over the pain in her mouth. Confusion because, hasn't she already been punished enough?

"I don't want to question your parenting, but I don't understand why she's grounded from the Wii. Don't you think what happened today was natural consequences?"

Considering our heated discussion the other day about our differences in parenting, I expect Elliott to get angry. Sometimes I forget she's actually one of the most level-headed people I know. I should give her more credit.

"Well, she definitely understands why we had banned that game in the first place. So yeah, there are some natural consequences. But they also disobeyed us, Abel. We've told them more than once not to play it. I don't think we have to worry about them kickboxing anymore, but maybe she'll think twice before not listening to me next time."

I rub my head, thinking about how different our thought processes are. It's not that she's wrong. She's not. But in a way, I'm not either. How do we get on the same page with the girls if we're so far apart in our thinking? Regardless, we can't sort it out if they aren't here.

"When are you guys coming home? I want to make sure we have enough medicine for her. I know I have ingredients for a few different smoothies while her tooth heals. I assume she has to be careful for a few days?"

The long pause on the other end of the phone makes my heart sink and my anxiety spike. Before she says it, I know, I *know* what's coming. I want to hang up the phone and go back to pretending she's still stuck at the dentist, so I don't have to feel this kind of pain and rejection.

"We're gonna stay at my mom's house for a few days."

My head drops and I breathe out, "Shit, Elliott."

"I need to sort some things out, Abel."

"What things, Elliott? That I'm a shitty parent who doesn't know how to discipline my kid? How are we supposed to learn how to navigate through things if you're not here?"

On top of all the other emotions I'm feeling, now I'm angry too. Angry that the person I'm closest to in the world hates my child. My daughter. The love of my life who I would do anything for. And even worse, Elliott hates her so much, *so much* she's willing to toss us aside.

"You knew I was a package deal when we started dating, like you are. I know you don't like Mabel right now, but you're going to cut and run when things get really hard?"

"Derrick is threatening to file for custody, Abel," Elliott interrupts and all the anger I was feeling disappears into a cloud of disbelief.

"What?" I breathe.

"Yeah. He's talking about filing a change of circumstance, saying Ainsley is in harm's way living there."

I'm stunned. I knew Derrick was a douche, but it never occurred to me he'd go this far. "But... he can't do that, can he? He can't just claim Mabel is dangerous and that's it, right?"

"I don't know. But the burden of proof is mine. Which means I have to find the money for an attorney if he pursues this. I can't risk it." I feel like my breathing has stopped thinking about the mess Elliott is now in. "Look, I love you, Abel. And I love living there, even when Mabel is obnoxious and I want to stuff a wet sock in her mouth, but I can't risk losing custody of my daughter. I won't."

As much as I hate to admit it, I understand exactly what Elliott is saying. Even worse, I agree with her.

"No. No, you can't lose her. She's the most important thing here."

We sit in silence for a few seconds, each lost in our thoughts. Thoughts that probably mirror each other's in wondering how everything went to shit so quickly and how long it will take to fix.

Clearing my throat, I try to push past my own shock and support Elliott as much as I can from a distance.

"Um, are you going to need help paying for an attorney? You know I can take on a few extra clients, or maybe pick up a part-time job for a while if you need. I don't need much sleep. The coffee maker's got it covered." I try to take some of the heaviness away from the situation with some of our normal humor, but she's too upset now.

"No, Abel. You don't need to do that. It's not your responsibility."

"I know it's not my responsibility," I lie, knowing I'm responsible for this. It's one thing for Mabel to be snotty and disrespectful. But now her behavior has affected someone we love in a very real and scary way. That's on me. "But we're a team, Elliott. I want to help you any way I can."

She pauses again, and I know about to experience another rejection from her.

"We can't be a team right now, Abel." I suck in a breath, willing the stabbing pain in my chest to stop. "Let me sort this out, okay?"

I nod, even though she can't see me. "Yeah. Yeah, okay. I understand. But, Elliott, please let me know if you need anything, okay? I love you."

"I love you too."

That's the last thing she says before hanging up the phone and leaving me stunned and speechless with that damn Wii still playing in the background.

CHAPTER THIRTY

ELLIOTT

E*lliott-*
As you know, I have concerns over the living arrangements you have made for Ainsley. Without my prior knowledge or even asking if it was okay with me, you moved her into a house occupied by a single man in his thirties.

Despite my reservations and brushing aside statistics showing personal trainers and bodybuilders have a significant increase in the use of performance enhancing drugs that can lead to symptoms like mood swings, irritability, and aggression, I didn't say anything. I trusted your judgement that this co-worker wasn't a danger to our child and that the home environment you have provided to our daughter would be safe.

In light of the circumstances of April 8, I no longer believe that to be the case. I'm sure you can understand how receiving a phone call that my daughter's permanent front tooth has been knocked out would be jarring. But to find out she's been kicked in the face while left unsupervised by her mother is cause for additional concern and warrants potential revision of our current custody agreement.

Additionally, I have seen the bill for Ainsley's emergency dental appointment and, given the circumstances, do not believe I should be held responsible for it. Had she been properly supervised, it would have never happened. This incident occurred while Ainsley was in your home and under your (lack of) care, and therefore, I believe the burden of paying for the resulting treatment rests solely with you.

I trust you will find suitable alternative housing or move back in with your mother to ensure our daughter remains safe and to prevent an incident like this from ever happening again, and that I won't receive a bill regarding this matter.

Thank you,

Derrick.

Clicking out of my emails, I stifle the urge to panic and cave to my anxiety over his ridiculous email. He always claims to have "concerns." Whatever. We all know what he's trying to do is create a paper trail that makes him look like a saint should he ever need to refer back to it. What he neglects to remember is I also have a paper trail that includes time and date stamped texts, and information on actual behavior, not just "concerns" that usually coincide to incidents where money is involved.

And he looks like a douchebag for always putting a period at the end of his name. Seriously. Who does that? Is it a subtle reminder that it's his way or the highway? "Derrick—period." How obnoxious.

One of these days, I'll find enough nerve and tell him to shove it. The problem is finding the guts to say the words. To be honest, the idea that he could get custody of Ainsley scares the crap out of me. It's not that he's a bad dad; he's just not a good one. If I was filling out one of those surveys, I'd click on the bubble that says "fair." That's about where he falls. I don't worry he's going to beat her, but I also don't trust he's going to nurture her beyond the bare minimum of keeping her alive.

. . .

Not to mention, my job affords me the ability to be home with her most of the time. His doesn't. If she lived with him, she'd go to daycare when it opens at six, then to school, back to daycare, and not get home until dinnertime. Forget activities during the week. And Derrick has proven time and time again that weekend activities are out of the question because he needs his "rest." What kind of life is that for a little girl when she can have so much more by living with me?

But half the time, instead of fighting it out with him and telling Derrick he isn't allowed to make me feel anxious anymore and I'm taking back control, I let it go. And by "let it go," I mean suffer in silence.

How's that for irony? Here I am, droning on and on to Abel about how he needs to be better about teaching Mabel to not be a mean girl, while letting the man I divorced crap all over me on a regular basis. On top of that, I'm hiding out at my mother's house and she's already driving me crazy.

"Do you want some help?"

Speaking of the she-devil, Mom comes into the kitchen as I'm pulling out the ingredients for Ainsley's lunch—a super delicious strawberry and banana smoothie with chocolate protein powder and vanilla almond milk. Hey, we may not be staying at Abel's house right now, but there's no reason to lose some of his healthy habits.

. . .

"There's really not much to do," I respond, while snapping the blender together. "Unless you want to start peeling a banana for me."

"I can do that." She grabs the most overripe banana on the bunch. Good choice. Once it's blended, Ainsley won't know the peel was starting to turn brown, which means I won't have to buy more as soon. "I'm glad you came back home, Elliott."

I take a deep breath and try really hard not to roll my eyes. It's already beginning. I don't need her to try and fix this for me. Plus, I'm not sure she really wants to. As much as she claims to want her single life, I think she's lonelier than she admits. And I'm no longer sure she ever grieved the loss of my dad; instead, she used us living here as a distraction from all the inner turmoil.

And there's more irony for you: Abel's been preaching to me about how Mabel is still struggling through her version of grief after the loss of her mother, which is part of her issue, and all I do is bitch about my mother, who is processing the loss of my father.

You know what sucks? When you've run away to your mother's house and suddenly realize you're a pot talking to a kettle. I hate when that happens.

"I knew it was a bad idea to move in with that man," my mother continues. "You never know how people are going to be behind closed doors."

I take it back. I'm not the pot. I'm the kettle. And I swear, if my mother doesn't stop with this crap about how I always make poor choices, steam is going to shoot right of my head and my top is going to blow off.

"He lets that child run wild and do whatever she wants."

Grabbing what I need and slamming the knife drawer closed a little more forcefully than necessary, I find myself defending Abel. "He does not, Mother. Both girls disobeyed. They both knew they weren't supposed to play that game."

She pauses and purses her lips. I know she's trying really hard not to say anything else, but this is a battle we both know she's going to lose. If she can get the last word in, she will. "And yet Ainsley is the only one who got injured."

"Well, it was kind of hard for her to kick back when she was screaming."

Pretty sure I just made things worse, but I don't want to talk about this with her. There's a reason I haven't told her about Derrick's email. She'd go off on a rant about how he's doing so much emotional damage to Ainsley and say something like, "Seriously, Elliott, I don't understand why you even let him see her until he gets his act together. Who cares about something silly like contempt of court and jail time for not adhering to a court order?" I can practically hear it now.

There may also be a tiny part of me that is afraid she will agree with him and pressure me to move back in. I don't know what we're going to do or where we're going to live, but I really don't want it to be here. I love my mother, but I prefer loving her from a distance.

I need to think about my options and the best course of action, and I can't do that with so many people chattering in my ear all the time about which direction is the best to go in.

Dumping the strawberries and the rest of the ingredients into the blender, I wait for the banana so I can finish making this drink and have an excuse to get out of this kitchen. Taking her sweet time, Mom finally walks over to me.

"I know it was an accident, but it's something you need to consider." Finally, *finally,* she puts the banana in the blender so I can pop the lid on. "This could be indicative of a bigger iss—"

Whiiiiiiiiiiiiiirrrrrrrrrr

I cut her off with a press of a button, the blender at the fastest speed so there is no way I can hear her.

Clearly unhappy, she leans against the counter and gives me the mom-glare. It's the same one I give Ainsley sometimes. The same one I used on Mabel.

Most effective when a child is being a little shit and knows it, the mom-glare incites a combination of guilt and fear, with a dash of the desire to stop whatever you're doing to shape up or ship out. Turns out, the mom-glare never loses its effectiveness and can also be used as a weapon against forty-two-year-old women who behave like brats, as I suddenly have the urge to keep my eyes downcast and apologize for being rude.

Or my mother is just that good and I have a lot to learn.

Regardless, part of me is hoping this smoothie never blends, so I never have to turn it off. Alas, the wonder of engineering works against me this time and I press the off button.

"That was really immature, Elliott." Mom's not mean about it, just factual. That's almost worse than if she'd yelled at me. At least then I could say she's crazy and not have to take responsibility for acting like a child.

Like I said, driving me bonkers or not, I've got a lot to learn from her.

"If you don't want to talk about it, you can just say so."

Pouring the now blended drink in a cup, I avoid her gaze. "I don't want to talk about it. I need to think and process, and I can't do that if I'm talking about it."

"Fair enough. Now that you've told me, I'll leave you alone with your thoughts until you need to talk it over with someone." She turns and walks away, leaving me with my mouth agape.

What was that? Has it always been as easy as just telling my mother how I feel? I don't think so, because the few times I've tried before, it hasn't really changed anything. That's why I started biting my tongue in the first place. It wasn't worth wasting my breath.

But maybe she's had a come-to-Jesus of some sort?

Shaking my head, I also shake off this strange turn of events. I still have a child to care for and the liquid diet isn't exactly filling her up. Which means she eats, err, drinks more often than normal. Plus, she's not getting sidetracked playing video games for the time being. That might actually be a bigger part of her hunger—boredom.

After popping a straw in the top, I make my way to the living room where Ainsley is camped out. I'm not sure how knocking her tooth out hurt her legs enough that she can't climb stairs, but she's made herself comfortable on the couch. Now that I think about it, I bet the kickboxing is why she can't climb stairs. Nothing good ever comes of exercising that hard.

Ainsley, meet Karma. If you're not careful and don't listen to your mother, you'll become the best of friends. But Karma is a back-stabbing bitch, so you really don't want to know her well.

I don't say that out loud. My child has had enough discussion about natural consequences to last her a while, I hope. Instead, I take the nice mom route. "Hungry?" I hand her the smoothie and quickly inspect the inside of her mouth. Everything looks good, although her gum is still a little bit swollen. Dr. White said that was to be expected for a couple days after a trauma like this to the area. I was a little ticked when he used the word "trauma" in front of Ainsley. She latched onto that word and now, everything is about the "trauma" she went through.

Honestly, the biggest trauma of the whole thing is the ding to my checkbook from the co-pay.

Taking a huge suck on the straw, Ainsley moans with approval. She licks her lips and smiles at me. "That's really good, Mom. Is it one of Abel's recipes?"

Hearing his name is like a stab in my heart. I miss him. It's only been a day, but it doesn't feel right to not have him here, laughing and throwing his personal brand of sarcasm around. I miss hearing him cuss at his coffee maker, although he doesn't really do it anymore since I got him the new one. I miss listening to him tell me all the benefits of some other healthy vegetable I've never of that he's making for dinner. I miss him sneaking kisses and pats on the butt when the girls aren't around. I miss *him*. And I still don't know what to do about it.

"Sort of." I stroke her long hair and try to school my features and cover the hurt in my heart so she doesn't know how hard this is on me. "I didn't have any avocado or veggie greens, but it's kind of the same."

. . .

251

"I like it." She takes another drink and shifts down a little farther on the couch. "When are we going home, Mom?"

It takes me a second to realize where she's talking about. It hasn't felt like we've actually had a home for a few years. Like we've been drifting through a long period of transition. At least, that's how I feel. I had no idea Ainsley had gotten so comfortable so fast in the townhouse.

"I don't really know, baby," I answer honestly. "Abel and I have some things to work out first."

Ainsley nods sadly and looks at the TV. Some Disney movie is showing, but somehow, I don't think she's really watching. I recognize that look on her face. I have a picture of myself from years ago making the same one. Derrick took it one night as "proof" that I don't always listen to him. In actuality, I was sorting through my thoughts after we'd had a fight. If she's anything like me, that's what she's doing right now.

"Mom." She says it so quietly, I barely hear her. Turning my head to look at her sweet face, I nudge her as way of acknowledgement. She swallows and looks back at me, sadness written all over her little features. "It wasn't Mabel's fault."

"Oh baby. It was an accident, I know that."

I settle in closer to her, my arm around her shoulder, trying to convey my support and appreciation for her desire to make this right.

. . .

"No, Mom. It was an accident, but..." she pauses, and I see a lone tear slides down her cheek. "Mabel didn't want to play kickboxing. She said we'd get in trouble. But I was tired of playing *WipeOut* so I made her."

I suck in a breath and find myself blinking rapidly a few times before I can say anything. "What?"

"I'm sorry, Mommy. I know you said we couldn't play it, but I didn't listen, and then I ran in front of Mabel when you called us, and then she got in trouble, and I don't want to not live there because it's all my fault." The words come out as fast as her tears as she bears her soul. Has she been carrying around all this guilt since yesterday? I didn't have to give her the mom-glare, which means this must have been eating her alive. No wonder she's stayed on the couch. I bet she has a horrible nervous tummy too.

"I think you did the right thing telling me," I say, trying to stay in mom-mode and not veer off into my own guilt. And I have lots to feel guilty over. I never once listened to what Mabel was saying. I assumed her defensive behavior immediately meant she started it. I let myself believe that because she is mouthy and defiant toward me the next believable step would be physical violence toward her best friend. I made assumptions that fit my own bias as to what the situation should be instead of gathering all the evidence.

I did the exact same thing Derrick does to me all the time. I may as well sign my name with a period.

. . .

The shame I feel over my own behavior renders me almost speechless. I basically accused Abel of being a terrible father and his daughter of being the worst kind of kid, when mine is the one who caused this preventable accident in the first place. And now I don't know how to fix it.

"Mabel isn't going to get in trouble, right?" Ainsley's innocent question brings me back to this moment. I'm kind of grateful because I don't know what to think of the rest of it.

"I don't know the answer to that. That's Abel's decision to make." Not mine. Because I'm not Mabel's parent, and no matter how crazy his lackadaisical parenting style makes me, Abel isn't wrong to recognize there is more going on than just Mabel being a brat.

But I am.

Ainsley turns back to the movie. "Tell him she didn't do it. It's not fair for her to get in trouble for something I did."

Like it's not fair I made unfounded assumptions.

Looks like I have a lot more learning to do than I realized. I don't think here, with my mother, is where it's going to happen. It's going to have to be at our house with the rest of our little ragtag family. I'm just not sure we're welcome there any longer.

CHAPTER THIRTY-ONE

ABEL

T he sweeping lights through the living room indicate my ride is here. Balancing the human burrito in my arms, I reach down to grab everything else.

Mabel's school bag—check
    Mabel's clothing bag—check
    My workout bag—check
    Our lunches—check
    Haven't dropped the child yet—check

I stabilize everything precariously as I step out the door, trying not to slam it too hard behind me with my foot. I fail, but what else is new? I've come to rely on Elliott so much, even the basics like leaving the house are difficult without her.

Or maybe I got spoiled with her here because she picked up so much of the slack I now have to do again. I fumble with my keys, partially from carrying so much stuff and partially from being distracted, wondering if she misses me as much as I miss her. Does she still need me to pick up Ainsley from school? Who will give my tiny dancer a snack and let her burn off some steam when she gets home?

Maybe that's a bad idea anyway. Burning off steam is what got us in this mess in the first place.

Climbing into the back seat of my favorite Ford Escort, like I do every morning, I settle us in and take the coffee from Marv, who is side-eyeing me in the mirror. I brace myself for the third degree.

"You have a fight with the new woman?"

I swallow my mouthful of lukewarm coffee, grateful he's not one to dig into things too deeply. "Sort of."

Marv eases us down the road like every morning. Except this morning he's more inquisitive. "Your fault?"

"Partially."

He nods once, probably in solidarity from years of been there, done that. "You gonna make it right?"

"Doing my best to."

· · ·

Another nod and he pulls up to the front of the gym. "Ladies don't want flowers anymore. That's too old school. Actions are more their speed. Listen between the lines when she talks and do something that's important to her. That'll win her back."

I hand him the now empty coffee cup back, trying but failing to smile. "Thanks, Marv. I'm working on it."

He nods once more and waits patiently until I can get Mabel and all our junk out of his car, slamming the door with my foot behind me. That's two for two on accidental slams. I'm definitely out of practice.

I see it the second Gina realizes I need help opening the door and watch as her brain comes to its own rapid conclusions as to why. She does this weird double take where her eyes get wide—well, as wide as they can get before her coffee—and she hoofs it over to help me. I don't say anything beyond "Thanks" as she holds the door open for us. Not even a morning greeting. I'm too busy dodging her gaping stare.

It's not just Gina. Everyone I normally greet when I first get here is openly staring at me as I carry Mabel by. It feels reminiscent of a year ago when I started having to bring my daughter with me to work. The rumor mill started swirling immediately about May leaving and how sweet it was that I was now taking care of my daughter alone. Being the center of negative attention sucked. No one wants people constantly staring at them and making assumptions about how they feel during a crisis. Nosy assholes.

Besides, I never knew what the big deal was about me bringing her, other than the inconvenience. I'm a parent, not a babysitter. It's what a father does. Or, at least, what he should do. Not like Derrick who only takes Ainsley on weekends, and if it's too inconvenient for him, ditches her at her Grammy's house.

Which reminds me that the eyes on me all throughout the gym are connected to the same rumor mill that is probably already spreading around that poor Abel is single again.

I don't know if it's being the subject of all the rumors or the possibility that said rumors are true that bothers me more this morning. I still refuse to believe it's over between me and Elliott. It's been thirty-six hours. In the overall scheme of things, that's almost no time at all.

As soon as Morgan sees me coming, she does the exact same double take Gina did and then hops to it. I'd laugh at the ridiculousness of it if I wasn't so pissed I'm in this position in the first place.

Fine. I'm sad. Not angry. Sad.

"I didn't expect to have to do this again," Morgan remarks as she spreads out the yoga mat on the floor under the desk. "Everything okay with Elliott?"

I know what she's really asking, even though she's too polite to be direct.

. . .

"Fine. She stayed at her mom's last night."

"Oh. You need to talk about it?"

"Nothing to talk about." I lay Mabel down carefully and begin adjusting her blankets. Suddenly, my little burrito's eyes are open and she's looking around, confused.

Quickly, her brain catches up. "Why am I at the gym, Daddy?"

"Elliott's not at the house, baby. I couldn't leave you alone."

Mabel blinks a few times and her eyes begin to well up with tears. "They're not home yet? They didn't come home?"

My heart breaks all over. Those are almost the identical words she said when May left. I can't imagine what kind of feelings this situation is triggering for Mabel, and the only person I can blame is myself. I'm the one who thought living with a single mom was a great idea. I'm the one who kept pushing Elliott to date me. I'm the one who crossed those roommate boundaries and slid so easily into tag-team parenting. And I'm the one who kept brushing off what Elliott was warning me about until the worst-case scenario happened.

Sitting down on the floor, I look up at Morgan. "Can you give us a minute?"

.   .   .

As my co-worker walks away, I pull Mabel to me. She curls up in my lap, sniffling. I hate this for her. I hate that one fight caused Elliott to run away. I get it, but I hate it.

"They stayed at Ainsley's Gigi's house last night." I'm hoping to soften the blow, but I don't think Mabel is falling for it.

"But they'll be home tonight, right? And Ainsley is all better? Her tooth got put back in?" Mabel's little voice quivers.

"Oh yeah. Her tooth is back in, and she has to drink a lot of smoothies right now. But she's going to be fine."

"They're coming home, right?"

This is the one I don't know how to answer. I'm almost a little surprised Mabel is as upset about it as she is. In a weird way, I'm glad. It means Mabel cares, which means we have a better shot of making this work. We just have one giant hurdle to get over first.

"Ainsley's daddy is really upset she got hurt. Like if it was you that got hurt and I wasn't there to see it, I'd probably be upset too." I don't take on that he's an asshole who is probably using this incident as an excuse to cause Elliott anxiety. She'll learn soon enough what the term "dickhead" really means. "They need a little time to sort it out and make sure he's not so upset, okay?"

I feel her nod against my chest, burrowing her little body as close as she can get to me—the one person who hasn't left her yet, no matter the circumstance. I worry she's afraid I'm next.

"I'm not leaving you, Mabel. You understand me?" She doesn't respond. "It's you and me, kid. No matter what happens. No matter who does or doesn't live with us, I'll never leave you. You're the most important thing in my whole life. More important than my job or the house or anything. Don't ever doubt that, okay?"

She nods again, and then I feel the wetness of her tears soak through my shirt. "I miss them, Daddy."

Sighing, I lean my cheek on top of her head. "I know, baby. I miss them too." Pulling back, I encourage her to shift over and look at me. "I have to say, though, I'm kind of surprised you miss them so much. You're not very nice to Elliott."

Mabel looks down at her hands and watches as they fumble with the zipper of my jacket. "She makes me mad sometimes. She doesn't do things the way you do."

"Of course, she doesn't, baby. She's not me. She has her own way of making breakfast and her own way of waking you up. Every adult has a different routine in the morning. That doesn't mean it's the wrong way."

Mabel is silent for a few moments, and I let her think about what her next words are going to be. Finally, quietly, she begins to get to the root of the issue. "Sometimes I really miss Mommy. Especially in the morning. Elliott isn't my mom, and she gives Ainsley hugs and kisses in the morning and my mom doesn't do that for me."

I look up at the ceiling and blink back my own tears, cursing May and her selfish behavior under my breath. When I'm confident I've bitten back all the horrible things I want to spout off about my ex, I ask, "Do you want Elliott to give you hugs and kisses in the morning too? I know she's not your mom, but I bet she would if you wanted."

Slowly, very slowly, Mabel begins to nod, until she's vigorously moving her head up and down. "Yeah. I want her to hug me too. And I know I already have a mom, but Elliott knows how to vacuum and do the dishes and make really good eggs."

I smile at her candor and also in relief that we're finally getting somewhere. "She does. And she's really nice, right?"

"She's the nicest lady I've ever known." Those wide brown eyes slay me with this admission. It seems Elliott leaving was an unexpected natural consequence for Mabel. Fingers crossed, we may be over the hump on some of her bad behavior because of it.

I kiss Mabel's little fingers. "I think maybe you need to tell her that. Tell her you want hugs too. Tell her she's nice and you like her. And stop being such a grumpy bear in the morning. You think you can do that?"

Another vigorous nod from her.

. . .

"We have to do better if they're going to come home. Both of us. Think we can do it?" I look down, locking eyes with her.

"Yeah. And I think I need to tell Ainsley sorry for kicking her in the face."

A laugh rumbles out of me. It feels good to know there's still hope for our little unit to get back together and make this work. "That is the first thing you need to say. But we'll do that when we see them. Right now, you probably need to go back to sleep for a little bit, so you don't fall asleep at school."

Wiping her nose with the back of her hand, she shakes her head. "I'm not tired. Can I play in the gym instead?"

"Sure. As long as you hang next to me the whole time but don't interrupt with my client, that'll be fine. What do you want to do?"

With the most serious face I think I've ever seen, Mabel adamantly says, "Not. Kickboxing."

"I agree. Why don't you take your clothes into the locker room and get dressed quickly while I set up for the day, and we'll find something for you to do when you get back."

She nods and grabs her bag, turning to walk away. Before she gets out of arm's reach, she turns back and jumps into my arms.

. . .

"I love you, Daddy." My girl clings tightly to my neck, not just a gesture of love, but an obvious gesture of gratitude for talking her through the feelings that have been plaguing her for months now.

"I love you too. We're gonna fix this. Don't worry."

One last squeeze and she trots off to get ready for the day. I feel much better now that Mabel is working through her issues and recognizing how ugly she's been. It gives me hope that things are going to be fine.

Now, I need to get Elliott on the same page. Grabbing my phone, I shoot her a quick text, knowing it'll be the first thing she gets this morning.

"We love you. We miss you. And we really need to talk."

She never responds.

CHAPTER THIRTY-TWO

ELLIOTT

Today has been the worst day. I should have known it was going to snowball into this madness when I woke up late this morning. I left my charger at Abel's, so my phone was dead. Then, as we were already scrambling to get to school on time, I realized we also didn't have very many clothes left here.

Thank goodness there was one box of leftovers I had planned to take to Goodwill still in the closet. They aren't the finest duds we've ever worn, but at least they're clean and they fit. Or at least sort of fit. Ainsley's a little kid. I can always blame her for having terrible fashion sense and me choosing my battles. That sounds so much better than admitting we raced out of my boyfriend's house while she bled from a traumatic injury and we haven't been back.

Yeah. We're sticking with the fashion sense argument.

By the time we got to school, we were barely on time. Unfortunately, it wasn't as easy as dropping her and running. Because of her nearly liquid diet, I had to talk to the school nurse, the principal, her teacher, and the school counselor explaining the situation when someone became "concerned" by Ainsley's injury. Once that was cleared up, I was able to write out my request to for her to drink smoothies for lunch, only because it's a temporary situation. Poor nutrition is apparently a sticking point at this school, which you'd never know by the sorry state of the vegetables in the lunchroom. I didn't bring that up though. I didn't have any more time to waste, not after having to wait for the one secretary in the building who is a public notary to get off her break to finalize the documentation they needed.

I understand the school policy when there are special dietary needs, but geez people. I'm just bringing her liquid food so her tooth doesn't fall back out. And who takes a break at the beginning of the school day?

For a split second, I actually wondered if we could forget all the red-tape nonsense, eat real food, and hope for the best. Maybe it was a little longer than a second. Maybe it was a solid two minutes while I listened to the school counselor jabber on about the importance of safety and supervision while children play.

I bit my tongue from telling her my ex-husband already beat her to the lecture. Period. See what I did there? Obviously, I fell into the pit of delirium as she droned on and on, that's what I did.

Finally, I was free to leave, but by this time I was so behind, I didn't have long to race to Abel's house and grab some clothes for work. Okay, fine. Maybe I had some time, but I got sidetracked staring at my favorite magnet on the dishwasher and trying not to cry over the half empty coffee cup sitting on the counter. The only reason it wasn't totally empty is because Abel didn't have time to drink it all. Because I wasn't home to do morning duties with the girls. Because I was hiding at my mom's house like a coward.

Like I'm still doing as I wait for Ainsley to get out of school. He never came to see me at work—not that I expected him to, since he normally doesn't—but between that and not having a phone to text Abel and ask if he was still picking her up, I had to assume he wasn't. I did leave him in a lurch this morning, after all. And now I'm afraid I'll see him, but I'm also afraid I won't. And I didn't know my brain could actually have rambling thoughts, but apparently it can.

"I see the cougar has gone back to her part of the jungle."

Huh?

I look over to see Tina, PTA mom extraordinaire and a shining example of who Regina George probably grew up to be, standing next to me.

"I'm sorry, what?" I honestly don't know what she's talking about. My attention is on the kids who are coming out of school now so I can intercept my daughter and get out of here quickly.

For whatever reason, Tina's focus is trained on me, not on her own children, one of whom is likely to end up in a fistfight if someone doesn't intervene soon.

"We haven't seen you around for a while and that—" She sucks in a breathe through her teeth, literally sucks it in as if she's trying to get her lady bits under control. It's weird. And creepy. "Tall drink of water has been picking up your child from school every day for a few months now."

Sure enough, I look over to where she's staring, and Abel is looking back at us. He's not smiling. He's not walking toward me. He's just... watching. My heart feels like it cracks a little and it takes everything in me not to allow tears to form in my eyes. It's not about Abel seeing me cry. Maybe my tears would be evidence of how heartbroken I really am. No, I refuse to cry in front of Tina. She's not the only shark in this ocean. I don't need them circling me the minute they smell blood.

Fortunately, we're interrupted by a pint-sized pixie with a giant, full-toothed smile. "Hi, Mommy! Am I going to the gym with you today?"

Smiling back at her, I turn my back on Tina. Unfortunately, that means I turn my back on Abel as well, but I try not to focus on that part. "You are! Is that okay with you?"

Thankfully, Ainsley begins jumping up and down. "Yay! I want to play on the big slide again! Is Mabel coming with us?"

I barely register Tina moving a tiny bit closer, trying to eavesdrop on my answer. Too bad for her, there's nothing juicy to know. "Not this time, love. Maybe tomorrow though. I need to talk to Abel about it."

There. Let her chew on that nugget for a while. It's a teeny tiny nugget. Really, it's not a juicy piece of information at all, and certainly not one that should be useful to the peanut gallery around here, but sometimes their ability to create stories out of nothing is pretty impressive.

"Come on. We're gonna be late."

I guide Ainsley as far away from Abel as possible and out the gate, moving with the crowd. He watches as we go, never trying to catch up to us. Never calling out. So, I guess that's it. I guess what we had wasn't worth fighting for that much. It hurts my heart, but I can't focus on that now. I still have more than half a day of work left.

Half a day may as well be a week long, because it has to be a full moon or something random. More than likely, it's because I'm completely off my game today and my mom whistle doesn't seem to have the same power behind it as it normally does. Add to it, the stations weren't set up in time for the kids to get here because I had to pick up Ainsley, so the older kids started bothering the younger kids, which lead to more frustration and fighting. This is what I get for staying at my mother's house.

Dramatic much, Elliott? Someone better leave some wine and chocolate on my pillow tonight after powering through this day. Of course, I don't know which pillow…

"Holy cow, is mercury in retrograde today or something?" Dinah's words mirror my thoughts exactly. "It's insane in here!"

"My fault," I grunt as I lift the last of the station tables up. "I should have planned ahead, but I wasn't thinking this needed to be done before I got back. I thought if I got Ainsley fast enough, I could beat most of them here."

Dinah grabs the other side of the table and helps me get it situated. "Yeah, that was weird. You picking up Ainsley today instead of Abel."

She's fishing. I know she's fishing. She knows I know she's fishing. But I don't have it in me to deflect right now.

"I know what you really want to know and, yes, we got in a fight, so I stayed at my mom's. No, I haven't talked to him about it yet. There hasn't been time."

Dinah makes a noncommittal "Ahh," which only makes me glare at her. I know she wants to say more and is not trying very hard to be polite and stay in her lane. Which of course means weaving right over into mine.

The awkward silence begins to make me uncomfortable, which I'm sure was always her plan. "Just say it, Dinah."

"Say what?"

Uh huh. She doesn't even have a pretend innocent look about her.

"Say whatever it is you're thinking about Abel and me because I need to get these kids under control."

She waves me off like it's no big deal that a couple of toddlers are drawing all over the walls with marker. "It's washable. Besides, it'll give me more ammunition to convince management we need another person in housekeeping."

I find myself nodding in agreement. She's not wrong. We really could use someone to come in and disinfect more often.

"I'm thinking how cute it is that it's your first fight."

"Seriously?" I place the supplies on the table and glance around for my big kids who prefer to do their math before going home. "You find this cute? It's been a mess. Angelica! Caleb! Station is ready!"

My two little math nerds come running, ready to knock out the hardest part of their day so they can go play again. Honestly, figuring out third grade math is the hardest part of my day too, but I prefer it to them taking over the train table now that our two-year-old train aficionado is finally content.

"You're gonna work it out. But you have to go home first, ya know."

"I can't," I grumble, rolling my head around to try and alleviate some of the tension in my shoulders. Abel would know how to rub it out if he was here. But he's not. And that sucks.

"What do you mean you can't?" Dinah looks thoroughly confused. She's not the only one.

"I can't until I work out something with my ex. He's threatening to sue for custody because Ainsley got hurt in my care."

Dinah laughs. She actually laughs. I'm not sure why she finds it funny. "He's trying to use the change of circumstance argument because of a childhood accident with her friend? He's delusional."

"Delusional or not, I don't have the cash to fight him on it if he pushes things to court. I have to get him to calm down or wait him out or something. I don't know."

"No. You need to beat him at his own game." Dinah reaches down and picks up one of our new crawlers who just made her way through the madness over to us. "How did you get over here, little one?" Dinah coos. "You were behind the gate in the baby room. Do we have a climber?"

"Beat him at his own game? How would I do that?" I ask, wiping down the counter with a disinfectant wipe. How it got sticky is unknown to me. I'm not sure I want to know.

Dinah looks at me, a smug smile on her face. "Think about his motivation. What's the most important thing in his life?"

"Easy," I say with a shrug. "Money."

"So, get creative. Show him how much he has to lose if he doesn't play nice."

That gets my brain thinking. Dinah's not wrong. Derrick gets to me because he threatens to take away the most important thing in the world to me—my daughter. All I have to figure out is how to threaten to take away the most important thing in the world to him.

Grabbing my paycheck off the desk, I open the drawer where my purse is and stash it inside.

I think I have an idea. And even better, I think it might work.

CHAPTER THIRTY-THREE

ABEL

S tanding at the bottom of the stairs, I bend down and put my hands on Mabel's arms. We've been talking about this all day. About how to give our girls a big gesture and show them that home is where they need to be, and we'll fight as a team no matter what happens.

We didn't really come up with anything grand. In fact, it's fairly... not grand. But we're at least here to fight for what we want, and what we want is our little unit back together.

Locking eyes, I do my best to pump Mabel up. "Are you ready to do this?"

She nods, eyes wide with excitement. "Yep. Let's bring them home."

We high five and trot up the steps to ring the doorbell.

I rub my hands together nervously. It's not cold out, maybe a bit chilly, but it's a habit I always have to break after so many months of winter. Apparently, Mabel picked up my habit because she's doing the same thing.

We only wait a few seconds, but it feels like hours before the door opens, and there she is. My Cutie. She's standing in the door, still in her work clothes, hair up in a messy ponytail and what appears to be dinner dripped on her shirt.

She's never looked more beautiful.

"Hi." Elliott is apprehensive and a little confused, but she doesn't slam the door in our faces. That's a good sign.

"Hi. We um…" I put my hand on Mabel's shoulder, knowing she's as nervous as I am. "We want to talk to you."

Elliott furrows her brow but pushes the door open. "Yeah. Of course." I'm sure she expected me to show up at some point, but the surprise is Mabel being with me. Like I said, though, we're a team. The four of us. Yes, there are times Elliott and I need to hash out things alone. Now isn't that time.

"Mabel!" A girly screech practically blows my eardrum out. Wow, that girl has some lungs. It's a small price to pay, though, to see my girl and her bestie jumping up and down hugging. Despite less than forty-eight hours apart and seeing each other at school, they squeal like they hadn't seen each other in years.

I make eye contact with Elliott and thankfully, she's smiling at the scene like I am.

We give them a few minutes for Ainsley to show Mabel her tooth and tell her about all the smoothies she's been eating. Apparently, her grandmother adds a scoop of ice cream to all her meals. The health nut in me is cringing over the information. The paternal instincts, however, are just happy she's been getting some form of nourishment in her body.

As the conversation starts to taper off, Elliott jumps into mother mode. "Okay girls. Why don't you go play so Abel and I can talk?"

Mabel turns her attention to me, and I can see the question in her eyes. She has something she needs to do first before she can let the adults work things out. From the look on her face, I think she fully understands how important it is too.

"Hang on." I hold my hand up to stop the girls from racing off. "I think Mabel has something she wants to say first."

Elliott looks confused by my words, and I'm grateful when she responds with, "Okay."

Mabel takes a deep breath and closes her eyes. She's nervous. I get that. It's never easy to own up to your mistakes. It's even harder when you're eight years old and it's the first time for it to really matter. But then she straightens her spine, opens her eyes, and looks right at Elliott.

"I'm sorry for being mean to you. And for saying ugly things. And for not listening to you. Sometimes, I'm grumpy in the morning. And then you hug and kiss Ainsley, and I remember my mom isn't home and it makes me sad." Mabel blinks back tears, and I squeeze her shoulder in encouragement. That's a lot of personal information for my girl to share with someone. Especially with someone who has the power to reject her.

Elliott's face softens and her own eyes well with tears. Shit. I really should have thought to bring tissues. If I'm going to live in a house with three women, I better make it a point to remember them from now on.

Elliott sits down on the couch and holds her hands out to Mabel. "Come here." She wiggles her fingers until Mabel moves forward, placing her tiny hands in Elliott's larger ones. "I know you miss your mom so much. There's nothing wrong with that. And I will never, ever try to replace her. I'm just going to be another adult in your life who loves you like your teachers and Miss Dinah and your grandma. Is that okay?"

Mabel nods and wipes a stray tear away. Poor Ainsley looks like she's not sure what to do, so I put my arm around her and hug her close to me. Her tiny arms wrap around me and the gravity of this moment hits me. This is when we move from a dating relationship and helping each other with our kids to being a family. It wasn't instant, but it was certainly inevitable.

"The one thing I need from you," Elliott continues, pulling Mabel closer to her so her arms are now around her protectively, "is how I can make it better for you. I know I can't bring your mom back, but I'm still the mom of the house. Which means my job is to help you any way I can. Can you think of anything I can do when you feel sad? Something that might make you feel better?"

Damn, I love this woman. To push aside everything for the sole purpose of taking care of my child's emotional needs? I think love might be too small a word. What's stronger than love? Really love? Obsessed with? Want to marry her?

Huh. That last one might be about right. I just won't tell her yet. I had a hard enough time convincing her to date me.

Mabel takes a shuddering breath and says, "I want you to hug and kiss me too."

"Oh honey, I can absolutely do that." Elliott immediately puts her arms around Mabel, whispering things in her ear I can't hear, but Mabel nods every once in a while. I take that as a good sign.

When they pull away, both are smiling and wiping tears from their eyes. I'd be lying if I said I wasn't wiping tears away too. Damn all this estrogen I've surrounded myself with. It's turning me into a sissy.

"Oh!" Mabel exclaims. "And I'm sorry I kicked Ainsley. I didn't do it on purpose."

"I know you didn't, baby." I watch as Mabel's eyes light up at the nickname. "But I need to apologize to you too."

This time I furrow my own brow. Why would she need to apologize to Mabel? Did I miss something?

"I assumed the accident was your fault, but it wasn't, was it?" Mabel shakes her head and now I'm thoroughly confused. "Ainsley is the one who made you play kickboxing, isn't she?" Mabel nods and Ainsley stiffens by my side. My own jaw drops open, but I close it quickly, instead opting to go into dad mode.

Looking down at Ainsley, I try to give her a disappointed look without being too stern. I don't know if it works, but Ainsley looks up at me and quietly says, "I'm sorry, Abel. I should have listened to her when she said she didn't want to play it."

I squeeze her shoulder and respond with, "Yeah, you should have. But I think maybe you learned a lesson on why you need to obey us next time, huh?" Ainsley nods and I continue. "You girls aren't just friends. You're roommates. Your job is to help each other make good choices. And when one of you isn't doing that, to find one of us."

Both girls nod vigorously.

"And one more thing," I add. "Ainsley, you already know this, but Mabel, both of you are grounded from the Wii for a month."

Mabel begins to protest but quickly stops when Ainsley responds with "Yes, sir."

"Good." Elliott claps her hands down on her lap. "Now that we have all that worked out, Ainsley, why don't you show Mabel your old room and some of the toys you have here until we're done talking?"

True to form, the two of them race off, loudly, clamoring up the stairs. We need to have a talk about going up and down the steps safely before someone knocks another tooth out.

When they are safely out of earshot, Elliott turns to me. "I'm really sorry, Abel."

"For what?" It's taking everything in me not to touch her and hug her. But I hold back, feeling like she needs to get this off her chest first.

"Well, I'm sorry for running away, because I know that's what it was. And I'm so sorry for hounding you about confronting Mabel when I realized being here means I'm doing the exact same thing, just with the adults in my life." I'm not sure what that means, but I can ask about it later. I'm too close to getting my little family back. I don't want to open up wounds that aren't necessary anyway. "But most of all, I'm sorry I accused Mabel of being the cause of all of this. I tried to give her grace, but I never once stopped to actually talk to her and hear her out. And I feel sick about how I was blaming an eight-year-old, when really it was me being a terrible person—" A sob escapes her throat, cutting off her rant. It also gives me the opportunity to jump in and pull her close to me.

"Hey, hey. Stop."

I run my hand down her back, so grateful to be enjoying the feel of her in my arms again. She doesn't have the same comfort though, shaking her head, rejecting my words.

"No, it's not, Abel. I didn't make her feel better. I made her feel worse. That's on me."

"We may have lived together for a couple months, but one thing you apparently don't know about Mabel is, I guarantee your lack of conversation didn't make her feel worse."

"But I didn't make her feel better either."

I shrug. "Neither did I. Elliott—" I pull back so I can look her in the eye. "There is no way we could've prepared to help her through a situation like this. When she was born, I didn't start trying to figure out how to explain to her that her mother's pending rejection had nothing to do with her. You did the best you could, and frankly, you held your tongue more than most people would or could have. It was actually kind of impressive to watch."

She smiles softly, not accepting my words as truth yet, but at least she's not letting the guilt eat her up as much anymore. "I could've done better."

"We can always do better. But we didn't do bad. Besides, I actually thought she was the one who decided to play kickboxing too. She's a little shit most of the time. This is the first I've heard it was actually Ainsley."

Elliott laughs lightly. "We're the worst parents."

"No. Derrick and May are the worst parents. We're just in the trenches, doing our best."

Her lips quirk to the side, and the relief I feel is palpable. We got through our first big fight and it was about our children. Longer relationships than ours have crumbled over kid issues. That's got to bode well for our future—assuming we actually have one.

Unable to wait any longer, I lean down and kiss her. She reciprocates without any hesitation, and my body immediately responds, wanting more. Wanting to wrap her legs around my waist, drop right on this couch, and pound into her. Fortunately, I have more self-control than that and keep it to lips and tongues. And maybe a stealthy ass squeeze and boob grab. So maybe I don't have *that much* self-control.

Pulling away, Elliott nudges me. "Come on. It's getting late. Let's grab the girls and go home."

I look at her quizzically. "But... wait—I thought you had to stay here until this thing with Derrick gets worked out."

"Oh that. Yeah, that's been worked out already." She bites her lip, and I feel a manipulative story coming on.

I grab her hips and demand, "Explain."

Elliott can't help the giggle that escapes from her. "It wasn't hard, actually. Dinah gave me an idea to remind him of how his one true love would be affected if he was raising a child."

Now I'm thoroughly confused. "His one true love? Himself?"

"Money."

"Ah, yes. I can see that. What did you do?"

She pulls away and begins folding a blanket that's on the couch. It looks like Ainsley must have camped out here in "sick" mode. I immediately begin helping her clean up.

"He came to check on her today, so as we were sitting here, I pretended to be searching for daycares since I'd obviously need to find a new job if I don't have a roommate situation going on. Can't afford to live on our own while working for a daycare."

The idea of her not being at the gym anymore makes me insane, but I let her continue, knowing she has a point.

"I started spouting off how much it would cost to put her in daycare full time. Especially over the summer—the cost is outrageous. Or at least the fancy places I was picking were. I could tell he was not expecting it to cost so much."

I stack the empty cups and put all the straws in the one on top, prepared to take them to the kitchen. "And that was it? He caved?"

"Oh no," she says, taking the cups out of my hand and putting them on the TV tray so she could stuff napkins inside. "He's much tougher than that. But we got paid today, so I conveniently had accidentally left my paycheck on the table. When I asked him to pass me my phone, which was also accidentally on the table, he took a good look."

I'm starting to understand how she got under his skin without ever saying a word about custody. "And he crunched the numbers."

She nods, a victorious smile on her face. "Of course, he did. And he quickly realized he'd pay more in daycare costs than he does in child support. And with how little I make, the fifty bucks a month he would get from me wouldn't even make a dent. He has more money if he leaves Ainsley where she is, and he won't have the added inconvenience of, you know, parenting and all that."

I throw my head back and laugh. "Oh my god, that's brilliant. I can't believe it was that easy."

She shrugs and puts her hands on her hips, clearly pleased with herself. "I wasn't sure it would work at first, but then he started talking about how he's been thinking about things, and he knows I'm a good mom and I just need to be careful and make sure the girls follow the rules. Stuff like that. That's when I knew it was over."

Still laughing, I wipe the tears from my eyes. They could be from laughing. Or they could be from the emotional last two days. I'm not sure. What I am sure of, though, is all four of us are going to be sleeping under the same roof tonight. That's a better outcome than I expected when I knocked on her door.

Grabbing Elliott's hand, I pull her to me and kiss her quickly. "I'm proud of you, babe."

"I'm kind of proud of me too. Now if only I could stand up to my mother."

I chuckle lightly. "One conflict at a time. If it's okay with you, let's get these girls and go home."

"I never thought you'd ask."

Within minutes, the kids are back downstairs, the living room is cleaned up, and everyone is grabbing their jackets to go. Elliott's mother is clearly not happy with this turn of events, but at least she doesn't say anything, instead giving me a tight smile, Ainsley a tight hug, and Elliott a quirk of an eyebrow.

No one else seems to notice and that's fine by me. As Elliott and I walk hand in hand down the sidewalk, the girls skipping happily ahead of us, all is once again right in my world.

EPILOGUE

ELLIOTT

Six months later

"What the hell are you making me watch, anyway?"

Abel looks down at me like I've lost my mind, which, according to him, I have. "Only the best movie series in the history of cinematography."

I snort a laugh. "Seriously? Not *Gone with the Wind* or *Casablanca. The Fast and the Furious?*"

"Those aren't movie series," he argues. "Those are standalone movies. I said series."

I grab a handful of buttered popcorn from the bowl he's hogging. When I made it my goal for him to relax a little on the healthy foods, I wasn't expecting him to take it to such extremes that I have to fight to get some. Don't get me wrong, he still rarely eats junk. But he doesn't scoff when I pop a bag of nitrates and preservatives disguised as microwave popcorn for movie night anymore. I've created a monster.

"And don't give me this crap that you aren't enjoying it," he prods. "You practically called out Vin Diesel's name last night."

I glare at him incredulously. "I did not! I was choked up from our emotional connection."

Now it's his turn to snort a laugh. "Babe, I love you. And I'm always making love to you when I fuck you. But you were bent over this couch with one leg hiked up on the armrest. I would hardly call that our most emotional love-making session."

He's not wrong, but I'll never admit it. I don't want him to have second thoughts about doing that again. It was really, really good. And since we are almost never alone in this house without at least one child racing through at any given moment, I want to make sure we take advantage of that again.

I turn my attention back to the movie. Seriously. I had no idea Vin Diesel was this hot. Add the criminal element covering up a heart of gold and I may have to add him to my hall pass. Not that Abel would agree to that—not after last night.

A knock at the door interrupts fantasy, err, movie time. The girls come racing down the stairs, excited to be part of the action. Me? I'll let Abel do the heavy lifting this time.

"It's here! It's here!" The girls are jumping up and down while Abel answers the door, before he finally yells, "Girls! Move before you get hurt!"

The delivery man chuckles as he pushes the giant box through the door. "Twins, huh?"

"Yep," Abel grunts as he strains to help push it up the stairs.

We gave up a couple months ago trying to explain that the girls aren't twins, nor are they sisters, nor are they step-sisters. Yes, it's such a blessing they're so close, blah, blah, blah. Now we just say yes to the twins question and move on with our lives. It's not like it's anyone's business anyway, or that we'll even see any of these people again.

I should probably do my part to help, though. I'm the one who actually picked this monstrosity out.

"Come on, Beast!" I yell. "Put your back into it!"

There. I helped. Abel's responding comment of, "Good thing she's cute," would indicate he might not agree I'm actually being helpful. Oh well. It's not like I can move a king-sized mattress up the stairs. My contribution was buying new sheets for it and washing them in advance.

Yes, I said mattress. Ainsley and I have lived here for almost a year, and I've finally come to the realization we're not leaving. This is it for us. This is our family. It's our home. It's time to stop trying to separate things out and let things work out the way they should. The first step to that is Abel moving back into the master bedroom with me and the girls having their own rooms.

Now that we're going to have a lock on our bedroom door, maybe I need to suggest getting a couch in there too. If the noises I heard from behind me last night are any indication, I don't think he'd frown on that suggestion.

Following everyone upstairs, I take a peek at the progress the girls are making. They've been working all day, the goal being to get their rooms set up. Well, Ainsley was to get her room set up. Mabel was supposed to get hers put back together. Instead, I discover they have completely different plans.

"Um, Abel?"

He shakes the hand of the delivery guy and watches as he heads back down the stairs and out the door before responding. "Yeah."

Pointing to Ainsley's new light blue bedroom, formerly Abel's room, I ask, "Do you know about this?"

The confused look on his face gets even more confused—if that's even possible—when he sees what I'm looking at. Both twin beds have been moved in and are pushed against perpendicular walls, the heads of each strategically placed for minimum whispering distance at night.

At the same time, we look across the hall into Mabel's bedroom. Both the girls' dressers are in there. Clothes on hangers are all over the floor. And then I realize the full-length mirror from my room is in the corner.

"Huh," Abel finally says, probably as stumped and impressed as I am. "I guess they want to share a room."

"Hey girls!" I call to my bedroom, where I'm sure they're

jumping up and down on my new bed. I'd be mad, but I'm going to breaking it in myself later on anyway. Seriously, having a younger boyfriend has some pretty awesome advantages.

The girls come running, big smiles on their faces.

"What's going on here?" I ask, pointing to one of the rooms.

Ainsley opts to speak first, and she speaks fast. "Me and Mabel were on Pinterest and we found this super cool room this girl had. It's like a giant closet where she can get dressed and sit on chairs and she can even dance in there if she wants. It's so big. So, Mabel and I decided to make one."

"Yeah!" Mabel interjects and rushes past us into Ainsley's supposed new room. "This is going to be the bedroom where we both sleep. See?" She twists and turns in various poses like she's on a game show. "And we have all our stuffed animals in this corner and our toys are all organized in the closet."

"And in here," Ainsley mimics Mabel's model moves, "are all the dressers. And all our clothes will be here in here. We need a chair to sit on when we put on shoes."

"Why can't you sit on the floor?" Abel asks. He obviously doesn't understand how influential a good Pinterest board can be.

Both girls gape at him like he's lost his mind. "That's not what girls do, Daddy." My little sassafras bonus kid puts her hands on her hips. No surprise there.

"I watched you sit on the floor to put on your shoes yesterday. I don't get what's changed."

Patting him on the back, I feel empathy for the man. He thought he was in trouble when he was raising one girl. He's even more lost when the two of them have an idea and run with it. Periods are going to blow his mind.

"Pinterest changed, honey. Girls! I think you've done a nice job." They giggle and jump up and down excitedly. "But you have more work to do." The jumping stops and the faces fall. "From here until dinner time, you need to be in the closet room putting clothes away."

"Closet room?" Abel questions in my ear.

"It's easier than putting everything back. Give it six months, and they'll be ready to have some space."

He flashes me a look that says he doesn't believe me. I have my own reservations about whether or not I'm right, but I also don't think this is a battle we necessarily need to fight. I don't think Abel does either.

"Get a move on, girls," he orders, as their legs get more and more sluggish and slow. "Mabel, you're supposed to FaceTime your mom in a couple hours."

She rolls her eyes and sticks out her tongue. "Do I have to?"

It's the same question every week, and it usually ends with the same conversation.

"Do you want to?" Mabel ponders his question for a second, so he asks another. "What does Elliott always say?"

Mabel and Ainsley both answer simultaneously. "You can love someone while you're mad at them."

"And?"

"Not every relationship looks the same," they repeat, sounding bored out of their minds. But at least the knowledge is sticking.

After that one big incident, things have been pretty smooth sailing around here. We still have our frustrations, and Mabel is still not at all a morning person. But we've made lots of headway. I realized the same things I was trying to instill in Ainsley are exactly what Mabel needs to hear too. You can love your parent even if you don't trust that they're going to be there for you like you want. You can love someone and still be angry with them. And that my or Abel's feelings won't be hurt if they have a strong bond with their other parent as well. We want them to feel secure and loved. Mabel has a strong relationship with her dad, and Ainsley has a strong relationship with me. That doesn't mean the other situations don't have merit or their own value.

The separation will always be painful, but we're going to help them decide how to navigate through it all. We won't let them go it alone. And we won't let each other go it alone, either.

Yet another benefit of moving into the same bedroom—more stability and permanency for all of us.

And sex. All the sex.

Speaking of, I better get my new bed ready for tonight.

Abel trails me as I head to our room. *Our* room. I like the sound of that.

"Wanna help me make the bed?" I ask as I grab the freshly washed gray fabric off the dresser. I barely have time to shake out the fitted sheet before I feel him behind me, wrapping his arms around my waist and moving my hair out of his way so he has easy access to my neck.

"I'd rather help you unmake it," he murmurs into my neck, his teeth lightly nipping, leaving goosebumps in their wake.

"I'm more than happy to let you do that once we have something to unmake."

"Mmm…" He continues to assault the sensitive area of my spine. If he doesn't stop soon, we're going to have to sleep without sheets tonight. "Is it bedtime for the girls yet? I'm ready to snuggle."

"You want to snuggle? That's why you wanted the largest California king, so it's easy to snuggle?"

"I can starfish and snuggle at the same time."

Turning in his arms, I wrap my arms around his neck. All the turning gets us tangled up in the sheet, but I don't mind. It's just a precursor to getting tangled up in them later anyway.

"I don't care if we starfish or snuggle or sleep right on top of each other," I murmur against his lips. "As long as I get to sleep in bed with you."

"Always," he says, and presses deeper into our kiss, putting every ounce of emotion into it that he can. I know that's what he's doing because it's exactly what I'm doing.

That, and ignoring the giggling from the doorway.

We're definitely locking the bedroom door from now on. Especially after we get that new couch.

The End.

Did Joey make you laugh as much as he did me? Turns out, he and Rosalind have a crazy story. You don't want to miss the plot twist that makes you gasp before laughing out loud. *Get ready for Rosie Palm and Her Five Pictures*. Coming in the next Smartypants Romance launch! Here's a sneak peek:

ROSALIND

"I get off in three hours. Where do you want to meet?"

Funny how Joey's tone over text changed the minute I dropped the "p" bomb on him. I admit I'm a tiny bit impressed he didn't immediately ask if the baby was his. I'll give him a little credit for that. The rest remains to be seen.

My one-night stand with Joey was supposed to remain just that— one night. If he'd been any good in the sack, I would have extended it to another night, but he was a pretty selfish lover. I hadn't expected much more than just scratching an itch with a stranger. I definitely hadn't anticipated falling on my head.

All I did was bend over and touch my toes. It's a good angle. But the idiot thought I was trying to do some sort of circus trick and suddenly my legs were wrapped around his waist and my head banged against the wall.

It was weird. And pretty much cemented that our one night together would be our last. It ended up being my last night with anyone at all. There was no particular reason for my celibacy, except maybe a bit of PTSD from my near-concussion. I just didn't meet anyone who caught my eye. Not that you typically meet many quality candidates in the audience of The Pie Hole. Usually it's a group of drunk frat boys who are barely over age, a bunch of guys old enough to be my dad, or an honest to goodness pervert who sits by himself, trying to hide the fact that his hand is stuck down his pants for most of the night.

But Joey was different. I don't know if it was the man bun he was sporting or his green eyes. Hell, it could have been those impressive guns he calls biceps. He just didn't look at me like I was a piece of meat on stage. He looked at me like I was a person. A person who deserved respect.

Okay, okay. That's taking it a bit too far. He was merely polite enough to hand me a twenty without trying to tweak my nipple when I got close to the end of the stage. And yes, I know how cheap it makes me sound to be impressed by someone keeping their paws off of me, but seriously—have you been to a strip club before? It's not like those guys have tons of boundaries. The wedding rings half of them sport are proof of that.

So I went home with Joey for the night. I had a good—okay, fine —decent time and thought I'd never see him again. Unfortunately, his swimmers had other ideas. How those little shits got through a condom and my birth control pill, I will never know. But I'm already preparing myself for a toddler who runs across parking lots the second I take my hands off him. He or she is already proving himself to have some sort of super speed.

"Do you know where Blessings Chicken is?"

"I don't eat fast food."

"I don't care. I have a craving and as your baby mama, you need to meet me at Blessings Chicken."

The three little dots populate and then disappear, populate and then disappear, populate and then disappear, before I finally have an answer.

"I'll meet you there at five."

Hmm. No denial. No arguing. Not even a conflict over my choice in food. Maybe Joey isn't quite as selfish as I'd thought.

ACKNOWLEDGMENTS

I don't know how I ended up surrounded by such an amazing group of people but I will forever be grateful for the women of Smartypants Romance. The encouragement, fun, and integrity this amazing organization exudes has been a breath of fresh air. Every one of you, from Penny and Fiona to the newbie authors are truly incredible. Thank you for loving me as I am and making sure there is always a "loud room" in the hotel just for me.

Andrea Johnston and Marisol Scott, thank you for your initial feedback and love of this book.

Laurie Darter, one again you prove how much you know about everything. Next time I go on vacation I'll make sure to ask you where all the awesome places are to visit.

Erin Noelle, I hope your computer feels better. Especially since we're scheduled to do this again soon.

Karen Lawson, I'm glad you saw Elliott's perspective on such a common situation. And no, my mother won't read this one. Lol

Rebecca K, thank you for being the last set of eyes on this baby!! Fingers crossed we caught everything!

Thank you, Carter's Cheerleaders and Nerdy Little Book Herd for your absolute unwavering support, and The Walk for your unwavering prayer.

And thank you Lord for allowing me to fumble so I can grow along the way.

ABOUT THE AUTHOR

My name is ME Carter and I have no idea how I ended writing books. I'm more of a story teller (the more exaggerated the better) and I happen to know people who helped me get those stories on paper.

I love reading (read almost 200 books last year), hate working out (but I do it anyway because my trainer makes me), love food (but hate what it does to my butt) and love traveling to non-touristy places most people never see.

I live in Houston with my four kids, Mary, Elizabeth, Carter and Bug, who was just a twinkle in my eye when I came up with my pen name. Yeah, I'll probably have to pay for his therapy someday for being left out.

* * *

Website: http://www.authormecarter.com
Facebook: https://www.facebook.com/authorMECarter/
Goodreads: https://www.goodreads.com/author/show/
9899961.M_E_Carter
Twitter: @authormecarter
Instagram: @authormecarter

Find Smartypants Romance online:
Website: www.smartypantsromance.com
Facebook: www.facebook.com/smartypantsromance/
Goodreads: www.goodreads.com/smartypantsromance
Twitter: @smartypantsrom
Instagram: @smartypantsromance

OTHER BOOKS BY M.E. CARTER

The Hart Series

Change of Hart

Hart to Heart

Matters of the Hart

The Texas Mutiny Series

Juked

Groupie

Goalie

Megged

Deflected

The #MyNewLife Series

Getting a Grip (Getting a Grip Duet, Part 1)

Balance Check (Getting a Grip Duet, Part 2)

Pride & Joie

Amazing Grayson

The Getting a Grip Duet: Complete Box Set (Includes Little Miss Perfect)

The Charitable Endeavors Series (co-authored with Andrea Johnston)

Switch Stance

Ear Candy

Model Behavior

Cipher Office Series through Smartypants Romance

Weight Expectations

Cutie and the Beast

Kissmas Eve

OTHER BOOKS BY SMARTYPANTS ROMANCE

CPSIA information can be obtained
at www.ICGtesting.com
Printed in the USA
BVHW030953060420
576973BV00001B/47